The Satin Squeeze Play

In This Series

That First Heady Burn
True Vermilion
The Dark Shill
A Stack of Sawbucks
The Hillside Roble
The Peroxide Pomp
The Incidental Twin
Brawl in Bardo
The Window-Shade Job
The Convenient Patsy
The Artisanal Grifter
Shrink in the Shadows
Project Chartreuse
From a Desert Playa
The Tired Canary
A Desperate Frame-up
Trail of the Blue Agave
The Saucer-Heads
The Satin Squeeze Play

The Satin Squeeze Play

The Satin Squeeze Play

George Bixley

DAGMAR MIURA

LOS ANGELES

Published by Dagmar Miura
Los Angeles
www.dagmarmiura.com

The Satin Squeeze Play

First published 2024

ISBN: 979-8-89195-020-7

ONE

T HE FIRST TIME SLATER heard from the doughnut slinger was on one of the last warm days in October before the cool weather set in. He was at his house, out on the deck enjoying the late-afternoon sunshine and the view of the hazy hills north of Downtown Los Angeles.

His phone buzzed in the pocket of his jeans, and he pulled it out to check. It was a cell number without a name attached. He picked up anyway.

"Hey, Slater—it's Nathan."

"OK. Do I know you?"

"We met a while back. A hookup."

"Nathan." Slater thought about it. "Do you work at the Baltimore Downtown?"

"No—I'm Filipino, slender build, good cheekbones."

"That doesn't really narrow it down."

"We have a mutual friend. Kyle. He says you look into things for a living. People problems. I might have some work for you."

That wasn't a great referral—Kyle was a civilian, a clueless little trash bag who was married to one of his operatives. But he could use the work. Things had been quiet, and the insurance company he contracted for hadn't summoned him in a while. The desk jockeys usually called him in when they suspected fraud but didn't want to dirty their own hands in the field. That was the downside of working freelance—he never knew if a gig

1

was going to be the last time they hired him. He had to take what he could get.

"We should meet," Slater said. "Where are you?"

"It's not too late in the day?"

"I work when there's work."

"I'm in Reseda right now," Nathan said.

"Do you ever come into the city? I have an office downtown."

"Reseda actually is part of the city."

"If you say so."

"It doesn't matter anyway. I live downtown. I'll head out now. Where's your office?"

"In the Fashion District," Slater said, and rattled off the address.

He sat there for a minute longer, gazing at the California fuchsia he'd planted in wooden boxes along the low wall that surrounded the deck. It had bloomed all summer, and the bugs and the hummingbirds loved it, but it was well past all that now. He'd have to cut it back soon to prep it for next year.

Pushing himself up from the lounger, he went inside, and through the kitchen, and down a flight of stairs to the bedroom. Pike was back from work, standing in front of the closet, getting undressed. Built beefy, with a perfect little paunch, Pike wore his dark hair slicked back. Slater's heart beat faster at the sight of his naked torso.

Laid out on the bed were a pair of tan cargo shorts, a ball cap, and a white sports jersey with a big blue number on it.

"Did you turn hetero on me in the night?" Slater demanded.

Pike chuckled. "Lots of gay guys like spectator sports."

"I can see the appeal of the cute little outfits, but beyond that." He gestured helplessly.

Stepping closer, Pike embraced him, and Slater

rested his hands on Pike's waist, and kissed his jaw. The warmth of his bare skin was electric. Leaning in, Pike ravished him, and Slater tilted his head back, relishing the feeling of his mouth on his neck.

"You're getting me revved up," Slater said. "Why are you all naked?"

"I need to shower. I'm supposed to leave soon." Pulling him closer, Pike pressed into him and mouthed his jaw and his ear. "I don't have time for this, forty-niner."

"Your dick says otherwise," Slater said.

Finally he pulled away. "To be continued," he said, and walked toward the bathroom.

"I'm headed out too," Slater called after him. "I'm meeting a potential client at my office."

It was still too warm for a jacket, he decided, and trotted down the stairs to the garage. This house was a boxy modern structure, out of sync with the neighborhood's century-old bungalows. He hadn't been in it for long—he'd bought the place when he'd started things with Pike. He knew he'd need room to get into it with him, room to expand, room for their relationship. It wouldn't have worked in the grimy one-bedroom he'd lived in before.

As he hit the button to roll up the garage door, he caught sight of movement outside. A pair of tennis shoes and denim-clad calves quickly stepped to the side, moving out of view.

Shoving his car keys back in the pocket of his jeans, he ducked under the rising door. Standing near the front door was a guy in a dark jacket, hands in his pockets. He was tall, and looked well built, his Black hair in knobby twists.

"The fuck are you doing skulking around?" Slater demanded. "You can't camp here."

The guy frowned. "Do I look homeless to you?"

Slater stepped closer and slapped his face, left and then right, a rapid kovac. "I said hit the bricks."

Taking a step back, he pulled his hands out of his pockets, his fists balled. That familiar look of surprise was there on his face, and the usual anger, but there was something more. Slater might have misjudged the situation—this guy looked like he could be dangerous.

"Why would you do that?" he demanded, scowling at him. "I've got thirty pounds on you. I could flatten you in a heartbeat."

Slater jutted his chin. "Big talk."

"You're Pike's guy, right?"

He raised his eyebrows. "Am I? Or is Pike my guy? And how do you know Pike? Has he been handing out sandwiches at the soup kitchen?"

"I'm not homeless, you dick." He huffed. "I heard you were a handful."

"The fuck are you?"

"The name is Davis. Pike and I work together."

"So you're a fed. Are you packing?"

"Lucky for you, I'm not. We're supposed to go to the game tonight. Pike said the stadium was walking distance."

"You could have mentioned that up front, instead of creeping around like a window peeper." Slater waved a hand. "He's in the shower. He shouldn't be long."

Davis raised his eyebrows. "Can I wait inside?"

"I suppose you'd bust me if I said no." Stepping to the front door, he dug out his key and unlocked it. "He's one flight up. There's nothing to steal."

As he stepped to the door, Davis frowned at him. "Thanks for your hospitality."

Slater jabbed a finger at him. "No monkey business."

"What's that supposed to mean? You think I'm going to hit on Pike?" He laughed. "That's never going to happen."

"For your sake, I hope not."

He strode back into the garage. That was the one thing you could always count on: stupid people.

Digging out his car keys, he climbed in behind the wheel of the Thunderbird. It was a classic, black and sleek, and he loved that it was in cherry condition. The only downside for his work was that it didn't lend itself to stealth. But just sitting in it and feeling the rumble of the engine made the world feel balanced.

Backing into the street, he waited for the door to roll down, then drove to the Fashion District, on the other side of Downtown LA, just a few minutes away. He parked across the street from his office building in the surface lot, mostly empty this late in the day. Once he'd hustled across in a break in the traffic, and rode the elevator up to the ninth floor, he walked around behind it and admired the names on his office door:

SLATER IBÁÑEZ

MAXIMILLIAN CONROY

INVESTIGATIONS

Most of the suites in the century-old tower were garment factories, but he and his business partner, Max, had three little offices—one each, and between them a front office with a desk that their operatives sometimes used.

As he stepped in and flicked on the lights, he eyed the small statue that sat on the front desk, a rendition of Rey Pascual, a skeleton wearing a crown and holding a scythe. A gift from the woman who sold him pupusas, it had become an unofficial office mascot.

"How you doing, Rey?" he said as he went past.

Their operative Etta had painted the walls, and brought in deco-era furniture from a movie prop house bankruptcy sale, and even put in hanging deco light fixtures. It was a huge upgrade from the utilitarian space it had been, to the point that Max said the place looked too good for them.

Sitting behind his desk, Slater started to go through the stack of mail, and before long came a knock at the door. He went to pull it open and found a guy dressed in a stretchy black athletic top and rust-colored trousers.

Nathan beamed at him. "Slater."

"I totally remember you now," he said, and waved him in. "It's been a while."

His encounter with Nathan dated to the before time—the era before Pike, the dark days before the sun came out, when the highlight of his daily grind had been mindless hookups and bourbon.

"I almost didn't come up," Nathan said. "This building is all sewing factories."

"That helps us keep a low profile," Slater said, stepping into his office and sitting behind his desk. "Plus the rent is half what it is over where the lawyers and the accountants work." He waved for Nathan to take the guest chair across from him.

As he sat down, Nathan lifted the plaster statue that sat next to his computer monitor, a naked guy standing with a horse. "Who's this?"

"It's written on the base."

Nathan turned it around to read the inscription. "Pollux. It looks like a bookend." He set it down again. "Where's Castor?"

"On my man's desk. He gave me that."

"Kyle said you were in a serious relationship."

Slater raised his eyebrows. "That word isn't quite adequate to describe what we have. It's a multidimensional narrative complex."

He chuckled. "What's a narrative complex?"

"In broad strokes it's similar to a relationship, only with more layers to it, more dimensions, more moving parts."

"That does sound serious."

Slater waved a hand. "How do you know Kyle?"

"A hookup. We became friends."

"I'm surprised he had anything good to say about me."

"He said you were a booze hag," Nathan said, holding his gaze, "but that you weren't afraid to use your fists when it came to your work."

"A booze hag." Slater scoffed. "Kyle is a pompous little rat in desperate need of a tune-up. One of my operatives actually married him. For the life of me I haven't been able to figure out why."

"Andy. I know him too. Kyle told me he does research for you. On your door it says investigations—are you a PI?"

"I'm not. My business partner is."

"That's the other name on your door."

"So why do you need someone who can throw a punch?"

Nathan's expression clouded. "My husband, Ben, is an electrical engineer. Do you know the company Ekragen?"

"I've heard of it. I've seen that name plastered on more than one office building along the 105."

"Right. It's a big defense contractor. Rockets and missiles and stuff that explodes. They were ready to hire Ben, and they made him an offer. He was talking to HR, reading about his benefits, filling out forms. It was happening. He even passed a background check. Then the process suddenly stopped dead. Ekragen said there was a conflict of interest. They said Ben had worked before at an aviation company in Palmdale, and he had a nondisclosure agreement with them, and Ekragen couldn't hire someone in that situation."

"Corporations do things like that, don't they?" Slater said. "Treating people like indentured servants. That's why they make you sign the NDA."

"The problem is, it's not true." Nathan leaned toward him. "Ben never worked for that company, and he never worked in Palmdale. He never signed anything for anyone. There's no NDA."

"It sounds like a paperwork mix-up."

"We had a lawyer look into it. She said Ben's signature is on the NDA. This company in Palmdale told her they have employment records for him. But Ben has never heard of any of them."

"That is curious." Slater watched him for a moment. "So why are you here and not Ben?"

"He's not really great at advocating for himself."

Slater nodded and sat up. "I can look into it, but I'll need cash up front."

"I figured you were that type of guy." Nathan dug in his pants pocket. "I've got three grand. Is that enough to start?"

He'd planned to ask for a lot less than that. As he reached for the sheaf of bills, he said, "That'll do."

Not counting it, he folded it and tucked it into his front pocket, then pulled out his phone to make notes.

"What kind of business are you in?" Slater said, as he thumb-typed *Nathan*, and *Ben*, and *NDA*.

"I manage my family's doughnut shops."

"I thought those were mostly run by Cambodians."

"Not all of them," Nathan said. "We do vegan doughnuts. It's a small chain called Miss Healthy Donut."

Slater looked up and raised his eyebrows. "I know her well. Sometimes I detour down Broadway just to look in the window. They're like dope. Really good dope."

Nathan laughed. "Which one do you order?"

"I get a different one every time."

"OK." He nodded. "You're one of those."

"The boyfriend likes the bear claw. He once said it was transcendent."

"I like those too."

"What's the name of the company in Palmdale?" Slater said.

"Desert View Rocketry. From what I can find out online, they custom-manufacture replacement parts for old tech."

"Actual rockets?"

"The name might be aspirational. To me it looks like they work on military aircraft and weapons."

"Who's Ben's contact at Ekragen?"

"Ben could tell you."

"I'm going to need to talk to him in person," Slater said.

"I know. I'll make him call you."

"Is Ben not interested in getting help?"

"He's just a little reserved." Nathan gestured helplessly. "You know how technical people are."

"Get him to call me early tomorrow. We need to get a jump on this."

He rose and followed Nathan out to the hallway, and they rode the elevator down to the street together, and crossed to the parking lot. Nathan stepped up to a new Bronco, with a muddy powder-blue paint job, parked along the fence.

"Sweet ride," Slater said, pausing to look it over. "Is this the electric version?"

"It's a hybrid."

"Either way, it's a total dick magnet."

Nathan laughed at that and climbed in.

TWO

WHEN SLATER GOT BACK to his house, he trudged up two flights to the mostly empty room between the kitchen and the deck. There was a sofa and chairs, and he sat to pull off his boots and socks, then wriggled his toes in the artificial grass. Pike had chosen it to go under the coffee table and the lounge furniture instead of an area rug. The absurdity of it, the lifelike plastic turf, still made him smile. Stretching out on the sofa, Slater could see the glittering lights of the city beyond the French doors, and soon drifted off.

He woke sometime later when he heard Pike come in and call out a greeting. When he got upstairs, Slater saw that he was dressed in his cargo shorts and the blue-and-white sports jersey. He swung his feet off the sofa, and Pike sat next to him, leaning in to kiss him. Slater folded his arms around his torso and nuzzled his neck.

"How was the ball game?"

"Unfortunately we lost. That's it for the season. They tried a squeeze play in the ninth inning and blew it."

"In my business a squeeze play means extortion."

"In baseball it's about bunting when there's a runner on third," Pike said. "It's a risky move. Someone's going out no matter what."

"Were you the only person in Albuquerque who was a Dodgers fan?"

"There were lots of fans. We used to have their farm

team. Plus I think it's historical, about what people had access to. My pop was an Oakland fan because when he was a kid, the only pro ball games he could listen to were on an Oakland AM radio station that had a powerful transmitter. Davis grew up here. That's why he's a fan."

"That fricking guy."

Pike shifted to meet his gaze. "He said you assaulted him."

"That's a lurid distortion. It was a kovac. Low impact. Meant to focus attention, not cause any damage."

"You can't hit my friends. He could have decked you, or arrested you."

"It's his own fault," Slater said. "He was sneaking around. I thought he was trying to steal copper wire. Next time tell him to ring the damn bell."

Pike chuckled. "You're a lot of man, Ibáñez."

"Listen, do you need to sleep, or are you going to read, or am I? I want to find out what happens to Odysseus on that island."

"I'm not that tired. I only had a couple beers." Pike grabbed the book from the coffee table and got comfortable next to him, one leg draped over Slater's.

Slater wasn't especially interested in Greek mythology, but Pike had been reading about it when they'd met, and it had become one of their things, first reading the *Iliad* together, and now the *Odyssey*.

"Having lost all his clothes," Pike began, "Odysseus finally reached the shore. He staggered up the beach in the darkness, and concealed himself in a pile of leaves ..."

Listening with his eyes closed, Slater followed the story and the rich tone of Pike's voice, until he closed the book and tossed it on the table.

"I can't keep my eyes open."

Slater massaged his chest. "This shirt totally flatters your body."

"Oh, yeah? What are you going to do about it?"

"I'll fuck you, baseball boy, if that's what you want." He frowned. "I thought you were falling asleep."

"I'm too tired for Odysseus, but I'm not too tired for you." He pulled him closer, and with one hand deftly unbuckled Slater's belt, and leaned in to mouth his neck.

"We should go downstairs," Slater said, and rose, and Pike followed him.

In the bedroom Slater ditched his clothes, and watched as Pike dropped his shorts, then started to unbutton his shirt.

"You have to leave it on," Slater said.

Pike chuckled, and stretched out on his back on the bed, and grabbed his cock, already getting hard.

Once he was undressed, Slater took the lube from the bedside drawer and moved beside him. He shoved Pike's knees apart, then leaned in to meet his mouth as he worked a thumb into him.

"You're hard," Pike said, massaging his cock.

Shifting closer, Slater pressed into him, and Pike gasped with the intensity of it.

Kneading his chest through the shirt, Slater started slow, then built up the tempo, thrusting harder. When Pike met his gaze, that look in his eye was enough to send him over, and he came. Sinking on top of him, breathing hard, he buried his nose in Pike's hair and inhaled the heady scent of his sweat.

After a minute he pulled back, and shifted down the bed, and took Pike into his mouth.

"I'm not sure it's going to work," Pike said, "what with the beer."

Slater met his gaze. "There's no expectations, and there's no rush."

It took some time, but Slater could feel him gradually building up to it, getting harder, and he coaxed him along with his hands and his mouth. Eventually Pike climaxed, straining into him.

Slater shifted beside him and lay on his back, folding his arm over his eyes.

Once he'd caught his breath, Pike ran a hand over his chest. "I'm amazed that you can be such a hothead, and then have the patience to make sure I'm happy."

He moved his arm to meet his gaze. "It's because it's you. I have unlimited time for the man with the million volts in his pants."

Pike chuckled. "At some point I'm going to have to get up and take off this shirt."

"You should get the whole uniform. Especially the pants. Order them a size too small. You'll look amazing."

"I guess it won't matter if they're tight. You're just going to rip them off me."

"You know the drill."

IN THE MORNING SLATER woke to the sound of his phone buzzing on the bedside table. He was alone, as Pike was long gone to work. Scrabbling for the device, he peered at the screen. The caller ID showed no name, but it was from a cell phone, a 213 number.

"This is Ben," a deep voice said when Slater picked up. "You met my husband, Nathan, last night."

"We need to talk."

"So I heard. I'm in Hollywood today. Do you know that breakfast restaurant with the courtyard?"

"I'll find it. What's the name of the place?"

Once he'd ended the call and looked up the joint, Slater forced himself out of bed, and took a quick shower to wake up. Yesterday's jeans passed the sniff test, and he pulled on a clean shirt, buttoning it on the way upstairs. There was coffee still in the pot. That had become another routine—Pike always made it and left some for him.

At first he hadn't known how it would all go, whether Pike would get sick of him and go back to Albuquerque, and punt his heart into the trash. That still could happen, but right now they had a groove. His initial round-eyed awe of the guy, the euphoria of the new relationship, was gradually wearing off. But the next phase was still really, really good. At this point he couldn't imagine not having him around.

Trotting down to the garage, he backed the Thunderbird into the street and waited for the door to roll down. Navigating onto the freeway, he exited a few miles north in Hollywood, and parked at a meter up the block from the restaurant.

As he walked back to the place, he saw that it was fronted by a tall hedge with a gap in it that served as the entrance. He paused to look over the foliage. This was a wax myrtle. It was a little surprising that someone had planted that. Privacy hedges were usually eugenias, or ficus, with the gnarly roots that busted up the sidewalk.

Walking inside through the gap in the hedge, he found the host, a woman with long brown hair, standing behind a lectern.

She smiled as he stepped up. "You like the hedge? I wondered if you saw something wrong with it."

"It's in great shape. Happy and thriving. It should be—it's a California native."

"Good to know. Table for how many?"

"I'm supposed to meet someone at the bar."

She gestured across the open space. "It's on the other side of the courtyard."

Most of the tables were occupied, he saw as he walked through, even on a weekday morning. A couple of people were sitting at the bar, but it wasn't a place that served booze. Instead an elaborate brass expresso machine sat behind it, along with racks of coffee cups.

Slater stood at the service area and waited until the barista, clad in a white apron, stepped over.

"Can you make me a soy latte?"

He nodded and turned to the machine.

Stepping back, Slater scanned the courtyard. A big burly guy was walking toward him, looking right at him, a smile on his face. At least six feet tall, Slater thought, giving him the once-over, and built for rugby. His African hair was short and unkempt, and he wore a plaid shirt and tan chinos. A little bland, he decided, but basically fuckable.

"Slater?" he said as he stepped up.

"Might be. You are?"

"I'm Ben." He extended his hand and gave Slater's a firm shake. "It was easy to pick you out of the crowd."

"I'm not the only brown guy here." He gestured toward the kitchen. "Look inside and you'll see the cooks and the busboys."

Slater had his father's dark Latin coloring but none of his cultural background, which made it especially grating when people made their assumptions about him.

Ben's brow furrowed. "That's not what I meant. Kyle said you always wear jeans. Everybody else in here is in yoga pants and shorts." He looked around the courtyard. "Although I kind of get it. I might be the only Black guy in here."

"And yet you picked this place anyway."

He chuckled. "I like the food."

"Do you want to get a table?"

"I already got one." He gestured for Slater to follow, and walked toward the middle of the courtyard, to a little table with two chairs.

As they sat, the server stepped up and tucked her hair

behind her ear. "What can I get you?"

"A short stack of buckwheat pancakes," Ben said.

"What's vegan?" Slater said, eyeing her.

"Nothing, really. I could bring you some fruit."

"I was waiting on a soy latte at the bar. You can bring me that."

Once she'd stepped away, Ben spoke. "Why are you vegan?"

"I'm not in the education department, toots. Do a web search."

He frowned. "I'm just curious. Man, chill out."

"Nathan told me a little about what's going on," Slater said, shifting his chair closer to the table. "The issue with the NDA. Tell me about that. What do you know about Desert View Rocketry?"

"Nothing," he said intently. "I'd never even heard of it before the HR person at Ekragen told me about it."

"Who's your contact at Ekragen?"

"I can text you her name and number, but I don't think she'll talk to you about it. Confidentiality and all. She wouldn't even tell me where they got this NDA. She did say she was certain it was me—the signatures on the NDA and on my employment application matched."

"How close were you to getting hired?"

Ben raised his eyebrows. "I was hired. I'd already negotiated the salary and benefits. I was really looking forward to working there. They have a whole range of contracts with the government, so lots of money for research and development. Then they said I'd lied on my résumé, that I hadn't disclosed the NDA."

"So you don't know who told Ekragen about Desert View Rocketry."

He shook his head. "Ekragen told my lawyer they saw employment records for me for the last two years. It's insane."

"What were you really doing during that time?"

"After I got my master's degree, I took a couple years off. I needed to decompress. This year I was ready, and I started job hunting."

"Two years to decompress?" Slater frowned. "People who've had their legs blown off in combat recover quicker than that. It seems lazy."

"You sound like my father." He folded his arms. "I had the luxury of not needing to work. Nathan makes enough to support us both."

"Vegan doughnuts."

"It's a lucrative business," Ben said. "There's lots of vegans around. That's why I was curious about your reasons. The shops are beautiful, and people love the vibe. They love coming in. Everybody in there always looks happy."

"It's where the hep cats go to groove?"

He chuckled. "That might be an exaggeration."

"Give me your driver's license."

"Why?"

"It has all your vitals. I'll need that."

Reaching for his back pocket, Ben pulled out his wallet and handed over the card. With his phone Slater snapped a photo of the front and the back, then handed it back to him and studied the images.

"Your full name is Benoni."

"Nobody ever calls me that. Not even my mother."

"It sounds a little hebe-y," Slater said. "Are you Jewish?"

"I'm not, and that term sounds a little racist."

"I'm allowed. I'm Jewish."

His brow furrowed. "You're Jewish."

Slater scoffed. "Text me your Social Security number and the name of your school. You did a master's in science?"

"That's right." He pulled out his phone and tapped at

it, then glanced up. "I thought it was a bad idea to give out your Social Security number. You'll know everything about me."

"I'm not a lowlife, Ben. I'm working for you. I need the details to compare to the records at Desert View. I'm thinking someone might have stolen your identity."

He sat back and grinned. "So you believe me."

"You're paying me to believe you."

"I don't think it's identity theft. If they'd used my name and Social Security number, I'd see income from those years on my tax records. There's no sign of that. Plus our signatures wouldn't match."

That was actually sound logic, Slater realized, watching him talk. Maybe that's what Nathan meant when he said Ben was a technical person.

"I'll need a sample of your signature to compare to the one on the NDA," Slater said, "and then I'll need a copy of the NDA. An expert might be able to tell if it's a forgery."

"My signature is on my driver's license."

"Those are all shrunk and distorted. I need a firsthand one, on paper. A scan or a photo is good enough."

"I haven't actually seen this notorious NDA," Ben said. "Ekragen wouldn't show me what they had. They said I should have kept my own copy."

He paused as the server set down his plate of pancakes and Slater's coffee.

"At this point, they've basically stopped responding to me," Ben said, reaching for the syrup bottle. "They think I'm a liar."

Slater sipped from his mug, glad to find the java was hot, despite how long ago he'd ordered it. "So how do you know the document even exists?"

"My lawyer reviewed it. She talked to somebody at the Desert Rocketry place in Palmdale. You should connect with her. Her name is Sybil Álvarez."

"Lawyers aren't cheap. What did Sybil achieve?"

"I just asked her to look into it," Ben said, "not to sue anybody. I figured she'd know what to say to get people at that company to talk. To cut through their confidentiality bullshit. But a lawyer can only get so far."

"So you called in the ruffian."

He grinned and finished a mouthful of pancakes. "You don't seem that rough to me. Although Kyle said you were definitely the stick."

"The fuck does that mean?" Slater demanded.

"You know, the carrot and the stick." He waved his fork. "Persuasion versus force. You're the stick."

Slater slurped at his coffee and stood up. "I'll be in touch."

Walking out to his car, he thought about that. The guy wasn't wrong about the stick, but was that really the only way he did things? Surely he used the carrot sometimes, played all nice, soft-soaped the chumps. But thinking about it, he couldn't come up with any instances when that had actually happened.

Once he was behind the wheel of the Thunderbird, he texted Max:

You around today?

A moment later came his reply:

In office

Slater had to chuckle. Max was terse by necessity. He could picture him at his desk, typing with his thick fingers, his phone dwarfed in his big meat hooks. They worked well together, even though Slater regularly wanted to punch him in the face. Most significant was that as a PI, Max had access to tools like criminal databases that he didn't.

Ben had sent a series of texts, he saw, and he read through them, then sent a text to the lawyer's phone number:

My name is Slater Ibáñez. I need to see you today about Ben Clague.

Starting the engine, he pulled into the street and got back on the freeway, and headed downtown.

THREE

S LATER PARKED ACROSS FROM his office building, and when he got upstairs, he saw that Rey Pascual was still facing the front door, his bony empty eye sockets ever watchful. That meant their operative Etta wasn't around today. She always turned him to face the desk so that he could watch her work, then faced him in the other direction to watch the door when she left.

Slater stuck his head into Max's office. Its walls were warm yellow, a contrast to the taupe in the front office and the turquoise in his own. Max was a chunky guy with short mousy hair, today wearing his gray checked suit, a red necktie loose at his collar. He'd hung his jacket on the coatrack in the corner, revealing the straps of his holster over his shirt and his weapon under his arm.

"Can I bug you for a minute?" Slater said.

"Always." Max waved to the chairs in front of his desk and leaned back.

"I picked up an odd one," Slater said, dropping into one of them, and told him a little about the case. "I want to make sure this guy isn't crazy and lying to me."

"You already know he's lying to you."

"About some of it, sure. Hopefully not about the primary ask."

Max sat up and pulled his keyboard toward him. "What's his name?"

"Benoni Clague," he said, and spelled it.

Max pecked at the keyboard with his thick fingers and

peered at the screen. "I can see that the guy exists, but he's never been in trouble with the law."

"That fits. Apparently he passed a background check to work for a defense contractor."

"When the military's involved, they go beyond checking for felonies," Max said, meeting his gaze. "They make sure you don't know too many foreigners. Do you need his vitals?"

"I have all that." Slater rose. "Thanks, buddy."

"Listen—I think we've got a problem. We're getting gentrified."

"What are you talking about?"

"I saw two white girls," Max said. "Lots of hair. They look like models. In the office down the hall."

He frowned. "What are they up to?"

"We call ourselves investigators, man. I think we need to go find out." Rising, he reached for his suit jacket and shrugged it on. Max didn't care about looking formal, but he needed to conceal his handgun and its holster.

Slater followed him out and waited while Max locked the deadbolt. He led the way down the hall and around a corner. The doors of a couple of the factories were open to get the cross-breeze, with the noise of sewing machines cycling on and off filling the air. A row of several women sat at machines under the windows in one, and in the next were several rolling racks of clothes.

"Here," Max said, under his breath, pausing at a door that was propped open with a cardboard box. Taking a breath, he stepped inside. Slater stood in the doorway.

Several stacks of moving boxes were piled along the wall, and past them was a rolling clothes rack hung with what looked like dresses in a sheer pink print. Bolts of fabric were propped against the back wall, and in the center of the room was a big cutting table. Behind it stood a woman with a coiffed blond mane that tumbled to her shoulders. Westside thin, she wasn't yet forty, and wore a striped Breton shirt.

"So this is where they put all the windows," Max said, affecting a cheery tone.

He was right—tall tattersall glass filled most of one wall. The view was mostly of the building next door, plus a glimpse of the sky and the street below.

She beamed at them. "We took it because it gets such good light. We're still moving in. You work in the building?"

"Right up the hall."

"It looks like you're in the schmatta trade," Slater said.

"Guilty. I run a clothing line. I'm Cassidy."

Max introduced them both. "We have the office behind the elevator."

"The investigators," she said, raising her eyebrows. "I saw the sign on your door. How cool is that? You get to shoot at people."

"I actually don't," Max said, and laughed. "Although I won't say I don't get the urge to do that on a regular basis."

"Can I see your office?"

"It's just an office," Slater said. "It's like this one only a lot smaller. And we don't really have windows."

Max threw up a hand. "It can't hurt. Come on."

The three of them walked back to their office, and Max unlocked the door, and held it open for Cassidy with a palm. She stepped inside and looked everything over, then stepped into Max's office, then across to Slater's.

"There's not a lot of room in here," she said, "but you've done it up really well. I absolutely love the art deco furniture. Who's your designer?"

Slater was standing in front of Rey Pascual, his hands on his hips. "We flew him in from Berlin. Part of our contract with him was that we couldn't reveal his name."

"I've been there," Cassidy said, and nodded. "We make couture for big-name celebs. Some of them insist on that too."

Slater raised his eyebrows. "Which celebrities?"

"You're funny." Cassidy chuckled, and looked from him to Max. "Listen, guys, I love this building, but I want to ask management for a couple of upgrades."

"Good luck with that," Max said.

"There's strength in numbers. Maybe you guys can chime in too. Be my backup."

"You signed a hard lease, right?" Max said. "That means you're responsible for everything in your suite. Even the wiring and the plumbing."

Cassidy waved a hand. "In theory, sure. But I'm going to try to negotiate. I won't get to it for a while. There's tons of stuff to do to settle in. Plus there's orders we need to produce."

"You have staff to do that?" Slater said.

"Our work is too irregular for full-timers. We hire day laborers. It's not hard to find seamstresses, but pattern graders are a pain. They're always fully booked." She looked from him to Max. "So is anyone up in here single?"

In unison the pair of them said, "No."

Cassidy laughed. "I get it. Let me know if anything changes."

"I'm sure we'll see you around the place," Max said, following her toward the door.

Once he'd closed it behind her, Slater eyed him. "It's not very often somebody hits on you and me both."

"Happens to me all the time," Max said.

"I've actually witnessed that myself. It's weird. For some inexplicable reason straight women dig you."

He waved an arm. "'Come with me to pester the landlord,' she says. 'Let's negotiate.' She's a gentrifier."

"At least they're in the fashion business, like everybody else in the building. They're not going to attract the wrong crowd. Influencer trash or tech industry grifters."

"White folks means a rent increase, Slater. You know it's true."

"You know you're white, right?"

Stepping into his office, Max called back, "I blame my parents."

Slater's phone had buzzed a minute ago, and he pulled it out to check. It was a text from Sybil, the lawyer:

I'm in my office today if you want to stop by.

A second text had a street address. He knew that neighborhood, over by that stupid stadium. Sybil's office number was 2804. On the twenty-eighth floor. It had to be in one of those glassy new towers between Flower and Fig.

Calling good-bye to Max, he went down to the street and across to the parking lot. A few minutes later he was cruising Sybil's block, and he slowed down to troll for parking, but there were no open meters. Eventually he gave up and turned onto the ramp to the garage under her building, and grabbed the little paper ticket from the machine. It was totally annoying to have to pay for parking.

Interesting that there were no security cameras in the garage, he thought, climbing out of the Thunderbird, even though this was a new building. There was a subtle camera in the corner of the elevator car, he noticed, as he hit the button marked 28.

Sybil's door was blank, with the suite number on a plaque next to it, and when Slater knocked on it, she soon pulled it open. Not very tall, she was built lithe, like a runner, with copious breasts that were way out of proportion with her frame. Her tight silvery blouse was open a few buttons to reveal her cleavage, and he could see a black bra underneath.

She pushed her dark hair back with a hand and greeted him in Spanish.

"No comprendo, sister," Slater said, elongating the vowels to make it sound as Anglo as possible.

"I made an assumption," she said. "People do that all the time about me. I'm Sybil. Come in."

The place had big windows and a glass door onto a little balcony, he saw, as he followed her inside. The view from this high up was dramatic, toward the south, of the low-rise neighborhoods stretching toward the port, the hills of Palos Verdes poking above the haze. This room had a messy desk and a row of file cabinets at one side, and closer to the windows a set of lounge furniture. Sybil gestured to the club chairs and sat opposite, on the sofa.

"I thought this was a residential building," he said as he sat down.

"Mostly it is. I'm using it as a live-work space. This room is my office."

"From your name I thought it might go either way, Anglo or Latin, but you speak Spanish."

"And I look Latin," she said. "That's the part you're not saying out loud. White folks usually assume I'm the maid or the nanny."

"With that rack? No one could have done that on a maid's income."

She held his gaze. "You like what you see?"

"They're impressive," Slater said. "But I'm on dick."

She absently adjusted her shirt collar. "Story of my life."

"I don't actually mind the view. Obviously you're proud of them. Lean into it."

Sybil pushed her breasts up with both hands. "How do you know nature didn't bless me with these?"

"Nature has a more consistent sense of balance. At least you didn't go nuts, and stuck to the single letters. In LA they say as long as you can reach the steering wheel, you didn't overdo it."

She frowned. "Can we stop talking about my breasts?"

"So it's Sybil," he said, shifting in the chair.

"That's what I said."

"It's such an odd name. In the classics the sibyl helped Aeneas break into the underworld. She was basically his tour guide."

"I'm aware of her, but it's spelled differently." Rising, she stepped over to her desk, then returned and handed him a business card. As she sat on the sofa again, she folded one leg over the other.

Slater glanced at the card and tucked it into his shirt pocket. "However you spell it, it fits."

"What do you mean?"

"You're a lawyer. That's exactly who'd lead a civilian into the underworld." He waved a hand. "Lawyers are sleazy."

"Ben said you were kind of a dick," she said, and frowned.

"He called you since I met him this morning?" Maybe Ben was more on the ball than he'd expected.

"So why does a guy like you know about Aeneas and the sibyl?"

"You're making assumptions again," Slater said. "How do you know I don't have a PhD in literature, and speak classical Greek?"

She raised her eyebrows. "Do you?"

"Not even close. I got an associate degree in horticulture. When white folks assume I'm the gardener, they're not wrong."

Sybil chuckled. "The question stands."

"You're not going to let that go. You really are a lawyer."

He gestured vaguely. "The boyfriend and I are reading the classics. It's part of our multidimensional narrative complex."

Her eyes narrowed. "A narrative complex."

"An intricate set of interrelated romantic and erotic events, operating in multidimensional space. It's roughly equivalent to what squares call a 'relationship,'" he said, waggling his fingers to put air quotes around the word.

Sybil's brow furrowed as she watched him for a moment. "Still, it doesn't quite fit that you're well-read. The *Aeneid* is a little high-tone for a gumheel, or a gardener."

"The stories aren't pretentious at all once they're translated into modern language. They're completely straightforward." He sat up. "Tell me about Ben. And use small words, so that I can understand."

"What do you need to know?"

"What's he like?"

"Nice enough. A little introverted, maybe. One of those people who doesn't know he's hot."

Slater nodded. "That's so incredibly rare."

"Girl," she said, and held up an index finger.

He chuckled at that. "How long has he been with Nathan?"

Sybil's expression clouded. "A few years. I don't know Nathan that well."

"Ben said he's your client. Why does he need a lawyer?"

"I can't discuss that. It's privileged."

"I can't help him if I don't have all the information." He sat back. "Do you think he's crazy?"

"That's subjective. I've looked into the NDA and his time at Desert View Rocketry. It seems pretty clear."

"Ben says he never worked there, never even heard of the place," Slater said. "The three obvious possibilities are that he's lying, or he's a deludenoid, or someone stole his identity."

"He's my friend. I don't want to disbelieve him."

"But you don't believe him."

She gestured helplessly. "There's evidence."

"Who did you talk to at Desert View?"

"It's a small company. I dealt with the owner. A guy named Cody Layton."

Slater pulled out his phone, and thumb-typed a note with the name. "I'll need to see your files on Ben and the NDA."

"I don't have any files, and I don't have a copy of the NDA."

"Didn't they teach you record-keeping at law school?"

"All I did was make some phone calls."

"OK," he said evenly, and got up, and stepped toward the door.

"Do you want me to validate your parking?" she called after him.

"Yes, Sybil, I do," he said, turning back. "I want that very much."

From her desk she picked up a paper ticket with a bar code on it, and held it out between two fingers, like a cigarette. Slater plucked it from her hand and rode down to the parking garage.

Once he was behind the wheel of the Thunderbird, he took a deep breath. He didn't want to deal with that rat-faced little toothache, but he had no choice. He texted Andy:

I need to talk to spouse B.

Next he texted O'Dowd, the lawyer he and Max used:

Do you have time for me today?

Her response came as he twisted the key in the ignition:

Can we do it on a phone call?

He thumb-typed a reply:

Better in person.

O'Dowd wrote back a moment later:

I'm in my office all day.

That was the right answer. She knew that sensitive stuff couldn't be written down or discussed on the phone.

Pulling up the ramp into the daylight, he waved the little ticket Sybil had given him under the reader, and the barrier arm swung up. That was the best validation of all: free parking.

As he nosed onto the street, his phone rang. The caller ID said REDDY KILOWATT.

"*Mi vida*," Slater said as he picked up.

"How would you feel about a poker game?" Pike said.

"I don't know how to play."

"Not for you. For me. Some of the folks from work have a regular game. I thought I should offer to host."

"Baseball, and now poker?" Slater said. "The only thing you're missing is cigars and hookers."

Pike laughed. "It's a coed poker group. No smokers or sex workers. We might indulge in some bourbon, though."

"Well, you live there too. You can do whatever you want. You don't have to ask me."

"A head's up, then. The game is after dinner tonight. We'll use the dining table."

"You're such a guy sometimes, you know that?" Slater said, briefly shoulder-checking as he accelerated to merge onto the 10.

"Will you be around?"

"Probably, but I'm not playing poker. I'm headed

over to my lawyer in Westwood right now. I can't figure out how the hell my life got this complicated. I have a lawyer and a mortgage and a ring on my finger."

"Why do you have a lawyer?"

"Max and I needed to figure out our finances and deal with the tax people."

"Maybe he can do my taxes," Pike said. "I haven't found anybody out here yet."

"She's not that kind of lawyer. More like when you find yourself in a murky gray area. She's the one who finds a way to weasel you out of it. She's not cheap."

"I get it. I need an accountant, not a tax weasel."

"We're not avoiding any of our responsibilities to your Uncle Sam, by the way," Slater said. "It's just that with a cash business, things get complicated."

"Those murky gray areas."

"So you don't need to mention any of that to your IRS buddies."

Pike laughed. "I don't know anyone over there."

"I'm glad you're making friends here."

"Wherever you are, it's all about the people. Relationships are the foundation of everything."

"Got it, Sunny Jim," Slater said. "The only thing I'd add to that is that people are basically fucking crazy. They're the foundation of everything that's wrong."

"And also everything that's worthwhile."

"I can't believe you think like that when you're in a job where people shoot at you."

"But you love me anyway," Pike said.

"Like a searing hot laser beam. My love for you could melt steel."

FOUR

CRUISING THE ASPHALT CANYON between the office towers along Wilshire Boulevard in Westwood, Slater turned in and parked under O'Dowd's building. From the glove box he took out his camera-jamming glasses, and clicked on the power switch, and pulled them on.

Andy had replied to his text, he saw:

Kyle is at his apartment today. You can drop by.

He thumb-typed a reply:

Where the fuck is that? I'm not allowed in your private life anymore, remember?

"Idiot," he muttered, and climbed out of the Thunderbird.

Upstairs he found O'Dowd's door, and knocked, then tried the handle. It was unlocked, and he stepped in. She had a lone small office with paper piled everywhere, on the cabinets and the credenza and two of the guest chairs. He wasn't even sure there was a desk under it all. Fluorescent-colored sticky notes protruded from the folders and binders and books, studding the room with flecks of color like confetti at a wedding. O'Dowd did lots of accounting work, and for some reason accountants were always messy.

Sitting behind the desk, O'Dowd, in her forties, had her African hair pulled back with a band. She was wearing a baggy gray cardigan with a black tank top underneath, and no jewelry—the casual look implied she had no meetings today. She greeted him as he dropped into the lone open guest chair.

"Those are quite the glasses," O'Dowd said.

Slater pulled them off and reached across the desk to hand them to her. "My Russian tech supplier built them. They're supposed to conceal my identity by broadcasting UV and IR from little lamps around the frames. That messes with security cameras, even though the human eye can't see it."

She turned them over in her hands, then tried them on. "They're heavy."

"That's the batteries. In the arms."

"They're certainly not subtle."

"The pattern on the frames is a third way to confuse surveillance. It injects mathematical confusion into facial recognition software, so it sees a different person than when I'm not wearing the glasses. I can get you a pair if you want."

O'Dowd grinned and handed them back. "I'll keep that in mind." Sitting back, she heaved a sigh. "This world we live in, Slater. What can I do for you today?"

"I need to find out what kind of lawyer this woman is." He handed over Sybil's business card.

"You mean her legal specialty?" she said, briefly scanning it.

"I mean is she on the level, or is she a crook? She's part of a case I'm working. I'm not sure who to believe."

O'Dowd nodded. "I can make some calls. Somebody in my network will know about her." She lifted a folder from her desktop to reveal a cell phone, and scooping it up, snapped a photo of the business card, then handed it back.

"Great," Slater said, and rose.

"I still need those expense reports from you."

"I was working on them this morning." He waved a hand. "I just need to add the finishing touches."

"You're lying to me," she said flatly. "The two people you should never lie to are your doctor and your lawyer. Just make something up. I could do it for you, but I don't know your business. I need a starting point."

"I'll get on it."

When he got downstairs to the Thunderbird, he saw a text from Andy. It was an address on Grand Avenue. That had to be one of those upscale apartments on Bunker Hill. Of course Kyle would live in a place like that, the fancy little poseur.

Half an hour later he was rolling up Grand, and nosed in at an open meter. This neighborhood was so sterile, just museums and theaters and dead-ass housing for rich folks. Walking into the courtyard of Kyle's building, he saw that it was one of the new ones. He found Kyle's name on the board outside the entrance and pressed the button. A moment later the lock buzzed open.

When he got upstairs and knocked on the apartment door, Andy was the one who pulled it open. Wearing shorts and a T-shirt, he was wiry, and had a perfect shaggy tangle of brown hair, and several days' stubble. Such a beautiful man. Flashing that brilliant smile, he waved him in.

"You've never let me come over here before," Slater said.

"There's never been any ... reason for you to."

Facing the entrance were wide windows looking east over Downtown. The lounge furniture in front of them was trendy, in blond wood with thin upholstery. A Scandinavian vibe, he decided. Typical Kyle: all style and no substance. At least there was zero clutter.

Parked beside the door was Andy's red mobility scooter. Slater gestured to it.

"You ride from your place?"

"It's too far to walk on my … sticks," Andy said, "and it's uphill all the way. But this baby … has torque."

Kyle walked in from the back of the apartment. The guy was in good shape, and always had a trendy haircut, today wearing a thin burgundy sweater with no shirt under it. Slater hated that he actually looked great in his pants, filling them out in the most satisfying way. Kyle's brow furrowed at the sight of him.

"Nice place," Slater said.

"I know," he said flatly.

"You recommended a client to me."

"You're welcome."

"How well do you know Nathan and Ben?"

"Let's sit." Kyle gestured to the lounge furniture, then he paused, and his eyes flicked over Slater's form. "You haven't been working outdoors, have you?"

"My heart is black and grubby, baby, but my jeans are clean."

"It's just the whole addict thing." Kyle waved a hand. "I worry that you woke up in a stupor, covered in your own vomit, then you'll track it in here."

"I promise not to sully your frosty Nordic world for too long." Slater dropped into an easy chair and watched as Kyle and Andy sat on the sofa opposite. "You look even paler than usual, Kyle. And that's saying a lot."

"We think he had the … flu," Andy said. "I managed to dodge it."

"I just assumed someone put a pea under your mattress, and you weren't getting any sleep."

"Speaking of looks," Kyle said, "surprisingly for a drunk, you don't look hung over."

"Even with the flu, cupcake, you look as sweet as a

whole bag full of candy sprinkles. Problem is, they're all vanilla, and they taste like plastic."

"Slater." Andy raised his voice. "Focus."

He huffed and sat up. "I know you're both fucking Nathan. Is Ben part of it too? The grand four-way?"

"They're our friends," Andy said.

"That's not an answer."

"I know that detail doesn't … matter for the work you're doing."

"So tell me about them."

"I don't see Nathan very often," Kyle said. "He's busy running his family's company. He's a decent guy. Smart. Plays keyboards."

"Where do they live?"

"Here—basically in the next building. That one with the red terra-cotta. It's how we met. We had remarkable proximity on the hookup app. It said he was two hundred feet away."

"Great," Slater said flatly. "More affluent zombies."

"I know you use a hookup app," Andy said.

"It's not about that. It's about living up here in the rarefied air, with the opera and the bougie private museums, looking down on the rest of us."

"This isn't really that kind of … neighborhood," Andy said. "And you're working for them. Why are you … trash-talking your clients?"

"What about Ben? Do you know him well enough to tell whether he's got emotional problems, or some personality disorder? Is he a habitual liar?"

Kyle held his gaze. "The only emotional wreck in this scenario is you."

"I can't believe you think … Ben is lying," Andy said.

"I don't actually think anything, one way or the other. Not yet. But I have to check."

"He's not that guy," Kyle said. "I don't know him well

either, but he's articulate, and has a sense of humor. I've never known him to be a storyteller or even to exaggerate. He's an engineering type. They see things in black and white."

"Do you think someone's running a … gimmick on him?" Andy said.

"I can't see how." Slater gestured helplessly. "Not yet, anyway."

Kyle frowned. "What's a gimmick?"

"It just means a con or a grift to … extract cash or services from somebody without … putting in a lot of effort," Andy said.

"You've been working in Slater's seedy world for too long."

"As much as you soar above it all, sweetheart, it's real," Slater said. "And it's always going to be down here. Why did Ben take two years off after he got his master's?"

"I guess he's that kind of guy," Kyle said. "He needed to relax."

"For two years? It doesn't wash."

"He said he traveled overseas for a while after … school," Andy said, "then it took six months just to … find the job at Ekragen. So it wasn't two years of just … sitting on his ass."

"Have you thought of identity theft?" Kyle said. "Maybe somebody used his name and Social Security number to work at the company in Palmdale."

"I'm looking into it." Slater glanced from him to Andy. "What's your gut instinct about Ben?"

Kyle raised his eyebrows. "He's not making it up."

"He's a solid guy," Andy said. "I hope … you'll try to help him."

Slater rose. "So am I ever going to be let into the cool kids' club again? The people you sleep with?"

"You know why that's not happening," Kyle said, rising with him.

He did know. They claimed it was because it messed with Andy's feelings. He'd been crushed out on Slater before he married this yutz. Still, it didn't seem fair.

"It's sexual shunning is what it is," Slater said, putting his hands on his hips. "You cast me aside like yesterday's worn-out tennis shoes. Dumped me in the gutter like so much street trash."

Kyle shrugged. "If the tennis shoe fits."

Andy followed him to the door, walking with his uneven gait. "No one can ever say … you're not intense, Ibáñez."

"It's too much for you fools, obviously," he said, and walked out.

Once he got downstairs, stepping out into the building's courtyard, the sun was low in the western sky. He sent Pike a text:

Did you eat?

His reply came as Slater was climbing into the Thunderbird:

Thai?

He started the engine and wrote back:

You order. I'll be there before the food.

His house really was that close, even in evening traffic, the next exit on the freeway. Soon he was nosing into his garage. Upstairs he found Pike in the other bedroom, where he had a desk set up for when he worked remotely, positioned under the window. The view was opposite the street, over the trees in the next yard and the hilly green neighborhood.

As he stepped in, Pike rose and folded his laptop

closed. He was wearing a bright hibiscus-print Hawaiian shirt and fugly cargo shorts.

"It looks like you're ready for poker night," Slater said.

Pike embraced him, and met his mouth, and Slater nuzzled his neck. After a moment Pike pulled back.

"Don't get me too wound up. The food is on its way, and my poker posse will be here right after."

Slater unbuckled his belt, and grabbed Pike's wrist, and shoved his hand down into his crotch, inside his skivvies.

"Feel that?" Slater said, holding his gaze.

"I'm familiar with your junk."

"That's what's waiting for you. When you're dealing cards and counting chips tonight, you can smell your hand and think about that."

Pike squeezed his cock and then pulled his hand out. "That is so damn nasty. It's also pretty damn hot."

He raised his eyebrows. "Don't wash your hands."

"I can't sit around all evening with your man-stank on me."

"Don't wash," he said intently.

Pike chuckled and cradled his neck. "Where did you come from?"

They kissed again, and pulled apart when the doorbell rang.

"That'll be the grub," Pike said, and headed down the stairs.

———◆———

AFTER THEY'D EATEN, AS they were dumping the remnants in the compost bin, the doorbell rang, and Pike hustled down. Loud voices and laughter came from below, and a moment later Pike emerged with one of his work colleagues. Slater had met her before—Brewster.

Her hair was tied back behind her prominent ears, and

she was wearing an olive drab jacket with a German flag on the shoulder. She greeted him with a smile, and they stood in the kitchen chatting until the bell rang again.

Pike trotted down and returned with Davis, the guy from last night's baseball game. He had a bottle of bourbon in hand. Slater recognized the label—it wasn't overly pricey stuff, but it was a couple of levels up from the applejack he bought for himself.

Davis frowned. "If it isn't Mr. Personality." Eyeing Brewster, he added, "This one came at me last night with the old paintbrush."

"West of the Rockies it's called a kovac," Slater said. "And to be fair, you were prowling around on private property, acting awfully suspicious."

"Let's not relitigate that one," Pike said. "Come on."

He waved them to the dining table in the space beyond the kitchen. Davis and Brewster sat at the table while Pike set out a couple of decks of cards and a tray of colorful poker chips.

"This is quite the house," Brewster said. "There's so much space up here."

"This floor is open-plan." Pike waved an arm at the empty room. "It makes it look bigger than it is."

"Have you ever thought of putting some furniture in here?"

"There's a sofa and a couple of chairs and a TV farther back," Slater said. "What else do I need? Sculptures on pedestals? A pool table? A popcorn machine?"

"It seems stark," she said.

"I like things simple. No clutter."

Brewster had picked up a deck of cards and deftly started to shuffle them.

"Hopkins must be running late," she said, eyeing Slater. "Do you want me to deal you in?"

"I've never played, so I'd only slow you down. I'll

come up after your game."

Downstairs, he stretched out on the bed, and folded an arm over his eyes. The doorbell rang again, and he heard Pike go down the stairs. That would be Hopkins. Slater had met him before too.

He listened to the drone of the distant conversation, once in a while punctuated by raucous laughter. Pike was so upbeat. He attracted people like bees to a yarrow in bloom.

Later the buzz of his phone in the pocket of his jeans woke him. When he checked the screen, he found a text from Pike:

Come on up.

Rolling off the bed, he climbed the stairs and stepped into the kitchen.

"Grab a drink," Pike called to him.

He didn't have to be asked twice. Slater poured into a lowball glass from the bourbon bottle Davis had brought, and took a big slurp, relishing the heady burn in his throat, the vapor in his nose. Once he'd poured another slug, he went over to the table. The poker chips were scattered all around now, and there was a messy pile of singles and fins at one end. Slater sat next to Brewster and took a deep breath. He needed to feign civility, and that took concentration.

Hopkins was a beefy guy, his Black hair in a natural style. He gestured with his glass in greeting. Slater could see it contained the bourbon, but diluted with way too much ice.

"I like your house," Hopkins said.

"Some trendoid gentrifiers built it, then they went broke."

"I told them they should get some furniture up here," Brewster said.

Slater swirled the contents of his glass. "It doesn't need more stuff."

"You're not alone," Hopkins said. "These big white boxes are all over the place now. It seems to be all that's getting built."

"I kind of like the clean lines," Pike said.

He wasn't quite slurring his words, but when he blinked it looked too slow. Pike was a little buzzed.

"It could be considered soulless and inert," Davis said, raising his eyebrows.

"I've got plenty of soul," Slater said. "I don't need it from my architecture." He waved an arm. "I needed the space for Pike, and I needed the simplicity to make room for our expanding narrative complex. This place was like a blank canvas."

"The mortgage must be painful," Davis said.

"I've almost got it paid off," Slater said. "Another few years."

Pike eyed him, his brow furrowing. "Seriously?"

"I had a couple big jobs this year."

"I need to get into the private sector," Pike said. "Money seems to be drawn to you. It swirls and piles up around you like drifting sand."

"I work plenty hard for it."

"For a while I wasn't sure you were real," Brewster said. "I heard a lot about you." She nodded toward Pike. "This guy has it bad for you."

"I know I'm antisocial," Slater said. "Plus it makes me nervous to have a bunch of law enforcement types around."

Meeting his eye, Hopkins raised his eyebrows. "What do you have to be nervous about?"

He threw up his hands. "And there it is. If I say anything more, you'll make me empty my pockets, and then I'm getting slammed on the hood of a prowl car."

Hopkins laughed. "We're not that kind of law enforcement."

"It's interesting that you're with someone who's afraid of cops," Davis said, eyeing Pike.

"I'm not afraid of cops," Slater said, holding his gaze, "and I'm definitely not afraid of you."

Pike gestured with both hands. "Sometimes when you love someone, you let them strike the match, and light the fuse, and you stand back as they get hoist with their own petard."

"Preach," Davis said, and reached over with his glass to clink it on Pike's.

Sipping his bourbon, Slater eyed Pike. "So this guy's got it bad for me."

"So bad it hurts."

"A pain in the neck, and a pain in the ass, I'm thinking."

"Not even a little, my sweet." A silly grin on his face, he rose and walked over to the powder room next to the kitchen.

"I can see the way you look at him," Brewster said. "You're right there too."

"I can't deny that," Slater said. "I'm obsessed with the guy. I'm finally kind of able to see what he looks like. Until now it was like staring at the sun. I had to just feel the brilliance without looking directly at it."

"You're a lucky man," she said. "He's a real catch."

"You think? I can't be objective about him. It's like standing on the beach and trying to assess the entirety of the Pacific Ocean."

Davis chuckled. "You have to see some of it. Pike is charismatic."

"I know he's an optimist. People seem to like him." He gestured helplessly. "You all seem to like him. It's actually weird."

Pike came back and sat in his chair. "What did I miss?"

"We did a rapid psych eval on you," Brewster said. "I think we've all got your number now."

"You need to put it in writing," Pike said, "and email it. I'll get to it eventually."

"I have to go," Davis said, and stood up. "I've got an early morning."

He said his good-byes, and Pike got up to walk him down to the door.

As they approached the head of the stairs, Slater called after them, "Bye, now. See you next Tuesday."

Pike shot him a look as he stepped out.

"What is your beef with Davis?" Brewster said, a wry smile on her face.

"There's no beef. But it's pretty obvious he wants into Pike's pants."

Hopkins folded his arms. "I can assure you that you're wrong about that."

"It doesn't really matter. It's simple — if he lays a finger on him, I'm coming for him."

"That sounds like a threat," Hopkins said.

"No threat." Slater shrugged. "Just cold hard facts. That guy needs to keep his grubby paws off the merchandise."

When Pike returned, Hopkins said, "One more hand? It'll help me sober up."

"Let's do it," Pike said, and reached for the pile of playing cards.

"I'm going to crash," Slater said, and got up.

In the kitchen he pulled out his own fifth of bourbon, the cheap stuff for his nightly ration, and took a few pulls from the bottle. His booze rules said he could have half an inch in a tumbler, but he wasn't going to measure it with all these people in the next room. He also didn't want to be piggy and drink more of what Davis brought, even though it was good stuff. Coughing at the burn in his throat, he closed his eyes to relish it. In the end maybe it wasn't all that different from Davis's version.

———◦———

SLATER WAS ASLEEP WHEN Pike came to bed. He felt him climb in, and draw close in the darkness, his warm breath on the back of his neck. He could smell booze. Pike had a hard-on, and pressed it between his thighs. Wrapping an arm around him, he squeezed Slater's cock.

He had to chuckle. "I'm usually the one who smells like applejack at this hour."

"You're awake," Pike said. "Can I fuck you?"

"I don't know, punk—can you? Let's see what you got."

"Copping an attitude, huh?" he growled, then rolled away.

A moment later he felt a handful of cold lube, then Pike pressed into him, drawing close with an arm around his chest. He must be loaded, Slater realized, because he was pushing hard, too insistent, not being gentle about it at all. Slater winced with the intensity of it, but then got into it, and soon Pike was pounding him. It took a minute, but eventually Pike grunted and strained into him as he climaxed.

"You're so fucking beautiful," Pike said, breathing hard.

Still inside him, he grabbed his cock in his lubed hand and stroked him. It took no time until Slater came, and he had to grab Pike's hand to get him to lay off.

As he drifted toward unconsciousness, Pike's arm was still around him. The electric warmth of his skin, the confident power in his grip, even his bourbon breath. It felt freaking perfect.

FIVE

WHEN SLATER WOKE, PIKE had already gone to work. They were sending him out of town less often these days, but he went in to his office early. Forcing himself out of bed, he went upstairs and poured a coffee, then sat out on the deck in a lounger to drink it and wake up, squinting in the bright daylight.

He could approach Ekragen, he knew, and try to talk to somebody there, but it was such a massive corporation. Nobody would know what anyone else was doing. Ben already said his HR contact had cut off communication. The root of the issue was the documentation that Ekragen had seen, the NDA and employment records, and that was about Desert View Rocketry. Small businesses were way more functional and accessible.

Slurping at his mug, he set it next to him on the deck and looked up the company on his phone. The website for Desert View Rocketry was spare, perfunctory, the design clunky and dated. The "About Us" section talked about legacy military aviation equipment. It wasn't spelled out, but it was easy to infer that meant missile systems.

He dialed the main phone number, surprised that a human picked up, a man's voice.

"What are your hours?" Slater said.

"For deliveries, it's nine to six Monday to Saturday."

"Is Cody Layton around this week?"

"He's in the office, but you'll need an appointment. Can I ask who's calling?"

Slater tapped the screen to end the call. No way was he going to give them a chance to stonewall him.

It was a long schlep to Palmdale, and he took a deep breath to steel himself for it, and went down to the garage, and climbed into the Thunderbird. As he accelerated onto the freeway, his phone buzzed in its dash mount—O'Dowd. He tapped at it to pick up.

"My favorite lawyer."

"I'm assuming I'm your only lawyer," O'Dowd said. "Listen, about your friend Sybil. She might be a little shady."

"How so?"

"She has more than one client, but the scuttlebutt is that she's working a lot for a sleazeball named Dragan. The guy claims he's a film producer, but his income is from running illegal gambling places. Those ones you find in backrooms in strip malls in immigrant neighborhoods."

"What kind of films does he make?" Slater said.

"He doesn't. It might be a front. My contact said he has nothing that's actually in production, just a lot of ideas and promises."

"So Dragan is a grifter?"

"When you call yourself an independent producer," O'Dowd said, "it means you're working solo, not part of a studio or a production company. There are no guard rails, no deadlines, lots of room to be incompetent or dirty. This guy may be both."

"There's unethical dirty, and there's illegal dirty."

"There aren't any lawsuits yet, but some of the people who invested in his movies are grumbling that nothing is happening. And the gambling is definitely illegal."

"Card rooms sound like syndicate business," Slater said.

"He's not connected to any syndicate, I'm told, and there's evidence for that."

"Like what?"

"When you don't have a syndicate, you have to launder your own money. Word is he works with small businesses to achieve that."

"What kind of businesses?"

"The kind that don't need receipts and can conceal the source of the cash," she said. "Retail is a cash business, and commercial real estate—lots of tenants pay in cash. The problem is, you have to change things up, and find new partners. Too much cash running through one mom-and-pop starts to look suspicious. My contact said that when Dragan finds a new partner, he delivers his 'investment' in a duffel bag."

"So what does Sybil do for him?"

"I'm told she's his fixer. As in when Dragan has legal trouble, she fixes it, and not necessarily through the judicial system."

"Sybil doesn't seem like the type who goes around busting kneecaps."

"It's about fixing things with cash and influence," she said. "Once a small business agrees to launder your money, you have them on the hook forever. Even if you don't work with them anymore, you can leverage the threat of exposing them. They'll do whatever you need them to."

"So she's a lowlife," Slater said. That exponentially increased the likelihood that she was lying to him.

"So I'm told. The caveat is that all of this is second- and thirdhand."

"Still, it's valuable information. Send me a bill for your time."

"Oh, you know I will."

The navigation app sent him on the 5, through the

Newhall Pass on the 14, eventually into the dusty mono-tone desert. The western edge of the Mojave was grubby and depressing compared to the more sparsely inhabited parts north and east of here, but the quality of the light was the same, that idiosyncratic Mojave brilliance.

On the outskirts of Palmdale he pulled up on the street address for Desert View Rocketry. The property was fronted by tall chain-link topped by coiling razor wire. The fence had wooden slats woven into it, broken and missing in places but mostly obscuring what was in-side. Nosing in the open gate, he found a dusty dirt lot. A long low building stood near the street, painted white and with the company's name on it in big letters. Farther back were a couple of corrugated metal–clad buildings and one with a big door and an arched roof. He parked just inside the gate with the dozen other vehicles and killed the engine.

Along the side of the main building was a loading dock, and he could see a bulky industrial machine sit-ting at the edge of it, under a crane that was mounted on a flatbed truck. From this side it was mostly blue-painted sheet metal, with what looked like sliding doors, and a control panel with a computer screen. It was attached to the crane by chains that were hanging slack. Standing next to the flatbed was a small group of guys in work clothes, one of them wearing a hard hat, seemingly in conversation.

Slater didn't bother with the stealthy glasses, and climbed out of the Thunderbird, stretching his back after the long drive. Walking toward the flatbed, he ap-proached the guys.

"Is that machine coming or going?" he said as he stepped up.

One of them turned and moved toward him. He had a scraggly beard and wore thoroughly scuffed yellow work boots, his red plaid shirt struggling to reign in his pot belly,

"You can't be in here," the guy said. "There's no copper and no empty cans. Go on back to your shopping cart."

"I'm not homeless, you moron."

He pointedly looked him up and down. "Are you sure about that?"

Stepping closer, Slater threw a left hook that snapped his head, then planted a palm on his chest and shoved him hard.

"Why do you make me do this to you?" Slater demanded, stepping after him. He threw up his hands. "Why do you do it?"

Surprise in his eyes, the guy quickly recovered from the punch and lunged for him. He was faster than he looked, and grabbed Slater around the neck with both hands. Struggling to break free, he punched at the guy's sides, but it was hard to land a decent blow, and it didn't seem to deter him or loosen his grip.

Then he felt hands under his arms, dragging him backward. Finally the guy let go of him as two other men behind him pulled them apart.

"You can't be fighting, man," the one with the hard hat said, pushing the loudmouth farther away. "You'll get yourself canned."

Slater ran a hand through his hair, then tucked in his shirt. "What a hothead."

The loudmouth jutted his chin. "Get the fuck out of here."

Eyeing one of the men who'd pulled them apart, Slater said, "You need to keep your ape on a leash."

He'd seen an office door back by the parking spaces, and he turned and strode toward the front gate, massaging his neck and his throat. It didn't feel like the idiot had done any damage. Pulling out his phone, he turned on the audio recorder, and dropped the device into his shirt pocket.

There was a camera high on the wall on this side of the building, he saw, trained on the office door. It wouldn't cover the patch of tan-brown Mojave dirt where the cars were parked, but it would have a good view of anyone who came to the door.

As he stepped inside, he saw another camera here, aimed at the entrance. It probably covered the front desk too. The place was utilitarian, a big room with some lounge chairs near the door. A desk sat at the back wall, in front of a credenza with a printer on it.

Behind the desk, standing at a tall file cabinet, was a lanky redhead with a messy coif, wearing a casual plaid shirt. In his thirties, maybe, his jeans weren't unflattering to his butt. Fuckable, Slater decided.

The guy turned as he stepped in. "Can I help you?"

"I need to talk to Cody Layton."

"Do you have an appointment?"

Slater put his hands on his hips. "You already know the answer to that, if you're the door troll."

His brow furrowed. "I'm not sure why you think you can just walk in here and get a meeting."

"Don't feel bad. Lots of people are stupid."

His face hardened. "If you don't have an appointment, I'm afraid—"

"Spare me the chin music, toots," Slater said, raising his voice. "Tell Layton I need to talk to him about Ben Clague."

Something flitted through his expression—recognition, maybe, or concern. "You're kind of pushy."

"I can easily dial it up if that's what you want. Personally I don't want to have to punch you in the face."

"Dude," he said intently, his brow furrowing. "Cool

it." But he stepped toward the hallway that led farther inside.

Slater looked around the room. It was spare, with no art, and the walls weren't even painted, just drywall with a coat of white primer. This was what his office had looked like before Etta had decorated.

A minute later the guy returned. "Come on back."

Slater followed him into the hallway and through an office door. Another sizeable room, this one was also unadorned. Behind the desk was a window with a view onto the dusty side yard where the crane was loading that machine onto the flatbed.

Facing the door was a cluttered desk, and a nearby credenza bore several chunks of shiny machined metal. In intricate rounded shapes, they'd been precision-made for some inscrutable purpose.

The redhead stepped out and pulled the door closed behind him. The guy behind the desk had to be Cody Layton, and he rose as Slater stepped in. Gray-haired with a bald patch in front, he had a tidily trimmed salt-and-pepper mustache, and he was wearing a dark-blue work jacket, the kind of heavy-duty fabric tradespeople wore, with pants in the same material. Grinning at him, he exuded the confidence of the person in charge.

Layton introduced himself and said, "What can I do for you?"

Fishing a dog-eared business card out of his hip pocket, Slater handed it across the desk to him. "I'm sure your lackey told you it's about Ben Clague."

"Graham's not a lackey. He's a valued member of the team. He has his machinist's papers."

"He's also got an attitude."

Layton frowned and gestured to the chairs in front of his desk. "Sit down," he said, and sat himself, resting his elbows on the blotter as he studied Slater's card. "You're an insurance investigator. Did Ben make some kind of insurance claim?"

"It's not about insurance. I'm representing Ben."

He set the card on his desk and met Slater's gaze. "This whole thing with Ben is silly. I don't understand why he doesn't come in himself. I'd be happy to talk to him. Is he OK?"

"Do you build actual missiles here?"

Leaning back, he laughed, his tone deep. "We make parts for them sometimes. You'd be amazed at some of the equipment the military is still using. It dates back to the Cold War. We also make drilling and piping parts for the oil industry, and precision parts for civil aviation."

"So Ben worked here."

"That's right." Layton held his gaze. "I'm not sure why that's so hard to believe. His lawyer seemed skeptical too."

"What did he do?"

"Ben's an electrical engineer. He worked on control systems for the components we manufacture. Designing circuits, that kind of thing."

"Why did he leave?"

"He said he wanted to work in the city. I couldn't pay him as much as the big players. This was his first job out of college. I'd call it a natural career progression for him to move on. I was lucky to have him as long as I did." Layton raised his eyebrows. "The separation was amicable."

"I need to see the NDA he signed."

"Right. Same as the lawyer."

He sighed and turned to his computer screen, and tapped at the keyboard. A moment later the printer behind him hummed to life and spit out several pages. Turning to it, Layton pulled off the sheaf of paper and handed it across the desk.

Slater quickly leafed through it. "This isn't signed."

"It's the standard NDA that everybody signs. I don't need Ben taking ideas he developed here and giving them to Ekragen."

"I need to see the signed version."

Layton slowly shook his head. "That's buried in a banker's box in a storage facility on the other side of town. No way am I going to waste employee time digging it out. You can take my word that he signed that. Everyone signs it. Didn't he keep his own copy?"

Civilians did that when they were trying to project guilelessness, Slater thought, watching him talk. The way Layton was holding his gaze, furrowing his brow, trying to appear sincere. It didn't necessarily mean he was lying, but it definitely felt like it.

He folded the sheaf of paper in half. "What kind of person was Ben?"

"Personable," Layton said. "He worked hard. Popular with the women, although I understand he's married."

"Did you ever see any evidence that he was mentally unstable?"

"I'm not going to sugarcoat it, Ibáñez." He lowered his voice, even though no one else was in the room. "I'd have to say yes. Several times I saw him get into a lather about aspects of his work."

"What did that look like?"

"He just seemed stressed out. Like he wasn't sleeping, and cranky. He'd snap at people." Layton tapped his temple with a forefinger. "He'd get this look in his eye."

"Do you have photos or video from when he worked here?" Slater said. "Meetings or company parties?"

Not hesitating, Layton swiveled to the credenza behind his desk and grabbed a framed photo that was propped there, and handed it across. It showed five people crowded together in front of a dull-gray aircraft that loomed at one side and over their heads. The plane was mostly cropped out to focus on the people. Layton was at the left of the group, and beside him, standing behind Layton and the next guy, was Ben. His head and neck were visible, and part of one shoulder. The two other people to the right were a woman and a man. All of them were looking at the camera and beaming.

"That was taken at the military airfield right up the road," Layton said. "About a year ago. That's the team that worked on the job."

"You built parts for this airplane?"

"It's actually a drone, or a UAV, as the Air Force calls them. We worked on it, but I can't tell you any more than that. The military insists on its secrets."

"Can I take a picture of this?"

He waved a hand. "Knock yourself out."

Slater pulled out his phone. The audio recorder was still running, and he opened the camera and took a shot of the whole image, then a close-up of Ben. Tucking his phone away, he set the frame flat on the desk. Layton reached for it and put it back on the credenza, folding out the little stand.

"I'll need his personnel file," Slater said.

"No way." He swiveled around to face him again. "I wouldn't even give that to Ben himself. It's private information."

"Can I talk to your HR person, at least?"

"She won't tell you anything more than what I know. The buck stops here." Layton tapped his desktop with a fingertip. "I'm the boss."

"I need to talk to her anyway. She must have known Ben."

He looked away. "Her name is Patsy. I'll see if she's around."

"Who else was he friendly with?" Slater said. "Who was in his work cohort?"

"We have a lot of turnover here," he said, and raised his eyebrows. "Sadly we've had to lay some people off. But Graham out front knew him pretty well, and Patsy."

"The receptionist and the HR person?" Slater frowned. "He must have worked with other engineers, and the people who built the stuff he designed."

"True, he did." Layton watched him for a moment. "Maybe some of the guys in the manufacturing unit knew him. But I'd have to ask around."

"Who was the head of the shop when he was here? Ben must have known that person pretty well."

"A guy named Redge. I had to lay him off."

"Do you know where he is now?"

"In LA, as far as I know."

"Was Ben the only engineer?"

"His work partner was an engineer."

"So Ben knew him," Slater said. "What's his name?"

"It's a her. A woman named Lunelle."

"Last name?"

Layton frowned. "Archuleta. She's long gone."

"Where's she long gone to?"

"I have no idea."

"She'll be easy enough to track down. It's an unusual name."

"Don't worry about her. You can ask your questions here. With me and Patsy and Graham." He sat up and held Slater's gaze. "I don't know what Ben is up to, what his angle is in all this, what game he's playing. But it's starting to get tedious. I've got a business to run."

"Can you show me where he used to work? His desk or his computer?"

"We contract with the military, Ibáñez. That means the work is confidential. I can't show you around."

"Where's Patsy's office?"

His brow furrowing, he picked up his desk phone and punched some buttons. "I've got a live one for you," he said into it. "An insurance guy looking for Ben Clague. Can you talk to him?"

"I'm not looking for Ben," Slater said as he replaced the receiver. "I know exactly where he is. I'm trying to figure out why he says he never worked here."

"All I can say is that the human mind is a mystery." He waved to the door. "Patsy is the last office on the left."

SIX

R ISING, SLATER WALKED OUT. The door Layton had described was unmarked and stood ajar. He knocked and then pushed it open.

The woman behind the desk was wearing a white blouse and showing some cleavage. In her fifties, maybe, she had mousy brown hair in a puffy style.

She sat back as Slater entered. "You're looking for Ben."

"Not really."

"What's your name?"

"Ibáñez." From his hip pocket he produced a business card and handed it over.

"Sit down, if you want." She studied his card for a moment. "Insurance. Did Ben file some kind of insurance claim?"

"I need to see his personnel file," Slater said, dropping into a chair across from her.

She scowled. "I can't show you that."

"You can, but you've decided you won't."

"Even if I wanted to, that's illegal."

"I'm acting as Ben's representative."

"It doesn't matter. I'm not going to open my files."

"How well did you know him?"

"As well as any employee. I guess we had a professional relationship. I knew him to say hello in the hall."

"What kind of guy was he?"

She briefly looked away. "I'd say he was personable. Funny sometimes. Women thought he was good-looking."

"Did he ever seem unbalanced?"

"I know there were episodes when he got stressed out about his work. He'd show up looking like he hadn't slept. He had this odd look in his eye. The rumor was that he might have been hopped up on goofballs. But personally I never saw any evidence of drug use. It never became an HR issue."

"OK," Slater said evenly, watching her. "Did he pass his drug tests?"

"We don't do that here."

"I don't suppose you have a copy of his NDA."

"I could print one out for you."

"I need the signed copy."

Patsy shook her head. "That's in the archives."

"Across town, in a banker's box. I heard."

Rising, he walked out, and down the hall to the front office. Graham was sitting behind the desk now, and looked up as Slater walked in, and frowned.

"So you knew Ben too," Slater said, standing in front of his desk.

"Sure."

"Were you sleeping with him?"

His eyebrows shot up. "Why would you say that?"

"Well, he's not exclusive with his husband, and you're a slab of cream cheese, and apparently you were both here every day. It seems like it would be inevitable."

"How did you know I'm gay?"

"You're too good-looking not to be."

Graham scoffed. "I see what you're doing. Soften me up to get me to talk. You don't have to do that. I'll tell you whatever you want to know about Ben."

"So sing, brother," Slater said, and waved an arm. "What was he like?"

"Well, he's Black." Graham sat back. "He wore his hair short. Tall and thin."

"He was thin?"

He met his gaze. "You've met him, haven't you? He must be six feet tall, and he can't weigh more than a buck forty."

Slater frowned. Ben looked nothing like that now — he was built thick. "Do you have any photos with him?"

"I never took any. There might be some around the office."

"What about his personality, his work ethic, that kind of thing?"

"He was definitely personable," Graham said, "and he had a sense of humor."

"Why are you working reception when you have your machinist's papers?"

His face reddened. "Who told you that?"

"Who do you think?"

"They didn't need me in the factory anymore, so I came out here. The pay is the same."

That didn't sound right, Slater thought, watching him. A receptionist would be at minimum wage, and a machinist would be much better paid, like all the trades.

"You've done a really good job with your hair," Slater said. "I can't see any of the roots."

"This is my natural color, you dick." He scowled. "I've gotten grief about it my whole life."

"I'm just razzing you. I know it's real. And the harassment makes no sense. It's a great look."

"It's not like I'm working a look here. I don't have much choice about it. And in my experience, bias and harassment is the natural human state."

"That's a dark outlook, Graham."

He chuckled. "I probably shouldn't get so worked up about it."

"That's the stereotype about redheads. The fiery temper."

"I've heard that one too, trust me."

"Don't get me wrong—personally I think it's kind of hot. A quick temper keeps things interesting."

"Man, you can really lay the mack down."

"I'm not funning, son. I wouldn't say no to a taste of all that."

Graham stared at him. "What is happening right now?"

"I'm flirting with you, dumbass." He put his hands on his hips. "Is there somewhere more private we can go? I can smoke you. You won't even have to drop trou."

"Who are you?"

"The name is Slater."

"And you're looking for Ben Clague."

"I'm working for Ben Clague."

"You're also wearing a ring on that finger."

Slater rubbed it absently with the tip of his thumb. "I have a hall pass."

The sex rules he'd agreed on with Pike said he could hook up with other people if he was out of town. Slater was the one who was out of town right now. He wasn't sure if that constituted a valid exemption or if he was bending the rules.

"We could do something in my car," Graham said.

"That sounds uncomfortable."

"There's an empty shipping container out back. It's not going to be very comfortable either."

"Let's do that."

He didn't move, and sat looking at Slater. "Things like this don't usually happen to me."

"It would if you wanted it to," Slater said. "You're a total smoke show." He whirled a finger in the air. "Let's roll."

Graham rose and led the way out the front entrance. The flatbed truck was gone now, the loading dock abandoned and the yard empty.

"What's your ride?" Slater said, pausing in front of the parked vehicles.

"Why?"

"I'm into cars."

"Is that antique yours?" Graham said, jutting his chin toward the Thunderbird. "I've never seen it here before."

"It's a '78." Slater frowned. "That's not old. It's classic."

He chuckled and pointed. "Mine is the fifteen-year-old Wrangler. It's too young to be a classic. It's just a hooptie."

"What about Cody—what does he drive?"

"The pickup." Graham gestured to it. "The white Silverado with the racing stripes."

"Sweet ride, but it's not a pickup. It's a sedan."

"It looks like a pickup to me."

"Pickups have one row of seats. That's a sedan with an open back."

"Who knew the definitions were so precise?" He gestured to the far side of the building, and Slater followed, walking abreast.

Between the main building and the fence, a narrow dirt driveway led to the back of the yard. It would have been more direct to walk on the other side, where the loading dock was. They walked all the way around the building, and Slater pulled out his phone to stop the audio recorder. He didn't need a record of what was about to go down.

The shipping container sat near the building with the arched roof. Its yellow paint job was powdery with age, and it bore rusty scratches and scuffs, a faded serial number stenciled on one of the doors. They hung partway open, and inside he could see it was empty, with a dusty board floor.

Graham scanned the yard before stepping into the container, then pulled the doors partly closed once Slater was inside. The narrow gap left enough daylight to see by. As Slater stepped over to him, Graham took a deep breath.

Slater massaged his biceps. "You seem nervous."

"I don't know you."

Leaning in, Slater met his mouth, warm and intense, and explored it. The guy was good at this, his lips firm and pliable, his tongue confident. He could feel his dick tightening in his jeans. After a minute he pulled back.

"So what's your sex thing?" Slater said.

"What do you mean?"

"The stuff that turns you on."

"I don't know."

"Yeah, you do. Everybody has a sex thing. I'm the guy you can tell it to."

Graham hesitated, absently caressing Slater's shoulder. "Can I kiss your fingers?"

"I'd be offended if you didn't."

He took Slater's palm, and kissed it, and with his eyes closed, mouthed his index finger, then his thumb. Slater left his fingers limp as Graham manipulated them. His mouth was wet, and he went at it methodically, until he had almost his whole hand in his mouth.

Watching him, it was kind of hot, and giving him serious wood. But more interesting was how into it he was. Eventually Graham dropped his hand, red-faced and breathing hard. He wrapped his arms around Slater's waist, grabbing his butt and pulling him close.

"You've got a stiffy," Slater said, and massaged his cock through his jeans. Unbuckling his belt, he zipped down Graham's fly, and pulled out his cock. He was rock hard. He dropped to his knees and started to smoke him. Graham put his hand on the back of his head, guiding him. For a guy who claimed he didn't get much action, he knew exactly what he was doing.

After a minute Graham pushed his head back, and Slater looked up.

"I'm close. Let me do you."

He sank to his knees, and Slater started to unbuckle his belt.

"Let me," Graham said, and took hold of the buckle, then pulled open his fly, popping the buttons one by one. Leaning in, he took Slater into his mouth.

Shifting onto his butt, Slater leaned back and closed his eyes. The guy was so intuitive at this. A moment later he climaxed, his body vibrating as he strained into him.

Sitting up, he turned Graham around, and pulled him close, one arm around his chest, reaching with the other to grab his cock. As he stroked him, Graham got into it, leaning back on him, his head on his shoulder. Slater could smell his sweaty hair.

With his free hand, Slater pressed a finger into his mouth, then another, probing his tongue. With that Graham came, and Slater held his fingers there for a moment longer, even though Graham had inadvertently chomped on one.

Pulling away, he stretched out on his back, catching his breath. He could hear Graham's heavy breathing slowing now too. He saw that he was sitting up, leaning back on his hands.

"So did you ever hook up with Ben?" Slater said.

"I never even considered it. I didn't know he was into guys. He was kind of quiet."

"There was a machinist here named Redge. What about him?"

"Redge Black." Graham chuckled. "I always thought

that was funny, that his name was two colors, like 'red black.'"

"Where does he work now?"

Graham's brow furrowed. "I don't know where Redge is."

Lying on his back, he worked to zip up his fly and buckle his belt. Slater did the same, then got up and brushed the dust off his jeans. Graham peered out between the doors for a moment, then stepped outside, and propped them in the same position they'd been in when they got here.

That was a sign of a stealthy person, the instinct to remember the placement, to leave no trace, even though it was unlikely anyone else would notice a detail like the position of the doors. Given the container's disuse, it could hardly matter. What did this guy have to hide?

"We have to walk around the far side again," Graham said.

"I get it. You don't want to walk past Layton's window with me."

He didn't respond to that.

"Give me your number," Slater said, pulling out his phone.

"You want to see me again?" Graham recited it as Slater thumb-typed it. "Text me your number too."

"Done." More like he might want to interrogate him again, but he wasn't going to say that.

When they got around to the office door, Graham smiled, blushing a little, before he went inside. "Bye, Slater."

From the trunk of the Thunderbird, Slater found one of his vehicle trackers, tucked down beside the spare tire. About the size of a thick cell phone, it had a hard black plastic case with magnetic ribs studding one side. He concealed it in the trunk because using it to track people was completely illegal. Finding the recessed power switch along the side, he clicked it on with a fingernail.

Slater bought all his illicit tech from his supplier, Svetlana, in Glendale. She built an array of surveillance gear, often clunky, but it always did what he needed it to. This tracker didn't use GPS, so it didn't need a view of the sky—it could go under the vehicle. It used local Wi-Fi and cell signals to calculate its location, and that meant it used a lot less power than sniffing out faint signals from space, so the battery would last for days.

He only had one of these with him. Graham's movements wouldn't likely be very informative, but Cody Layton's might be. Walking over to the Silverado, he scanned the yard to make sure he was alone, then crouched at the back tire on the driver's side. Reaching up into the wheel well, he ran the side of the device with the magnetic ribs over the surfaces. Eventually he felt a satisfying tug as it adhered to a piece of steel.

Rising, he looked around again, but there was nobody out here to see him. He walked back to the Thunderbird and climbed in, taking a breath. He wasn't even sure what he was looking for with these people. At least not yet.

———•———

It was a long drive back to civilization, on the freeway winding down through the Newhall Pass, and when he got in the Thunderbird, Slater played the recording he'd made of talking to Cody Layton and Patsy and Graham. A few times he paused it to thumb-type a note about the other employees Cody had mentioned, keeping one hand on the steering wheel, trying to keep his eyes on the road. Besides Redge Black, the guy had named Lunelle Archuleta.

Listening to it now, it felt like Layton hadn't wanted to tell him about her, and Slater had pushed him into it. The guy could have refused to give him the name, but Layton knew that would make him look cagey. In the recording he also discouraged Slater from looking for her. That meant he definitely had to track her down. Layton hadn't given him the shop foreman's surname either, but Graham had dropped that.

All three of them had told him a very similar story about Ben, even using the same words. That alone was suspicious. People usually remembered things different-ly, and had varying impressions, not uniform ones.

As he started the long descent on the freeway in the Newhall Pass, the brakes felt a little spongy. He'd no-ticed that in town a minute ago, that they were less tight than usual, and now it was getting worse. It felt like they weren't working quite right.

The slope got steeper, and Slater pressed hard on the brake pedal, but this time all the resistance was gone—his foot went right to the floor. The vehicle wasn't slow-ing down at all. He was coming up fast on the rear end of a Civic, and he swerved into the left lane in front of an-other car. It was so close that the driver honked at him.

His heart was pounding now as the car gradual-ly picked up speed. He tried to think rationally. If he turned off the engine, he'd lose the steering, and be in worse trouble. The gearshift wouldn't even budge going this fast.

Coming up on another car, he weaved right, then had to veer into the left lane again, and almost clipped a Prius. It was miles to the bottom of this hill, and he was only gaining speed. The Thunderbird was a two-ton missile, and eventually he was going to hit somebody.

There was no choice—he saw that now. He proba-bly wasn't going to survive this, in a classic car with no airbags or reinforced cage, but he didn't need to take anybody else out with him.

The left side of the road overlooked the oncoming freeway lanes a dozen feet lower down. No way was he going to cause carnage down there. On the right was the countryside, savanna carpeting the rolling hills. He couldn't see what was immediately past the outside lane, as the road was graded high, but he knew it was undeveloped.

Watching for a spot to go over, he waited until he passed a copse of trees along the roadside, then maneuvered to the right, dodging the slower vehicles. He kept one hand on the wheel and lay sideways across the front seat, then took hold of the passenger-side seatbelt, and held on tight. The front tires bit into the gravel beyond the edge of the pavement, and then it was quiet—he was airborne.

SEVEN

SLATER REALIZED THAT HE'D stopped moving. There had been a lot of noise but it was quiet now. Looking around, he saw that the roof was several inches lower than it should be, and the windshield was opaque. Shattered, he saw now, into a mosaic of cracked glass. Maybe he'd lost consciousness. At least he wasn't dead.

His shoulder hurt, and his hand had rope burn from hanging on to the seatbelt. He couldn't see his face—the rearview mirror was gone. Running his hands over his cheeks and his forehead, then pushing his fingers through his hair, he didn't find any blood.

The car was right-side up, he decided, as his thinking got clearer. He tried the door handle, and it moved, but it didn't do anything. Unbuckling his seatbelt, he reached for the passenger door, but its handle wasn't working either.

The right side of the windshield was sagging away from its frame, and he gingerly pulled at the edge of the glass. The whole thing fell inward on him, and once he'd shoved it aside, breaking the mosaic sheet into myriad smaller chunks, he pushed himself up, and climbed out onto the hood, then rolled onto the ground.

Slowly getting to his feet, Slater arched his back. It might be messed up, as it hurt when he stretched it. His whole body felt achy. Looking over the car, the roof was crushed, and every other part of it was mangled. The front end was suspiciously higher than the rest of the body. That meant the frame was bent. There was no coming back from this—it was totaled.

He stood there staring at it for a minute, listening to the rhythmic ticking of the engine parts cooling off. There was traffic noise too. Looking around, he saw that he'd landed on the grass a few feet from a road. It was paved, but narrow and unstriped, disappearing in both directions around curves in the hilly terrain. There were no structures in view. The Thunderbird had landed parallel to the pavement, almost like he'd pulled off the road onto the grassy verge.

The freeway was quite a ways away, and a little higher up. He could hear it but he couldn't see the vehicles. His trajectory from the roadway was visible in the dry yellow grass. That's where he'd gone off the road, and he hit the ground there, and then the car had climbed up to this place. The uphill path would have reduced its momentum. The car had obviously rolled over, but he couldn't see evidence of that in the grass, just that it was torn up in a wide swath.

He pulled his phone out of his jeans, glad that it was working, and called his mechanic, Duarte.

"Hey, *cabrón*," Duarte said when he answered. "Car trouble?"

"Big trouble. I totaled the Thunderbird. I need a tow, and another car. Do you have some time for me today?"

"Are you OK?"

"I think so. A little shaken up."

"Text me where you are," Duarte said. "We'll be there as soon as we can."

Once he'd sent the text, he tucked his phone away, and leaned on the mangled front fender, and folded his arms. What a freaking mess.

He stayed there for quite a while, waiting for Duarte, gazing absently at the grassy hillside, thinking it through.

He'd made the right choice, even though it was at the cost of his beautiful beloved Thunderbird. There hadn't been any other way.

A pickup came into view on the road, and as it approached it slowed down. The driver, a woman wearing a baseball cap, rolled down the window.

"Are you doing all right?"

"Just waiting on a tow truck."

She waved and drove off. Not far behind her was a motorcycle, and as it got closer, Slater saw that it was the CHP. He watched the guy park at the side of the road, a few yards behind the Thunderbird, and climb off the bike. He wore his uniform tight, revealing a little paunch. This guy was totally fuckable.

Once he'd pulled off his helmet, he came over to Slater.

"Is anyone else in the vehicle?" He stooped to peer inside the car.

Why would he ask that when he was checking for himself? But he couldn't snap back. He had to resist antagonizing this guy.

"It's just me," Slater said.

"Are you injured?"

"I'm not. Looking at this wreck, I can't quite believe it."

The guy met his gaze. "I didn't believe it when they said somebody went off the freeway. There was no sign of it up there. No skid marks. It took a minute to find you."

He'd been unconscious—it might have been longer than he thought. "I can't see the freeway from here, so you probably can't see the wreck from up there."

"What happened?"

Slater gestured helplessly. "I was headed southbound on the 14. I lost control of the vehicle. I think it rolled. I landed here."

"It rolled at least once, I'd say. Show me your license."

He dug it out and handed it over, and the cop gave it a cursory look, then met his gaze.

"When's the last time you had anything to drink?"

"Yesterday. I'm sober."

"What about cannabis? Are you on any medications?"

"Nothing like that."

He stepped closer. "Follow my finger." Holding a hand in front of his face, he moved it left and then right, peering at his eyes. Next he said, "Stand with your feet together, and close your eyes. Tell me when thirty seconds has passed."

Slater sighed but did as he was told, and counted in his head. He opened his eyes and said, "That's thirty seconds."

"OK." But from the look on his face, the cop wasn't completely convinced. He stepped away, and grabbed his radio from the front of his shirt, and started talking into it.

Another vehicle was approaching—Duarte's familiar tow truck. It was red and white with an amber light bar on the cab. He passed the motorcycle cop, and the Thunderbird, and pulled onto the grass at the side of the road. Rolling behind him was a cloudy-blue classic Lincoln Continental. That would be Vera, Duarte's wife. She was driving his loaner.

They got here fast—they must have dropped whatever they were doing. Slater knew he was a good customer. He'd given them a lot of business, spent a lot of dough on this car over the years.

Duarte climbed out of the cab and greeted him, then eyed the cop standing over by his bike. Lanky, Duarte was wearing cargo shorts and a Hawaiian shirt despite the season, his long black hair bound behind his head.

Once she'd parked the Continental a few yards past the tow truck, Vera stepped over to them. She was curvy, wearing tight jeans and a stretchy dark blouse, and had voluminous black hair and black eye makeup. The way Slater understood it, Duarte did the wrenching, and Vera handled the clients.

"You're not injured?" Vera said, her brow furrowing.

"I don't think so."

"Losing a classic car is like losing a family member." She briefly glanced at the wreck. "How are you feeling right now?"

"I'm not sure. A little scrambled."

"You're in shock. When the weight of this sinks in, I want you to call me. Later today, tonight, anytime. We can talk it through."

She was serious about that, he could tell. "I appreciate your compassion."

"So what happened?" Duarte said.

"I was coming back from Palmdale, and I got onto the downhill grade in the pass." He gestured toward the distant freeway. "It was the brakes. They totally failed. The pedal went right to the floor. No resistance at all."

Duarte frowned. "I know this rig. The brakes were in good shape."

"I can't explain it."

"I want to look at them. Is the cop going to take the vehicle?"

"I told him I lost control," Slater said. "I didn't say anything about the brakes. I don't think they'll bother to investigate, especially with your tow truck sitting here."

"Do you have any enemies in Palmdale?" Duarte said.

"You think it was sabotage?"

"I can find out. It's more likely than mechanical failure."

"Let me pay you now for the tow, and for the loaner. What do I owe you?"

"It's pretty far. Let's say six dollars."

"I can pay you for looking at the brakes too." Slater dug out his wad and peeled off the C-notes.

"I'm not sure how much work it'll be. I'll let you know."

The cop walked over and handed Slater his driver's license. "It's your lucky day."

"I would have to disagree."

"I can't hit you for speeding, even though the drivers who called it in said you were moving awfully fast. I was going to cite you for reckless driving, but I don't have my ticket book."

"So can I have the car towed?"

"Knock yourself out," he said, and walked back toward his bike.

"I'm going to hook it up before he changes his mind," Duarte said. "I'll take it to the shop."

"Should I clean out my stuff?"

"Not now," Vera said. "You've been through enough today."

"I'll get it all back to you." Duarte walked toward the tow truck.

"You shouldn't watch," Vera said. "It can be painful."

"You're so good at this. Like a concierge grief counselor."

She laughed. "I can be a hard-ass when I have to. That's not what you need right now. Listen, I want to introduce you to someone." She gestured for him to follow her, and they walked past the tow truck to the Continental.

"It's the Mark IV," Slater said. "It looks like a '73 or a '74."

"It's a '73." She met his gaze. "You know it has the same chassis as the Thunderbird, and the same engine."

"It looks longer, and wider. But I see it." He gestured

to the front end. "It has the same hidden headlights, and the opera windows."

"You'll find another ride. For now this baby should feel familiar. It'll take good care of you."

He looked back toward the wrecked Thunderbird. Duarte was backing his truck up to it.

"I should say good-bye."

Walking over, Slater put a palm on a mangled fender. "So long, old friend. You've done right by me. I'll never forget you."

Duarte stepped out of the tow truck's cab. "Do you have your keys?"

Once he'd handed them over, Vera gave him the keys to the Continental.

"You should head out now," she said. "Let us handle the rest."

Slater eyed the cop, still sitting on his bike and idly watching them. "Do you think he'll give you any trouble?"

"He's just waiting to make sure we clear the roadway," Duarte said. "Go on—I got you."

He took a breath. "You two are amazing. I'd be lost without you."

Climbing in behind the wheel of the Continental, he looked it over. The interior was dark red, with velvet seats. The steering wheel and the control panel were remarkably similar to the Thunderbird. He adjusted the mirrors and the seats and got comfortable.

When he started the engine, it sounded smooth and tight. Like everything Duarte did, it was as close to perfection as possible. He pulled onto the road, and tapped the brakes a few times, just to be sure. They felt solid and responsive.

Following the road down the hill, he found a freeway entrance, and hit the gas as he drove up the ramp. The big engine responded instantly, accelerating to match the speed of the traffic. He never got stressed out about driving, but he was feeling it right now, feeling unsettled, like it could all happen again. He took a few deep breaths to try to dispel it.

On the highway the Continental felt a lot like the Thunderbird. The steering handled the same. If anything, it was a little quieter.

Duarte kept the Thunderbird in top condition, he had no doubt about that. But sabotage seemed unlikely. If it happened in Palmdale, it would have been when he was inside talking to Cody or with Graham in that shipping container. That would have left plenty of time to mess with his brakes. Anyone working there would know which vehicle was his—it stood out. Graham had pegged it as his right away. But the only person there with a motive was that loudmouth idiot he'd scrapped with at the loading dock.

Maybe it was just a mechanical failure. The car was almost fifty years old. Duarte couldn't believe it because he didn't want to own it.

Once he was on the 5, he tried to shift his focus back to his case. Digging out his phone, he called Ben.

"We need to talk," Slater said when he picked up.

"Do you want to meet me at Miss Healthy Donut on Broadway?"

"There's nowhere to sit."

"The city put café tables outside on the street."

"OK," Slater said. "I'll be there in half an hour."

The freeway was still moving fast as he hit Burbank, and he tried to get comfortable cruising in the left lane. The Continental was smoother than the Thunderbird despite being older, maybe geared a little differently. His phone buzzed in its dash mount. The caller ID said REDDY KILOWATT.

"Hey, forty-niner," Pike said when he answered. "Sounds like you're on the road."

Slater considered telling him about the wreck, but he could do that later. Pike didn't need the stress. "Are you with Davis right now?"

"I'm in my office. Why would I be with Davis?"

"I'm pretty sure he's into you," Slater said. "I wondered if he was sniffing around."

"He's actually married. To a woman."

"That would make him even more desperate to get into your pants."

"You are so crazy," Pike said, his tone intent.

"I'm just putting it out there—he'd better keep his paws to himself."

"Back here on Planet Earth," Pike said, "I talked to Doris. She couldn't get us tickets for that dance performance, so I told her we'd see her tomorrow."

"That was tonight."

"You forgot."

"You know you don't have to hang out with her," Slater said.

"She invited us after I said it sounded interesting. She'd already bought tickets for her and Albert, but by the time she checked for us, it had sold out."

"Lo, once again god shows us his *rachmones*."

"It actually might have been fun. I can't quite figure out why she wants to see hip-hop dance anyway. That seems so far from her world."

"It's the teacher mind-set," Slater said. "Always ask questions, always expand your experiences. She says you have to keep learning or you atrophy."

"That is such a good attitude."

"I think it's more like a shark type thing. You have to keep swimming or you drown."

Pike laughed. "Doris is no shark."

Once he got downtown, he found a meter on Broadway. The Continental was about the same size as the Thunderbird, the steering and the mirrors familiar, so it was easy to back it into a parking spot. He walked up the block to Miss Healthy Donut and found Ben behind the counter with a staffer. The woman was in the shop's familiar uniform, but Ben was wearing a blue polo shirt that flattered his pecs, and smiled when Slater walked in.

"You look a little rattled."

"Car trouble," Slater said. "Do you work here?"

"I don't, but I'm married to the boss, so they let me hang out. It's worth it—I get free doughnuts."

"Hey, smoke 'em if you've got 'em." Slater dug out his wad of cash, and extracted a fin, and set it on the counter. "Give me a cruller."

"I can give you one on the house," Ben said.

"Put it in the tip jar, then."

The woman with him reached into the display case below the counter and pulled out a cruller, handing it to him in a little swatch of waxy paper. Ben lifted the gate in the counter to step out, then followed Slater out to the street.

Across the sidewalk sat a couple of metal tables protected from the traffic by heavy wooden planter boxes. This used to be a parking spot, Slater realized. They did a lot of this during the pandemic, creating outdoor spaces. He had to admit it made the street feel more livable, despite the graffitied steel shutters and the grime and the piss-stained sidewalk.

Once they were seated, Slater took a bite of his doughnut. "So what do engineers do?"

"All sorts of things," Ben said. "I'm an electrical engineer, so I design circuitry, electronic controllers, anything with wires or chips or circuit boards."

"That's what your old boss at Desert View Rocketry said."

Ben scowled and leaned toward him, raising his voice. "I never worked there."

"I met three people today who remember you well." He gestured with the doughnut. "I saw a photo of you with the staff."

"Bullshit."

Eating the last of the cruller, he wiped his fingers, then pulled out his phone, and found the photo. He turned the screen to Ben.

Peering at it, Ben's brow furrowed. "It definitely looks like me. That's how my hair was when I was in school. They must have lifted it from social media." He met Slater's gaze. "I've never seen those people before, and I never posed for that photo. It's a fake."

"That's what I figured. It also confirms that it's not an identity theft situation. No way would an identity thief also be your doppelgänger. Something else is going on."

"Did they show you the NDA?"

"Not yet."

Ben folded his arms. "So what's next?"

"I'm going to get a specialist to check into this photo, to see if he can detect that it's fake. And I'm going to get my hands on that NDA."

He sat back and sighed. "This whole things is so fucking weird."

"I hear you, brother."

Standing on the sidewalk nearby was a guy who'd caught Slater's attention—it felt like he was watching them. He wasn't sure at first if he was homeless, as he had a decent haircut and a reasonably clean jacket, but looking him over, the shoes were the giveaway—they were a tattered mess, one of them without laces.

The guy stepped closer to their table, and Slater

caught the unmistakable tang of homelessness, ammonia and vinegar and piss.

"Spread out," Slater said, eyeing him and jutting his chin.

"Can I borrow a dollar?"

"No," he said, raising his voice. "Beat it."

He took a step closer, right next to the table. "You don't own the streets."

Rising, Slater delivered a rapid kovac, slapping him right and then left, and shoved him back. The guy stumbled a few steps onto the sidewalk, startled and wide-eyed.

"You're a damn bully," he said, and turned to shuffle away.

"Keep walking," Slater said through his teeth.

Ben was on his feet now, his face contorted with alarm. "I can't believe you hit him."

"Too much for you, princess?" He turned to face him. "I thought I was the guy you needed. Someone who could handle the rough stuff."

"You can't just hit people."

Slater looked him up and down. "Nobody ever dared to take a swing at you, am I right? It's because you look like you can fight back. You're soft because you're big. That doesn't mean the real world doesn't exist. It just insulates you from it."

Not waiting for a reply, he strode away, back toward where he'd parked.

EIGHT

SLATER NEEDED TO TALK to Sybil too—he could walk to her place from here, and skip the slowing afternoon traffic that clogged the streets.

When he passed the Continental, he admired its smooth lines, and for a second it didn't click that this was his ride now. The Thunderbird was gone forever. That was just too much to comprehend. Maybe he really was in shock, like Vera said.

He walked the few blocks to Sybil's building, and rode the elevator up to 28, and knocked on the door. Sybil pulled it open and frowned at him. She was wearing a stretchy black athletic top and leggings, her hair bound tightly back, like she'd been at the gym. The top had a pink band across her chest, emphasizing her breasts.

"You should have called first," she said.

"I figured you live in your office. The odds were good you'd be here."

"I'm busy. What do you want?"

"An Italian soda water, if you have it, or a double espresso. With a twist of lemon peel."

Her eyes narrowed. "Are you kidding me?"

"You need to show me the signed copy of Ben's NDA. All I got from Desert View was the boilerplate draft version."

Sybil sighed and pulled open the door. "Come in."

He sat across from her as she stepped behind the desk, then spent a minute messing with some files on her desktop, moving them from one place to another before she sat.

Was she stalling to give herself time to think? That was never a good sign. You didn't have to think too hard to tell the truth, but lying took a lot of concentration and brain processing time to keep everything straight.

Finally she met his gaze. "I only saw the unsigned version too."

"So why did you believe Ben signed it when he said he didn't?"

"I spoke to Ben's HR contact at Ekragen. She said she had a signed copy of the document, and the signature matched the one on Ben's employment application."

"She wouldn't send you a copy? Isn't the paperwork kind of fundamental with you people?"

Sybil raised her eyebrows. "What people?"

He waved an arm. "Judicial system lowlifes. Prosecutors and judges and lawyers."

"The woman at Ekragen said it was my client's responsibility to keep copies of his own documents. I have to agree with her. I wouldn't distribute copies of a confidential document either." She shrugged. "I took her at her word, especially after Desert View told me the same thing."

"Could you get it with a subpoena?"

"Only if there was a court case filed. There's no reason to do that."

Slater watched her for a moment. "OK," he said, and rose to walk out.

"Oh, good-bye, then," she called after him.

Ignoring that, he walked back to the elevators. Where had the signed version of the NDA come from, and how had Ekragen obtained it when Desert View said it was buried in an archive? That might just be what Cody Layton told him. Or maybe Ben did sign the fricking document and he was playing them all. But it was interesting that nobody outside those two companies had seen the damn thing. It made him suspicious of Sybil too—if not her motives, then her skills at her job. O'Dowd said she was a lowlife. Maybe she was incompetent too.

He walked back to Broadway and to the cloud-blue Continental, climbing in behind the wheel. It felt familiar and new at the same time. Before he started the engine he pulled up Svetlana's app on his phone to check on the tracker he'd put on Cody Layton's Silverado. It was working, with the map showing a green circle with the vehicle's location. Zooming in, he saw it was still at the factory in Palmdale.

Nosing into the traffic, he drove to his house and pulled up to the garage. He didn't have his remote opener, he realized, and climbed out, and let himself in the front, and hit the button to roll up the garage door. When he hustled up the stairs, Pike was in the kitchen, his hands in a big aluminum mixing bowl on the counter. Stepping closer, he saw that it was full of little wrapped packages—candy bars, cookies, chewing gum.

"What's all this?" Slater said, embracing him.

"It's for Halloween. I'm trying to get a uniform blend of treats."

"Is that today? Isn't it bad luck to let children into your house?"

"I won't be inviting them in," Pike said. "I'm going to hang out in the garage and distribute the goods. There's a neighborhood list you can sign up for, so people know who's handing out candy."

"You already signed up, didn't you."

Pike chuckled. "I love Halloween."

"Are you going to dress up too?"

"I didn't have time to make that happen. Do you want to join me?"

"I should probably be around. Rugrats have sticky fingers."

"You're worried they might touch the Thunderbird? Or damage it by looking at it?"

"About that," Slater said, and leaned back on the counter. "The Thunderbird died today."

He explained what had happened, about the brakes failing, and flying off the freeway, and being rescued by Duarte and Vera.

Once he'd heard it all, and asked some questions, Pike stepped closer and cradled Slater's head in his hands. "You're sure you're OK?"

"Just some bruises. I got lucky today."

"I guess that's the downside of driving an old car. Like my mom's Crown Vic. They break down."

Slater kissed his neck, and met his mouth, and lingered in it for a minute. Eventually Pike pulled back.

"Candy time," he said. With the mixing bowl in hand, he led the way down to the garage.

"Whoa." Pike stopped to look over the car. "This looks a lot like the Thunderbird."

"It's a Continental. At the time it was the upscale model. The Thunderbird was the sporty one."

"I like the color."

"It's just a loaner." He hit the button to roll up the garage door and took the bowl while Pike went out to his SUV to grab a couple of lawn chairs.

The house had no front yard, as the blocky hulking structure had been built right to the sidewalk, and when they sat at the garage door, the street was just a few feet away.

Slater dug through the bowl and studied the wrappers of the various candy bars. "Some of these are vegan." He unwrapped one and took a bite.

"Those are for the children."

"This is my dinner," he said through a mouthful of dark chocolate. "It's actually really good."

"Damn it," Pike said, reaching into the bowl. "Now I want one."

A trio of children appeared on the street and approached them. One was dressed in green, like a turtle, and one as Spider-Man. The third was in pink with a blond wig. Pike got to his feet and greeted them loudly, then asked each one to explain their costume. A couple of parents hung back, beaming at the interaction. He gave each of them a big handful of candy, and they went on their way.

Dusk was setting in, and it was cooling off. A surprising number of costumed children were walking around, a group of them appearing every few minutes. Slater could see how into it Pike was, how much he enjoyed the kids. He felt a lump in his throat, for some reason, watching this guy interact with them, how animated he was, getting them to speak up, making them laugh.

As a group was walking away, Slater waved an arm. "That's like the tenth fricking Spider-Man."

"It's a mystery," Pike said. "You should ask one of the parents what's up with that."

A lone adult appeared on the street, hands in her jacket pockets, walking toward them. Slater recognized her—she lived across the street, but her porch was out of view from here, obscured by a hedge.

"I love that jacket," Pike said as she stepped up.

It was basic black nylon, Slater saw, looking it over. There was nothing to love about it. But that was Pike's way of connecting with people. He should probably be grateful that the guy did the work of interacting with the neighbors, rather than getting annoyed by it.

"Tilly, this is Slater," Pike said.

"Nice to meet you," she said, and smiled. "I see your

old car sometimes."

"It's actually a classic car. Or it was. I totaled it today."

"Ouch." Her brow furrowed, and she gestured to the Continental. "You seem to have replaced it quickly enough."

"That's a loaner."

"Have you shut down candy distribution for the evening?" Pike said.

"I think the kids are done. How many did you have?"

"I didn't count," he said, "but there were a lot."

"Where did you advertise this?" Slater said. "These half-pint chiselers are sucking us dry."

"He just wants the candy bars for himself," Pike said, eyeing Tilly.

She laughed, and chatted with Pike for a minute, then looked down the street.

"There's no more kids around," she said. "I think that's a wrap for me."

"We can shut it down too," Pike said as she walked away.

They folded the lawn chairs and waited for the garage door to roll down.

Pike carried the much depleted bowl up to the kitchen, and Slater leaned back on the counter, drawing him close with his hands on his waist.

Pike mouthed his neck. "Better than chocolate," he murmured, then pulled back.

"You're good with kids."

"They're fun."

Slater met his gaze. "Do you want to have your own?"

His eyebrows shot up. "Is that an offer?"

"It's impossible. I'd break them. Ruin them. You know that. They'd all turn out to be jailbirds."

"I know that's not true." Leaning in, he met Slater's mouth, exploring it for a minute. "Do you want to read to me? My vision has gone blurry from all the high-fructose corn syrup."

"There's nothing on this earth I'd rather do. As long as I'm in your arms."

They went to the sofa, and Slater pulled off his boots and socks, and put his feet on the fake grass. Pike leaned back on him, resting his head on his chest.

"Where were we?"

Slater shifted to get comfortable and flipped open the book. "Odysseus got washed up on the island of the Phaeacians. After they all had dinner, the blind singer tells the story of the Trojan Horse. Odysseus totally breaks down and reveals his true identity."

"I remember. For a war hero, he's a pretty emotional guy."

"You'd be an emotional wreck too if you weren't able to make it home for ten years. He's actually smart to express it. You have to feel it to heal it."

Pike chuckled. "Did you read that on a cereal box?"

"Those are the words of one of the many shrinks Doris sent me to in my youth."

"I'm glad some of it stuck."

"I don't think it did. I just learned to parrot the key points from one shrink to the next. It seemed to keep them off my back."

"On that theme," Pike said, "do you need to talk about the Thunderbird?"

"I don't think it's sunk in yet. I'm just kind of numb."

He reached up to put a hand on the back of Slater's neck. "Whatever you need."

Flipping open the book, Slater found the page and started to read: "His hosts and their dinner guests listened with rapt attention as Odysseus recounted how storms had blown his ships off course after he left Troy …"

Eventually his eyes were getting heavy, his throat dry,

and he set the book down, and caressed Pike's chest.

Pike stirred awake. "I got something today. I think you're going to like it."

"What? Spill it."

"Some baseball stuff."

"The pants?"

"Among other things."

"You know what I like," Slater said. "You have to put them on. Like, now."

He sat up. "You're not too tired?"

"Not for baseball pants."

"Give me a couple minutes," he said, and pushed himself up off the sofa.

Slater heard him trot down the stairs. Just thinking about it was making him chubby, and he adjusted his dick in his jeans. Setting the book on the coffee table, he rose and headed down to the bedroom.

He found Pike wearing the ball cap and the jersey he'd worn to the game, plus the pants to match. He had a band of black under each eye. Slater stood in the bedroom doorway to take it in.

"You're so fucking beautiful."

"You like?"

"Those pants are pretty damn tight."

Pike jutted his chin. "You want to make something of it?"

Stepping closer, Slater grabbed his ass, and pulled him close, running his hands over his back. As he pressed their mouths together he inadvertently knocked his cap off. Pike unbuckled Slater's belt and pulled his fly open. Slater pushed him back onto the bed, then pulled off his shirt and shoved down his jeans, stepping out of them.

Pike leaned back on his elbows, grinning as he watched him undress. Climbing up to straddle him, Slater grabbed the back of his head and ground his cock into his face. Pike took him into his mouth and worked him for a moment.

Moving off, Slater lay on his side. "Come here."

As Pike stretched out, Slater ran a hand over his legs and squeezed his cock. He unzipped the baseball pants and reached inside.

"What's this?"

Pike folded his arms behind his head. "What does it look like?"

He quickly unhooked the fly. Pike was wearing a jock-strap.

"Oh, man. Why do you do this to me?" He yanked the pants down, and massaged his junk through the fabric, and mouthed his neck and his jaw, inhaling the heady scent of his hair.

Sitting up, Slater unbuttoned Pike's shirt, and straddled him, and mouthed his chest and his belly. Pike reached for his cock.

"You're hard. You need to fuck me."

Slater rolled to the side table to get the lube, massaging it between his legs. Pushing his knees up, he moved in and gradually penetrated him. The black under Pike's eyes was smudged all over his face. He winced as Slater pushed harder, starting slow, eventually working up to pounding him. With his arms under Pike's shoulders, he pulled their bodies tight together.

Pike spoke softly in his ear. "Is that all you got?"

He pounded harder, and then climaxed, burying his nose in Pike's hair.

Once his breathing had slowed, he rolled onto his side. Pike's cock was distorting the fabric of the jockstrap, and he pulled it out.

"I'm close," Pike said. "Want to blow me?"

Shifting position, Slater took him into his mouth and worked him. Pike ran his fingers into his hair, guiding him, and a moment later he came, his body shuddering.

Slater moved up beside him and shoved an arm under Pike's neck, relishing the proximity, the feeling of his skin, the heat of his body.

"Why do you do this to me?" Slater said. "Why do you make me feel like this?"

"I got eye-black all over your face."

"It's all over your face too. You look like a gilded-age chimney sweep."

"Right now I'm the happiest chimney sweep in town."

NINE

W AKING IN BED, SLATER squinted at the bright sunlight streaming in the sheers. Pike was already gone, and he grabbed his phone and checked the tracker on Layton's car. It was parked at Desert View. Looking through the event history, last night the marker had moved a few miles into a residential neighborhood. That must be where he lived. This morning it returned to the factory. That wasn't really informative.

Duarte had texted:

I've got your stuff from the T-Bird. I'm downtown later. Can I drop it at your office?

Slater wrote back:

I'll be there today.

Next he sent Andy a text:

Are you at your place? I have work for you.

Forcing himself out of bed, he showered and pulled on a clean pair of jeans and a tan linen shirt. He was upstairs slurping on coffee and munching a bagel when he got Andy's reply:

I'm working today. You can stop in.

"Idiot," he muttered.

The tone of it grated, like Andy was gatekeeping

91

him, granting permission. That's just the way it was with him now, and there was nothing he could do about it. "Healthy boundaries," the junkies in Andy's twelve-step group had called it.

Trotting down to the garage, he drove to Broadway, and parked the Continental in the surface lot behind Andy's building. He walked around to the entrance and went up to Andy's loft. When he pulled open the door, Andy was dressed in boxers and a white tank top, and he flashed that easy smile. Even so lightly dressed, he kept the place cold because his CP made his metabolism run hot.

It was mostly one big room, with tall windows overlooking the square, and ancient board floors from when it was a textile warehouse, updated with a coat of hard resin. He followed him in and waited as Andy got settled in his big gaming chair. He claimed he spent so much time in front of his screens that he needed the comfort of it.

"It was weird to see you in Kyle's lair," Slater said.

"Most people just call it his … apartment."

"It's so sterile and icy, though. Like a Scandinavian serial killer did the decorating. It felt like you were trapped. Like you were a hostage with Stockholm syndrome."

Andy scoffed. "Kyle and I have a partnership. He's not … controlling me."

"Do you sleep over there every night now?"

"We usually sleep together, either … here or over there."

"If you decide you need to escape the situation, remember that I can help." Slater held his gaze. "I'm just a phone call away. You can use a code word—let's say 'Stockholm.' If I hear that, I'll come and extract you, no questions asked."

"You are such an asshole."

"And if Kyle ever needs to learn a lesson, I'm the guy." He swung a fist in the air. "*Bam.*"

"You never loved me, Slater. Not … really. You have no reason to be … jealous of Kyle."

He could feel his heart start to pound. "We had a groove, you and me."

"I want love in my life. Not just sex."

"It was pretty great sex."

"Yeah, I remember." Andy looked him up and down. "White hot."

Slater put his hands on his hips. "Kyle must be a cold fish, huh. Does he just lie there like a frat boy and make you do everything?"

"Stop talking about him. You only love … the type of guys who can throw you in jail. Conrad the cop, and now … Pike the G-man."

Watching him, Slater thought about it. "Fuck that."

"Slater, focus—what do you … need from me?"

He huffed and pulled out his phone, then sent him the group photo from Desert View and the close-up of Ben.

"I want you to look at a couple of pictures. I just shared them."

Andy swiveled to his array of screens and pulled on his black plastic gauntlets. An input device for his computer, they somehow compensated for his lack of fine motor control. Soon he'd pulled up the images.

"I recognize Ben," Andy said. "Are these people from the … company he didn't work for?"

"It's called Desert View Rocketry. In Palmdale. I already know the guy on the left, Cody. He's the boss. Can you use facial recognition to identify the others?"

Andy resized the photo and zoomed in. "They were working on an airplane?"

"It's a drone, I was told."

"Is it weird that they're all ... white folks, except for Ben? And there's ... only one woman."

"It's hard to say. Here it would be odd, but once you leave civilization, the rules are different."

"I can't believe in Palmdale it's ... still 1952," Andy said.

"Can you also check for signs of forgery? Maybe somebody glued Ben's head in there."

"I'll run it through some software. It would have been ... better to get the original."

"Well, this is what I got."

"It seems pretty damning," Andy said, swiveling to face him. "Ben standing there with ... people he says he's never met. Does it make it harder to ... believe him?"

"He's paying me to act like I believe him. I'm not even sure his lawyer believes him."

"Seriously?" He frowned. "I thought she'd be on his side. They're ... old friends."

"Like school friends?"

"I think they lived together, if I'm ... remembering it right."

"I wonder why nobody told me that," Slater said. "I talked to them both at length."

"Does it matter?"

"I'm the one who gets to decide what matters. Not the lowlifes."

"Ben's not a lowlife."

"Maybe, maybe not. One other thing—there's a film producer mixed up with these people. A guy named Dragan. Can you look into him?"

"Text me the name," Andy said. "I have some time to ... work on it today."

"Good answer." He held his gaze for a moment. "Bye, beautiful."

Walking out to the street, he phoned Nathan, glad that he picked up.

"We need to talk," Slater said.

"About what?"

"I'll tell you when I see you."

It took longer to meet people in person, but he needed to see how they reacted to questions, to new information. It wasn't always easy to tell when they were lying, but he got a lot more information face-to-face.

"I'm at the Broadway store," Nathan said.

"Man, I was just in there."

"Well, I'm working. I can't really take off."

"Fine," Slater said, and ended the call.

He nosed the Continental out of the parking lot, and drove the few blocks to Miss Healthy Donut, and found a space at a meter. When he walked in, the same uniformed staffer was behind the counter as yesterday.

"Where's Nathan?" he said, eyeing her.

As she stepped over to the door into the back, a couple of customers walked in, and came over to the counter, and peered into the doughnut case. A moment later Nathan appeared and flashed a smile at the sight of him. Eyeing the customers, he lifted the gate in the counter and waved him in.

"We can talk privately back here."

The back room was a narrow office with a computer and paperwork piled on a little desk. Farther back were a couple of lockers and a sink. Ben took the desk chair and gestured to the folding chair against the wall, and they sat with their knees almost touching.

"There's not a lot of room back here," Slater said. "Where do you make the doughnuts?"

"Reseda. We truck them in every morning. So what's going on?"

"Ben and Sybil. What's the history there?"

His eyebrows shot up. "They're old friends. They used to live together."

"Romantic friends, or sex friends, or just roommates?"

Nathan looked away. "They were in a relationship."

"So Ben is bi, or he hadn't come out yet when he was with her?"

"Officially he's bi." He sighed. "That always rubbed me the wrong way. Made him feel less trustworthy."

Slater frowned. "Why? He's either committed to you or he's not, regardless of what puts lead in his pencil."

"It doubles the number of people who could lure him away from me."

"Do you think that's likely?"

He laughed. "We're solid. It's not an issue. Just my irrational thinking."

"He'd be foolish to walk out on all the gravy," Slater said.

"What gravy?"

"You. You're a man who runs a profitable business. You're his meal ticket. He's unemployed."

Nathan shook his head. "It's not like that. We're in it for the long haul. He's going to be working soon enough, and he'll probably earn more than I do. It's what couples do. Share the burden."

Slater rose. "Two years without a job. You're a patient man."

Following him into the store, Nathan stood behind the counter.

"I'm not going to let you leave empty-handed. Pick a doughnut."

He looked into the case below the counter. "Why don't you pick for me?"

With a little sheet of waxy paper, Nathan grabbed a sugary brown ball and handed it to him.

"Thanks," Slater said, gesturing with it, and walked out to the street.

His phone had buzzed in his pants a minute ago, and he pulled it out with his free hand to check. It was a notification from Svetlana's tracking app—a proximity alert. It meant one of his vehicle trackers was close to his current location.

The only tracker he was running right now was on Cody Layton's Silverado. It was interesting that he'd left Palmdale and come way down here, the densest part of the city. Pausing on the sidewalk, he looked at the screen and watched the green dot reposition itself. It really was just a block away, and getting closer. He could walk there.

As he set off, he took a bite of the doughnut, then another, savoring the oily sweetness. It was overstuffed with strawberry jam, and as he took another bite, a big blob of it dropped onto his shirt, dripping down his right pec.

"Damn it," he snapped. Of course this would happen when he was wearing a light-colored shirt. Leaning forward to take another bite, he stopped at a trash can and tossed what was left of the doughnut. Leaning over the can, he wiped the jam off his shirt with the little piece of waxy paper. It left a wide dark-red stain from his pec almost to his navel.

Looking at the screen again, Layton's vehicle hadn't moved. It was just a block away. As he watched, the green dot went gray—the app had lost its signal. In this neighborhood, that meant he'd gone into an underground parking garage. The device reported its position via the cell network, and those signals faded underground.

If he could get eyes on him before he got out of that parking garage, he could follow Layton on foot. Jogging up the street, he dodged around the pedestrians. When he rounded the corner, he recognized the parking lot—he knew where the street entrance was. He was almost on it when the door swung open and a familiar person stepped out, dressed in a blue jacket and dark pants. That helmet of hair—Patsy, Desert View's HR person.

Slater slowed to a walk as he watched Patsy pause on the sidewalk. Her head swiveled as she scanned the street, likely getting her bearings after emerging from underground, then set off in the opposite direction. She'd glanced toward where he was loitering, but she hadn't spotted him. It looked like she was alone. Why was she driving Cody's rig?

He waited until Patsy turned the next corner, then hustled to follow her. When he was almost at the corner, a uniformed cop stepped in front of him. He had that dumb cop haircut, and his torso was inflated by a ballistic vest, but he was basically fuckable.

"Sir, hold up."

Slater couldn't dodge him—the guy had his arm out, and he was looking right at him. Another uniform stood a little behind him and to the side, her hair pulled tightly back. They looked dead serious, and they were focused on him.

"I'm in a rush," Slater said, and stopped on the sidewalk, scowling at him.

"Do you need medical assistance?"

"Why would I need that?" he demanded.

"Someone called in a shooting. They said the victim was running up Broadway."

"It's not me."

He gestured to Slater's shirt. "That bloodstain says otherwise."

"It's strawberry jam. I was eating a doughnut."

The other cop spoke up. "It looks like blood to me."

"Listen," Slater said, "am I being detained?"

"I'm going to call the paramedics," the guy said, "and

get that wound attended to."

He growled in frustration and quickly unbuttoned his shirt, then yanked it open, exposing his bare chest. "No bullet holes, see? It's strawberry freaking jam. Smell it."

The guy wrinkled his nose. "No thanks."

Slater eyed the other cop. "You—come here. Smell it. It's jam."

"I'm not going to smell your shirt, you weirdo."

"Did you witness the shooting?" the first cop said.

"I didn't see anything like that," Slater said, raising his voice.

He frowned. "All right, then. On your way."

Slater scoffed and buttoned his shirt as he strode away, rounding the corner. They'd delayed him too long—Patsy was nowhere in sight. He walked to the end of the block, scanning the doorways and shop windows, but there was no sign of her. After a few minutes he gave up and walked back toward his ride.

It probably wasn't significant anyway. Most likely Patsy was going to the bank or buying clothes or meeting some idiot for lunch. It would be meaningful if she'd gone to one of Ekragen's buildings out by the airport.

A thought struck him, and he paused on the sidewalk to look at his phone. But he was wrong—there was no listing for any Ekragen office downtown.

TEN

CLIMBING INTO THE CONTINENTAL, Slater drove to the Fashion District and parked across from his building. Upstairs he went into the restroom to wash the jam off his hands. When he unlocked his office, he flicked on the lights and double-clicked his tongue to greet Rey Pascual.

Max's office had a small wardrobe, and Max had convinced him to put a change of clothes in it, on a hanger next to his own. This was the first time he'd actually needed it. Pulling open the door, he found the clean shirt and changed into it.

Once he was at his own desk, he heaved his boots up onto the blotter and pulled his keyboard into his lap. A search for Redge Black was fruitless—there were just too many Reginald Blacks in this part of the world. The other name from Desert View was easier to track down. Not many people had a handle like Lunelle Archuleta.

Slater found several mentions of her working at a company in Santa Fe, and when he looked it up, the website described it as a purveyor of modern lighting design, "creating upscale bespoke fixtures." It sounded like they were decorators, not engineers. The pay couldn't be anywhere near as lucrative. What would drive Lunelle from building missile components to wiring chandeliers for rich idiots?

The company's site had a staff directory with the names of employees and their photos and office phone numbers. That was so small-town, putting it all out there.

In her portrait, Lunelle had short blond hair with dark roots, and a round face, and a smile with dimples. Her hair was different, but this was definitely the woman in the group portrait with Cody and Ben and the drone. He dialed her office number, surprised that she answered: "Lunelle."

Slater sat up. "My name is Ibáñez. I'm an insurance investigator. I have a few questions for you."

"I thought that was all done with," she said, her tone sharp. "The body shop fixed the quarter panel. You can't even tell it was ever damaged."

"That's not why I'm calling you."

"Listen—I can't really talk. I'm on a deadline. Can I come to your office?"

"That's not going to work."

"I can meet you anywhere near my office, then," she said. "It's right by the plaza. Are you around after six today?"

"I can't do it today. Can you give me your cell number? We'll set up something later this week."

"You sound like a busy man." She rattled off her number. "What was your name again?"

"Ibáñez," he said, and spelled it, then ended the call.

He wasn't even sure he'd follow up with her—it was a hell of a long way to go to interview a witness. But Layton had told him not to bother with her, which meant that he really should.

There was a knock at the door, and when he got up to pull it open, he found Duarte standing there with a grocery bag in hand. Cracking a smile, he handed it to him.

"It's mostly just paperwork and junk."

"I definitely need the garage door opener," Slater said, "and the parking pass."

"How's the Continental behaving?"

"I kind of love it. It already feels like an old friend. Any chance you'd sell it to me?"

He raised his eyebrows. "For the right price."

"What would that be?"

"You're a good customer, Ibáñez. I could let you have it for thirty."

"That seems reasonable for what it is. Let me think about it."

Once Duarte had gone, he settled into his desk again and did a search for Dragan, Sybil's shady client. Andy would find out more, but he wanted to see what was out there about him that was easily accessible. He had a business-card website that mentioned several upcoming projects, with links to flashy video clips. They looked like low-budget slasher movies. None of them showed a release date or a production timeline, just "upcoming."

Pushing his keyboard aside, Slater sat back. O'Dowd said Dragan used commercial real estate to launder his card room earnings. He knew someone in that business. They'd only met once, and it hadn't been an amicable meeting—the guy had actually punched him in the face. But it was worth a shot.

Once he locked up the office, he went down to the parking lot and drove to Koreatown, nosing the Continental into a meter space near Goh's office building. He was taking a chance that the guy would be in, but then Goh would never agree to a meeting if he called first.

Unusual in this dense neighborhood, the office tower was set back from the street, behind a sprawling green lawn. That was really irresponsible nowadays, maintaining all that water-hungry turf. Along the sidewalk were mature ginkgos, their leaves still on the trees but bright yellow for fall. Walking under them, he looked up through the golden canopy at the deep-blue sky and the mottled sunlight filtering through.

The security guard glanced up at him as he walked past the desk in the lobby, but they usually didn't hassle people during office hours. He checked the directory next to the elevators for the suite number, then rode up to Goh's office.

He knocked and tried the door, then stepped into the front office. It was roomy, with basic lounge chairs, and behind the reception desk was a woman with long black hair. She looked up as he walked in.

"If it's a delivery, you can just leave it inside the door."

"I'm not the help, toots. I want to talk to Goh."

She frowned. "Can I take your name?"

"Ibáñez."

Picking up the desk phone, she murmured into it, then looked up at him. "What is this regarding?"

"Real estate," he said flatly. "Goh will remember me. We met a while back."

As she spoke into the phone again, he realized the reason he couldn't understand her wasn't that she was mumbling but because she wasn't speaking English. Most likely it was Korean.

She set the phone down, and a moment later the door to the inner office swung open. Goh was lanky and fit, in his forties maybe, with his black hair slicked back in a neat mass. His luxy gray suit looked tailored, and the chunky wristwatch said he was a high roller, or aspired to be.

Goh's face clouded. "I actually do remember you. What do you want?"

"A minute of your time."

"Are you selling bibles or something?"

"I have a real estate question."

Goh frowned, and hesitated, but Slater could see the curiosity in his eyes. Finally he said, "Come in."

It was a corner office with tall windows on two sides

onto a dramatic view of the hills, the eastern part of Hollywood, and the towers on Bunker Hill. A conference table sat at one end of the room, and at an angle near the windows was a big desk.

"You've got a million-dollar view here," Slater said.

"It doesn't cost quite that much." Goh dropped into a lounge chair and waved at the others.

"When I was here before," Slater said as he sat down, "you used a hapkido move on me. I didn't know what hit me."

"As I remember it, you'd forgotten your manners."

"I do that sometimes."

Goh waved a hand. "What do you want?"

"A lawyer named Sybil Álvarez works for a film industry guy named Dragan. They do business with commercial real estate companies. Do you know either one of them?"

"Why are you asking?"

"I'm investigating one of her other clients. I get the sense that Sybil is shady as fuck."

"I know who she is," Goh said. "I'm not going to tell you more than that."

"Well, I've been told Dragan uses these real estate companies to launder his illegal income. Have you heard that before?"

He sat forward. "Whether I've heard that or not, I can't gossip about other people in my business. I will tell you this. She's not someone you can trust."

"You mean don't trust her to file court paperwork accurately, or don't trust what she says?"

"All of that and more. It's all poison under the gravy, Ibáñez. I wouldn't turn my back on her for a hot minute. You'll find a knife in it."

"Interesting."

Goh rose. "Listen—I'm a busy man."

"Thanks for your time," Slater said, rising with him, and walked out.

In the elevator on the way down, he checked his phone and found a message from Andy:

Got some stuff.

He drove back to Broadway and found a meter around the corner from Andy's building. When he got up to Andy's loft, he pulled open the door, and Slater followed him in, admiring his sinewy musculature.

"It was a wise decision to prioritize my ask," Slater said.

He dropped into his desk chair. "Just because it doesn't take long doesn't mean … it's going to be cheap."

"What have you got?"

"First, Dragan. It seems like he's a wannabe in the … entertainment industry. He hasn't achieved much, but he splashes … money around. He works to keep his name in the … trade papers. The guy should be charged with a felony for … the look he's working."

"You mean his clothes?"

"Have you not seen pictures of him?" Andy swiveled to his computer and pulled on his gauntlets, then pulled up a photo. "That's him."

Slater leaned in to peer at the screen. It was a red-carpet photo from some event. There were a dozen of these every week in this town, and the photos always looked the same, taken out front in the photo area with a literally red carpet in front of a white wall of corporate sponsor logos.

In the image Dragan stood with a woman in a slinky dress and lots of dark hair. She was smiling, but Dragan wasn't. His head was shaved, and he wore dark sunglasses, with a shiny silver lamé jacket and no shirt under it, exposing his hairy chest and the top of his belly. Several thick chains hung around his neck, along with a bulky gold medallion.

"The other men at this event were in … black tie," Andy said, clicking through a series of photos. "Dragan really stands out."

"He's definitely working a look."

"I'd call it Eurotrash meets … South Beach. When I saw him I had this … nagging urge to alert Interpol."

"Is he actually European?"

"He is. Here's a photo of him at a fund raiser when the … industry guilds were on strike."

In this image Dragan was wearing a skin-tight gold top and baggy purple-red trousers, with the same dark sunglasses, standing in a small group. Other people were in casual wear, polo shirts and T-shirts and jeans.

"His lawyer kind of dresses like that too," Slater said. "The shiny fabrics."

"You need a certain kind of body to … pull off that shirt. I don't think he's got it."

"It's not bad, though. He's chunky, but it actually looks good on him."

"But that shirt. It says ecstasy-fueled … dance party on Ibiza."

"There's magic in satin and lamé—you can see his nipples." Slater stood erect. "It's borderline, but I'd fuck him."

"I wouldn't call that a particularly … high bar," Andy said. "I guess half of it is … confidence, and he has that."

"You said he hasn't achieved much. I thought he hadn't done anything at all in the entertainment industry."

"Not the movies he's hawking, but he's producing … reality TV. Do you know that show *Snap Out of It?*"

"What the hell is that?"

"It's where people's houses are full of junk," Andy

said, "and they ... send a shrink and a cleaning crew to make you ... smarten up. Like an intervention for people who can't ... take out the garbage. It's actually filming right now."

"Do you know where?"

"I saw it in the trades. Let me check." He clicked around for a minute, then spoke. "They're working in Mid City this week. I'll text you ... the schedule. It has the times and locations."

He felt his phone buzz in his pants. "Got it."

"Next, your drone photo. The facial recognition site identified ... one other person in the group. He shows up in a ... social media image. He didn't post it himself, but someone else ... labeled him Reggie Black."

"That must be Redge Black," Slater said. "He worked at Desert View as a machinist."

Leaning in, he studied the image. The guy was standing behind a bar, grinning, wearing a straw fedora with a narrow brim set back on his head. Two young women sitting at the bar were holding beer glasses, posing for the camera and smiling.

"If he's behind the bar, it means he works there," Slater said.

"That sounds like a logical conclusion."

"This dude has a beard. In the drone photo he's clean-shaven. We're sure it's the same person?"

"Bearded or not, the software can still ... figure it out. It's way more accurate than the ... human eye. And the name is so close." Andy turned to meet his gaze. "This is your guy."

"I figured out who the woman is, but you can't identify the other guy?"

"Those two are in the shadow of the ... airplane. Redge and the boss on the left are clearer because they're ... in the sunlight. Plus there's reflection from the overhead light in … the room when you took the photo. It's possible those two aren't even real. They might be … AI-generated scalies. I'm still working on … whether the part with Ben has been manipulated."

"The fuck are scalies?" Slater demanded.

"Images of fake people. Designers put them in … architectural renderings to show the scale. You've seen them: fake people walking around … in front of buildings that haven't been built, or standing on … metro platforms that don't exist yet."

"What bar is this that Redge is in?"

"I'm not sure. There was nothing to identify it in the photo or … in the context. But I looked up Reggie Black."

"I tried that. There's dozens of them."

"There's only one who's white and fits … this guy's age," Andy said. "I found his address. He lives in Westlake."

"My old hood. That's easy. Text me the address."

"You're welcome."

Slater walked out and went down to the Continental. Checking his phone, he put the address Andy had sent into the navigation app. It directed him across the chasm of the 110 freeway into gritty Westlake, and he soon pulled up on Reggie's apartment.

There were lots of tired old buildings in this dense neighborhood, but this one had a new facade of trendy faux stone. Doing that to an old apartment building wasn't like renovating it. It was more like those elderly guys in Beverly who wore a jet-black toupee, or their wives with the cosmetic surgery. The building was still old once you looked past the facade, but now the owner could list it as "recently updated."

It would really suck if this hood was gentrifying, he thought, climbing out of the Continental. This was one of the few central places that newcomers could still afford.

Inside the front entrance, a letter carrier had the array of mailboxes pulled open, and stood there sorting the mail. Slater pulled on the door handle, finding it locked, then rapped on the glass with a knuckle. The woman frowned but pressed the latch to let him in, then went back to her task.

Slater trotted up to the second floor and knocked on Reggie's door, painted bright orange like all the others in another attempt to update the place. He listened, but no sound of movement came from inside. He pounded a few times with his fist to be sure.

As he stood listening, his ear close to the peephole, the door to the next apartment swung open, and a woman stepped out. Scrawny and bleary-eyed, she was wearing a sweatshirt and stretchy leggings, her hair tied back. A junkie, maybe, but she didn't look high right now.

"Can I help you?"

"I doubt it," Slater said, looking her over.

"What's all the banging?"

"I'm looking for Reggie."

"He's probably at work."

"Where does he work?"

Her brow furrowed. "Who's asking?"

"I'm an old friend."

"His friends would know where he works."

He dug in his front pocket. "Maybe you could explain it to my friend President Jackson." Briefly flashing a twenty, he palmed it, then extended his hand.

Not looking at it, she deftly retrieved it from his grasp, and it disappeared into her pocket.

"Reggie works at the bar in that deli on Melrose."

Slater waved an arm. "How hard was that?"

"Are you going to break his legs?"

"I said I was an old friend, not a gangster."

He turned away, and walked to the stairs, and out to the street. Interesting that she'd sold Reggie out for twenty bucks even though she thought Slater was going to mess him up.

Glancing at his phone, he checked the time. He needed to figure out Santa Fe. It was a steep hill to climb, going to another damn state, and it might not even be worth it. But maybe he could simplify the journey.

Once he was behind the wheel of the Continental, he found the number for the stable along the river in Downey, and called the front office.

"Is Big Mike there today?" Slater said when a woman's voice answered.

"He's riding right now. Can I take a message?"

"No need."

Ending the call, he started the engine and got on the freeway, headed south toward Downey.

ELEVEN

T RAFFIC WAS SLUGGISH, BUT before long Slater pulled up at the stable. It was clean and modern, with fresh blacktop and bright white lines delineating the parking stalls.

Farther up the river were the stables run by working-class guys from Durango and Zacatecas. The only thing they had in common with this shiny Waspy place was the horses—those guys wore jeans and cowboy hats, the parking lot was dirt, and the structures were ramshackle open framing and sheets of corrugated metal. This place could be a beach hotel in Maui.

As he walked into the main building, a woman behind the reception desk greeted him. She was clad in a checked western shirt with a little gold name plate.

"I'm looking for Big Mike," Slater said.

"I think he's in the tack room. He'll be out soon."

Slater walked away, and stood at the big windows with a view onto the show ring. He stepped outside to look it over. It had been used today, as there were lots of hoofprints, but nobody was using it now. The building beyond it, painted barn red, had a wide open aisle with stalls on both sides. Walking in, he picked up the familiar heady scent of straw and sweat and horse manure.

From one of the stalls a horse stuck its head over the gate. Slater stepped over. With a gray coat and a black mane, it was fully grown but still young. A filly, he saw, looking for its junk.

"Hey, girl," he said, and rubbed her nose.

The horse let him touch her, then batted Slater's shoulder with her muzzle. That made him chuckle, and he scratched her neck with his fingertips.

Reaching for the latch on the stall door, the horse mouthed it and then eyed him.

"You want out, huh? I wish I could do that. Unfortunately that would bring a world of hurt down on both of us."

As Slater scratched her vigorously under the chin, she stretched her neck out, seemingly enjoying it. From the direction of the show ring he spotted Big Mike walking toward him.

Mike wore his short graying hair in a side part, and today was clad in a white shirt and tan jodhpurs with English riding boots. Horses didn't care whether you dressed like the vaqueros up the river, or a polo player, or a dressage competitor. This outfit just made Mike look pretentious.

"It's the slappy gardener," Mike said as he stepped up.

Slater gave the filly a final pat on the cheek, then pointedly looked Mike up and down. "Christ, Mike, those boots."

"You liked them, I remember."

"They send me." Slater nodded to the horse. "Do you know this girl's name? She's bright. Knows how to communicate."

Mike chuckled. "You know horses?"

"A little. I got sent to a working ranch in Wyoming as punishment when I was a teenager."

"That sounds like a reward, not a punishment."

"There was a lot of work to do. It was supposed to straighten me out, but it was more like juvie in the middle of nowhere."

"What's juvie?"

"Juvenile hall. It's jail for minors. I can't believe you've never heard that word."

Mike raised his eyebrows. "Crime and punishment aren't really part of my life experience."

"That makes sense. Amassing obscene amounts of money isn't a crime."

"Why are you here?" he demanded.

"I wanted to ask you a favor."

"That's rich. As I remember it, the last time we met you slapped me and called me sleazy."

"That may have happened," Slater said, "but I also gave you the best pony ride of your life."

Mike took a breath. "I remember it well. I think about that day sometimes."

"So you're a fancy guy with a private jet, right? I need to get to Santa Fe and back without sitting in airport lounges for two days."

He laughed. "You've got nerve, Slater, I'll give you that."

"So how about it? When is your plane free?"

"It's not mine. It belongs to the company. And it's expensive to operate."

Slater put his hands on his hips. "We both know you are the company, big guy. And I saved your wife a lot of jack on that agave job."

"A few thousand dollars, if memory serves."

"It was seven large." He waved an arm. "As a favor, then, in memory of that time I rocked your world."

Mike groaned, and closed his eyes, and tilted his head back. When he looked at Slater again, he looked tired.

"Maybe we could come to an arrangement. Another tryst."

"That word means sex, I'm thinking?" Slater said. "I'll fuck you, Mike, if that's what you want. A few hours of airplane use in exchange for a pony ride seems completely reasonable."

"You make it sound sleazy."

"It's only sleazy if you want it to be."

"You know, I kind of do." Mike paused as a woman walked past them, the heels of her riding boots echoing on the concrete. "There won't be anybody here soon."

"I'm going to need the plane before the sex happens."

"You don't trust me."

"It's just business." He shrugged. "It'll give you something to look forward to."

Mike sighed. "I'll talk to my pilot and send you the details. I don't even have your contact info."

He pulled out his phone. "What's yours?" Thumb-typing it as Mike recited it, he sent him a text with his name.

"Now you've got my number," Slater said. "Where do you park the jet?"

"Van Nuys."

He pursed his lips as he tucked his phone away. "That's inconvenient, but I guess I can make it work."

Mike chuckled. "You're kind of an ass, you know that?"

"And you love it," Slater said, jabbing a finger at him, then walked away.

Driving north, he took the 710, along with all the freight trucks, next to the endless concrete river channel, under the multiple sets of electric pylons and the mess of wires overhead. Traffic was sluggish until he got into hilly Mount Washington and pulled up behind Pike's SUV, parked on the street in front of Doris's house.

Doris's Buick was in the driveway, and happily her stupid boyfriend Albert's stupid midlife crisis car wasn't. Walking up to the front door, he pulled open the screen and stepped in.

Pike was on a stool at the kitchen bar, one hand on

a coffee mug, and Doris was standing on the other side. She was petite, her dark hair graying, today wearing a blue jacket and dark pants. Greeting him, both of them were grinning like idiots.

Slater furrowed his brow. "What's going on?"

"We're just catching up," Doris said.

"OK." He eyed Pike as he stepped over to her and leaned in, and embraced her for a moment, and kissed her. "You look nice."

"My handsome son." Doris squeezed his hands and looked him in the eye. "What's this I hear about a car accident?"

He stepped around the bar to stand next to Pike. "I wouldn't call it that. When the Highway Patrol showed up they called it an incident. I'd call it a car wreck. The Thunderbird is toast."

"I know how much you loved that car."

"It's gone for good. I guess I need to adjust to the new reality."

"I'm so glad you weren't hurt," Doris said.

"Me too."

"So you just lost your brakes on the Newhall Grade? How did that happen?"

"My mechanic is going to look into it."

"To be fair, it was a fifty-year-old vehicle," Pike said. "It's not too surprising that it had mechanical problems."

Slater waved an arm. "So is that old croaker who's been schnorring off you still alive? His doll car isn't here."

"Albert contributes plenty. He's at work."

Pike gestured to the hall behind them. "Check this out. Doris is gearing up for a protest."

Propped against the wall were several big sheets of cardstock. The one in front was painted in big red letters: ¡FUERA JOSÉ!

"José is your city council member?" Slater said.

"My corrupt council member. Under indictment for a string of felonies for being on the take. He should have resigned already. We want him out. We're going to tell him that at his office tomorrow."

"Why do you need so many signs?"

"I'm not doing it alone," she said. "They're for my action posse. I want to make sure everybody has a message. We're going to make some noise."

"I love that you're doing that," Pike said. "Direct participation in democracy."

"Just don't get arrested," Slater said.

Doris raised her eyebrows. "How many times have I spoken those exact words to you?"

"What do you know about a company named Ekragen?"

"It depends on your perspective." She leaned against the counter. "If you think we need more machines to kill people, they're doing righteous work. Others might say they're villainous."

"But they're big, right?"

"Oh, yeah. They don't build fighter planes, but they make missiles."

He nodded. "Is there a time we need to be at the cemetery?"

"There's no schedule. As long as it's before dark."

"That's not for a couple hours. I've been neglecting your rosebushes. I really need to work on them."

"We can chat while you do that."

Slater pointed at each of them. "Don't be gossiping about me."

"He's worried that we're going to force him to go to rehab," Pike said.

"Can we do that?" Doris waved a hand. "It sounds like a great idea."

"Laugh it up," Slater said, "but know that if you ever try anything like that, I'll disappear." He raised his eyebrows and spread his fingers in the air. "Poof."

Walking out the back door and into the yard, he went to the gardening shed and pulled on a pair of heavy gloves, then grabbed the shears. He'd need to deal with the buds later in the winter. For now they just needed a trim.

He set to work, methodically cutting back the vines and the runners. It didn't take long, and eventually he raked up the cuttings and dumped them into the green bin, then pulled off the gloves.

When he stepped out of the garden shed, Pike and Doris were standing outside the back door.

Pike gestured to the rosebushes. "They look really sharp."

"Did Slater tell you why he planted them?" Doris said.

"I never heard that story."

"We were having a discussion, and he was exasperated. He said, 'What do you want from me, woman?' I didn't know what to say anymore. I threw up my hands and said 'roses.' A few days later he planted all these."

"We were actually having a blowout argument," Slater said, stepping over to them. "Not a discussion. And I was way beyond exasperated."

"Still," Doris said. "It was sweet."

"Planting roses was a squeaky-wheel type situation. A way to take the heat off me." He shrugged. "I was in school. I got the pots wholesale."

"It was still sweet, and caring, and sensitive, no matter how much you want to avoid those words. My sweet sensitive son." She squeezed his bicep.

"You see what I have to deal with?" he said, eyeing Pike.

Doris gestured to the plant beds. "You should cut some marigolds."

"I forgot." He went back to the shed for the shears, then went over to the beds in the part of the yard that got full sun, and started to cut the stems.

"Why marigolds?" Pike said.

"It's traditional for Día de Muertos," Doris said. "Slater has them timed to be ready for today. It works out every year that they're blooming."

He took the bundle of flowers, along with the shears and a trowel and a can of spray oil, and they went out to the street. Once he'd loaded the tools in the back of Pike's SUV, Slater pulled open the passenger door for Doris, then closed it for her and got in the back seat.

"I've been to the cemetery," Pike said, sitting behind the wheel and looking at his phone, "but I don't know what it's called."

Slater recited the name. "It's basically on Cesar Chavez."

"I'm so glad he took you," Doris said.

Pike tapped at the phone screen. "It was when I first started coming out here." Once he'd set the phone in its mount, he pulled into the street. "I love that you mark Día de Muertos. I saw the displays in Grand Park this week."

"Is that near your office?" Doris said.

"One of my colleagues wanted to go look at the *ofrendas*. They're basically massive artworks."

"Which colleague?" Slater leaned forward. "Was it Davis?"

Pike chuckled. "It was actually Brewster."

"Who's Davis?" Doris said.

"One of his coworkers who's trying to get with him."

"One of my coworkers who's actually not trying to get with me," Pike said.

Doris looked back at him. "It sounds like someone's jealous."

"Not jealous. But there's a smorgasbord of pain coming for that little shvantz if he lays a finger on him."

"Davis does some kind of Belgian boxing thing," Pike said. "He'd probably be able to deck you."

"Oh, yeah? Him and what army?"

"You don't need to be picking fights," Doris said.

Slater stifled a groan. It was like a broken record with her. Over the years he'd learned that the best response was just to hold his tongue.

There were lots of vehicles in the cemetery when they pulled in, unlike every other day of the year when it was mostly deserted, and lots of people were walking around. Slater told him where to park, then grabbed the tools and the marigolds from the back. Together they walked over to the squat stubby stone marked IBANEZ.

The grass around it was always dead and yellow, like every plot was, like the whole place. With the ongoing droughts they'd just stopped watering it. It was hard to fault anyone for that. But the crabgrass still managed to grow up around the marker.

Doris sat cross-legged, holding the marigolds, and Pike followed her lead. Kneeling, Slater dug out the grass around the stone with the trowel, then cleaned up the debris. With the spray oil and a rag he polished the smooth part of the stone, giving it a fresh luster.

Laying the marigolds on the marker, Doris dug in her bag and produced a bottle of Corona, and set it next to them.

"It's not much of an *ofrenda,*" she said.

Slater sat back. "It doesn't matter. He's dead. It's just a waste of good beer."

Eyeing Pike, Doris said, "The point of Día de Muertos is that the departed can hear us today. They're attracted by the marigolds, and they can enjoy the offerings."

"Once a teacher, always a teacher," Slater said.

"It's a nice custom." Pike leaned back on his hands. "It feels like it's spread more widely. Like it's evolving into something less traditional. Like those big displays in the park."

Doris nodded. "It's not really a celebration of death, even though that's the imagery for it. It's about remembering, and it's about the living, and our relationships." Her voice broke as she added, "It's to remind us that love outlasts losing people."

Pike sat up and put a hand on her back. Why didn't Slater have those instincts? It looked so natural coming from him, comforting her like that. Watching them, he realized it didn't actually bother him. It was fine that Pike was close to her. That felt meaningful—a positive development. Another curling tendril in their narrative complex.

"Tell me about him," Pike said.

"He was the salt of the earth," Doris said, and talked about him for a while.

Eventually the sun was getting close to the horizon, and Doris got to her feet.

"He loved you so much," she said, as Slater got up.

"I know." He wiped at the water in his eyes with the heel of his hand. "No love without pain, right?"

They ate at a taquería in the neighborhood, then Pike dropped him and Doris at her place. Walking out to the street, Slater looked over the Continental. In the golden light of the impending sunset it had a glow about it, a warmth, like it had character. Charisma, Davis had called it, when he was talking about Pike. He did like the elegant body and that curve in the trunk lid for the spare tire.

It was well after dark when he got back to the house.

Pike's ride was already here, and he found him upstairs in the bedroom, getting undressed.

"You take good care of Doris," Pike said.

"You mean the landscaping? She drives me crazy—taking care of her yard is just to take the edge off the constant grinding harassment."

"I wish I could detect that." Pike pulled off his shirt. "I can't quite see it."

"That's because I've learned how to avoid it. But she knows how to push my buttons." He scoffed. "It makes sense, right, she's the one who installed them."

"Is it about when your pop died?"

"I didn't take that very well."

"You were a kid."

"It actually made us closer, I think. All the tsuris. For a while it felt like we only had each other." Slater folded his arms, watching him dig out a T-shirt and pull it on. "I was a terrible son. Did terrible things. I made her miserable for years. I made her tear her hair out."

"She loves you anyway."

"That is a little odd. Most people would have cut their losses and run."

Pike chuckled. "She's your mother."

"I'm sure she would rather have had a kid who was halfway normal. Somebody who achieved something, made her proud, wasn't such a fuck-up." He met Pike's gaze. "Somebody like you."

TWELVE

SLATER WOKE EARLY TO his alarm, and quickly killed it before it woke Pike. Once he was dressed, he went upstairs to make coffee. Beyond the French doors sunrise was looming in the east, the first wan light shifting the darkness to gray. He never got up at this hour, but film production started early.

When he backed the Continental into the street, he flicked on the headlights and navigated onto the 10, exiting in Mid City. At the address Andy had sent for the *Snap Out of It* location shoot, things were already happening. Cruising slowly up the block, he saw the white box trucks and a couple of production trailers parked along the sidewalk, and people walking between them and one of the houses.

A block of low-rise bungalows with unfenced yards, these had been built during the development boom after World War II. One yard had xeriscape out front, but all the others had neatly kept lawns—except the one that was the focus of the production. That one looked neglected, hard-packed bare earth and patches of crabgrass, tall weeds growing in the shade along the side of the house.

Once he'd parked around the corner, he walked back. The plane trees along the block were well established, maybe even dating to that postwar era when the houses went up. They were mostly naked now. When they shed their big broad leaves in the fall it made a huge mess on the street, like a new layer of mulch on top of the asphalt, but that had already been cleaned up. There might have been a blight on them at some point that took a few of them out—a couple of much younger cherry laurels were interspersed among them.

The sun was casting its first golden rays on the treetops, and the door to the house with the neglected yard stood wide open, bright warm light spilling out. As Slater stepped into the yard, a security guard clad in black intercepted him.

"Sir, this is a closed set."

"I'm here for Dragan," Slater said.

"He's the producer, isn't he? He's not here yet. You should talk to the director." He pointed to a trio of people standing on the walk between the house and the street. "She's the one with the headset."

The woman had short black hair, and a big mike in front of her chin like an air traffic controller. The screen of the tablet she was gazing into illuminated her face in pale blue. As Slater approached them, one of the three turned and walked toward the house. The other person standing with the director was a guy with short hair, built solid, wearing a black shirt and jeans. Slater admired the way they fit. This guy was totally fuckable.

As Slater stepped up, the director turned to him and said something in Spanish.

"I've only got the one language, sister."

She frowned. "Who are you with?"

"Nobody. I'm looking for Dragan. I need to talk to him."

"Well, he won't be here for a while."

Eyeing the guy with her, Slater jutted his chin. "What's with the pancake makeup?"

It was thick and pasty, flattening out his features, with darker shades around his eyes.

"I'm on camera today." He looked to the director. "You know, this guy would totally work."

Her eyes flicked over Slater. "I see it too. He's already dressed for the part." Affecting a fake smile, she met his gaze. "Do you want to make some money today?"

"I doubt you can afford me, toots. What's the gig?"

"One of my cleaning crew didn't show up today," the guy said.

"I'm not interested in cleaning out somebody else's house."

The guy frowned. "Nobody's cleaning anything. You just have to stand in frame to make it look like I have a full crew."

"You make it sound like an acting gig," Slater said. "If that's the case, I get scale."

"Of course," the woman said. "Everybody gets paid scale."

He had no idea how much the guild scale was, or how it was calculated, but he knew it was an industry thing, as he'd heard actors mention it. Hopefully it made him sound like he knew what he was talking about. The work sounded easy enough, and it gave him a reason to hang around until Dragan showed up.

"What do I have to do?"

The guy clapped his hands together, beaming at him. "Excellent. I'm Tony. I have the only speaking lines on the cleaning crew. Your role is nonspeaking."

"I thought *Snap Out of It* was reality TV," Slater said.

"It is," the woman said. "We still have a script."

"You're the director?"

She smiled, for real this time. "Valéria. You'll look to me for instruction."

Tony jutted his chin toward the house. "This is Carol. She's the homeowner."

From the front door a woman was approaching, in

her fifties at least, curvy and wearing a baggy fuchsia sweatshirt and eyeglasses, her gray hair tied back.

"She's the hoarder?" Slater said.

"We don't use that word," Tony said under his breath.

Valéria raised her voice as Carol approached them. "We found another cleaning crew member, so there won't be any delays today."

Carol beamed and extended a hand. "What's your name, honey?"

"John Slade," Slater said, and gave her hand a gentle shake.

"Wardrobe did you right. You look the part." She briefly grasped his forearm and said, "Break a leg," then walked away.

"You need to talk to the production accountant," Valéria said, "and get on the payroll." She pointed out one of the trailers at the curb, then walked toward the house.

At the trailer, Slater mounted the pair of metal stairs, and knocked, then stepped inside. It was set up as a small office. Behind the desk, peering at a laptop screen, was a guy in his twenties. Built lean, he had a great pomp of thick black hair.

"Valéria wanted me to talk to you," Slater said. "She hired me to be on the cleaning crew."

"Great," he said flatly. "More paperwork for Butch. Sit down."

"Butch is your boss?" Slater said as he took the chair.

He frowned. "I'm Butch."

It didn't fit—he was too lithe, his skin too smooth, his movements too fluid.

"Did you pick that one yourself?"

"It's aspirational." He handed Slater a sheet of paper, then turned back to his computer screen.

It was a standard tax form, and he grabbed a pen from the cup on the desk that contained several of them, and wrote "John Slade" in the name box, plus a Social Security number that he knew would pass a cursory verification check. In the box for his address, he wrote "200 N. Spring St." That was city hall, but not many people would notice that. At the bottom he scrawled John Slade's signature.

Butch took the form, not even glancing at it, and set it in a tray.

"You'll get paid in about six weeks. We don't do deductions for union dues. That's on you."

"Sure," Slater said. He didn't care—he was never going to see the dough, and he was going to ditch the job as soon as he got a chance to talk to Dragan.

Butch handed him a sheaf of paper. "This is the on-screen agreement. Just sign the last page."

The top of the first sheet was emblazoned with EMPLOYMENT AGREEMENT, and he flipped through the document. It was a lot of legalese, paragraph after paragraph of dense text.

"Can you summarize this?" Slater said.

His brow furrowed. "Are you new? Everybody who appears on screen has to sign it. Basically it says you give the production company the right to use your image in perpetuity for any purpose."

"That's intense. People actually sign off on that?"

"One of the guild strikes was partly about that issue. So far, this is still standard. If you want to work today, you have to sign it."

Slater went to great lengths not to be tracked on surveillance cameras, but this wasn't about him, it was about John Slade. If they wanted to use his face to sell shampoo and hamburgers and car insurance, it didn't really matter. Once he'd signed it, he handed it back.

Butch set it aside and briefly met his gaze. "That's all I need."

"Do you know Dragan?"

"He's the producer. The man with the money—the big money. I deal with petty expenses on set during production, but I don't deal with him."

"You've met him?"

"I've seen him around." Butch waved a hand in a languorous gesture. "I know he's a good guy. Dragan was there for us during the guild strikes. We all lost so much. He helped raise money so people could pay their rent and feed their kids."

"Those went on for a while."

"It was hard on everyone."

Slater raised his eyebrows. "Did the world really suffer from mediocrity delayed?"

"So you're a cultural critic as well as an actor? You're part of it too, you know."

"I'm just here to clean up the trash."

Butch nodded toward the door. "If there's nothing else."

"So why do you want to be Butch? You're totally hot the way you are."

He scoffed. "All my life I've been that guy. The gunsel, *el passivo*, the twink. It's not who I want to be."

"Your whole life? What are you, like, twenty-five?" Slater rose. "You're hotter than you think you are. Besides, everybody likes twinks. Lean into it."

Not waiting for a response, he stepped out to the sidewalk. The sun was on the houses now, and he saw Tony over on the lawn, his boots planted apart, head down, gazing at his phone. The bulge in his jeans revealed that he was stacked. Just looking at the guy was making him chubby. Slater walked over to him.

"I like the look you're working," Slater said.

Tony frowned. "Apart from the stage makeup, it's just what I wear when I'm at work."

"It's more than that. They don't put unattractive people on TV—even reality TV. The jeans, and your haircut, and those fuck-me boots."

He briefly glanced down at them, and his eyes narrowed. "Are you hitting on me?"

"Is it working?" Slater said.

"No," he said flatly. "I've got enough problems without that."

"Hot people don't have problems."

Tony gestured to his face. "You haven't gone to makeup."

"Is that really necessary? I thought I was only going to
be in the background."

"If you don't do makeup, you look like a corpse. We
can't have that." He pointed to the other trailer. "Talk to
Terry."

The door was ajar, he saw as he walked over, and he
stepped inside. A woman stood at one end of the trailer,
between double racks of clothes that lined both walls,
flicking through the hanging garments. Curvy, she was
wearing jeans and had a single pink streak in her dark
hair.

"Are you Terry?" Slater said. "I'm told I need makeup."

She stepped out from among the clothes and smiled.
"Sit down. I'll get you fixed up in no time."

The chair had a reclining back with a neck rest, and
he got comfortable in it. Terry opened a bulky makeup
kit and pulled out a bottle, then poured a liberal blob of
brown goo onto a cotton pad.

"You're on the cleaning crew?" she said.

"Theoretically. It doesn't sound like we'll actually be
doing any cleaning."

"That's because we make reality TV, not real reality
TV."

"It feels like reality has become a malleable concept."

The product was cold as she started applying it to his skin, and he closed his eyes.

"It feels thick," he said. "Like crack filler when you paint the walls."

Terry chuckled. "It's just foundation. You'll look amazing."

"Do you know Dragan?"

"I know who he is. I haven't worked directly with him."

"What's he like?"

"He seems nice enough. Always professional when he's on set. Close your eyes."

"You don't have to be diplomatic with me," Slater said. "I'm not in the industry." He could feel the cold goop as she applied it on his eyelids.

"To be honest," she said, lowering her voice, "he scares me a little. He looks like a gangster."

"I've been told he's not."

"He likes to talk to the actors. The women. He talks about hiring them for his next movie. Nothing inappropriate, I've heard, just the big talk."

"I thought he hadn't actually made any movies."

"I wouldn't know about that," Terry said. "You can open your eyes."

"Are you finished?"

Her eyebrows shot up. "Goodness, no. I have to do your eyes."

She spent a minute with a thick pencil, then with a brush, working above and below his eyes. Eventually she rolled her chair back.

"Chin up."

Slater tilted his head back and looked toward the ceiling.

"Turn to the left."

Once he'd done that, and showed her the other profile, she nodded.

"I think you look amazing."

"Can I see?"

Terry gave him a hand mirror, and he studied his face. It was thick like clown makeup, but close to his natural skin color.

"I look like a photo with the soften filter cranked up to ten," he said.

"That's what the camera likes."

"At least my eyes really pop. Thanks for that."

"Break a leg out there," she said, and Slater got up and went outside.

As he walked toward the house, Valéria caught sight of him and waved him over.

"We're setting up for a shot of you and the other guys carrying trash bags out of the house," she said.

"I thought I wasn't going to have to do any cleaning."

"It's not actual garbage. We'd need a whole different permit to do that. The bags are full of clean textile fabric and polyester filler. You just walk out of the house carrying them. Follow the other guys. Then we'll do it again." She frowned. "Where's your hat?"

"Do I need one?"

"Ask Terry. She does wardrobe."

Back at the trailer, he stepped inside and hailed Terry. "I'm told I need a hat."

"Of course." She stepped back toward the racks of clothes. "I missed it because you're already in costume."

Returning a moment later, she handed him a powder-blue ball cap with IT'S CLEAN embroidered in black letters across the front. He pulled it on as he stepped out, and walked toward the house. Tony was wearing the same hat now, as were the two other guys on the cleaning crew. They looked like day laborers, and even from here he could see they were wearing the same stage makeup.

It wasn't just his clothes, he realized. His skin color fit with the immigrant labor aesthetic. That must be what reality television viewers expected.

THIRTEEN

S LATER WALKED TOWARD THE house as Tony followed the crew inside. A chunky guy wearing cargo shorts had a bulky camera on his shoulder now, aiming it at the doorway. Slater watched him futz with the controls and pan it around.

Someone was calling "John! John!"—the third time he heard it, he realized that was him. It worked better when they called him Slade—it was close enough to his real name that it caught his attention. Looking around, he saw it was Valéria, glaring at him now. He walked over to her.

"Have you got a hearing problem?" she demanded. "You should tell Butch. We can use it to fill out our diversity hiring quota."

"What's up?"

She gestured toward the house. "You're on. Inside. In this scene you grab two trash bags, then wait a few seconds before following the previous crew member. Tony will go first."

"Got it," he said, and walked over to the house, and stepped inside.

Everything about this production had been fake, but he saw now that the hoard was real. Piles of paper and plastic, food containers and clothing, boxes and shopping bags and big black trash bags—it was all piled several feet deep and stretched to the back wall, with a narrow trail of filthy carpet through it as a walkway. The smell was stale but not putrid. Whoever the real hoarder was, Carol or someone else, they didn't save food waste.

He greeted the other guys, and one of them, with a little mustache and visibly wrinkled skin even with the heavy makeup, beckoned for him to move.

"Step over to this side. You need to be out of the shot."

"We're ready," Tony said as he came in.

From a pile of black trash bags, he picked one up in each hand. The cleaning crew guys did too, leaving two for Slater. They weren't that heavy, he found, lifting them up.

Outside he heard Valéria call, "Action."

Tony walked out the front door, heaving up a trash bag in each hand. The guy with the mustache waited a few seconds, then followed him out. The other guy jutted his chin for Slater to go next, so he stepped outside with his two big bags, and walked toward where Tony was standing. He could feel the camera on him but didn't look at it.

Valéria had them do it twice more, then switched to bulky cardboard boxes, getting each of them to carry one out of the house. Whatever was in them wasn't heavy, and it didn't smell like garbage.

Afterward he stood in the yard with the other faux cleaners and watched Tony film a scene with Carol. The two of them stood just outside the house's front door, with the mountains of junk and garbage visible behind them.

Standing with the camera operator, Valéria called, "Action."

"You've got to choose between this trash and your life, Carol," Tony shouted, waving an arm. "This mess is literally killing you."

"Cut," Valéria yelled. "Tony, that was beautiful. Really professional work. But you're at a nine. Can we dial it down to a six?"

Tony nodded. "Of course."

When she called "Action" again, Tony repeated the same line, his tone intent but not shouting this time.

Carol's face contorted, and she teared up, and wiped absently at her eyes. "I know. It's just so hard."

It was impressive that she could conjure tears on demand, Slater thought. Whether she was the actual hoarder or not, Carol was a talented actor.

On the street he saw a sleek black Jaguar pull up behind one of the trailers. The security guard moved a traffic cone onto the verge to make room for it, and the Jag parked at the curb. Dragan climbed out from behind the wheel, wearing the dark sunglasses and a gray sport coat over a shiny green shirt, replete with his signature bundle of gold chains. The coat had a sheen to it too. This guy loved his satin.

As he walked toward the house, Dragan looked puffed up, swagger in his step. Slater went over to him, and Dragan paused in the yard.

"Is the camera rolling?" Dragan said, his accent thick. He sounded like his tech supplier, Svetlana.

"I think they're almost done with this shot," Slater said.

"OK. Where is Doctor B?"

"I don't know him."

"Doctor B is a her," Dragan said. "She's the psychologist who comes to help the crazy person in each episode. You'd remember her. She's very attractive."

Tony stepped up to them, beaming, and spoke in a low voice. "Looking good, Dragan."

"I thought Doctor B was filming today."

"Her scenes are scheduled after the midday break. She'll be here around ten."

"This is disappointing."

"You should hang around," Tony said. "We're creating some important content today."

"I know. I'll be back after ten."

Dragan turned to walk back to his car, and Slater trotted after him.

"Hold up," he said. "What can you tell me about Sybil Álvarez?"

Dragan stopped and turned toward him. He couldn't see his eyes behind the shades, but his brow was furrowed.

"I thought you were part of the shoot, with all that makeup. Who are you?" He raised his voice. "Are you working for the bunco squad? This is harassment."

"I'm not a cop," Slater said. "I'm on the cleanup crew. Moving fake garbage out of the house."

"Nobody gets to mess with my business." Dragan was shouting now. "You're spying on me."

He put his hands on his hips. "I don't know what you're on, baby, but you're buying from the wrong dealer. What does Sybil do for you, exactly?"

Dragan took a step toward him, looming just a few inches from his face. He was shorter than Slater, but he was trying to be intimidating, and he smacked Slater's shoulder with the heel of his palm, hard enough to make him involuntarily step back.

"Stay out of my business, trash man."

He knew he shouldn't react. Most of his teenage years had been spent in shrinks' offices trying to convince him not to. He was well aware of where the high road was. But in the moment, it was nearly impossible to step away. Slater threw a right hook that snapped Dragan's head.

"Why do you make me do this to you?" he demanded.

In a classic civilian reaction, Dragan held his arms up in front of his face. Slater hadn't been sure which way this would go, whether the guy could flatten him or not. He was built like he could, but it was obvious now that he didn't have any brawling chops. Dragan was strictly a white-collar lowlife.

He swung at Slater with his right arm, another predictable move that he easily sidestepped. At the same
time Slater struck with a gut punch—not too hard, just
enough to stop him in his tracks. Dragan doubled over,
wheezing.

"Dude," Slater said. "You shouldn't start a dust-up if
you don't know how to finish it."

Tony hustled over to them, his eyes wide. "What's going on?"

The filming had stopped, Slater saw, and a lot of eyes
were on them.

Straightening up, Dragan took a deep breath. "Who
is this monkey?"

"He's an extra," Tony said. "He's nobody."

Dragan jabbed a finger at Slater. "You'll never work
in this business again."

"I sincerely hope you're right about that," Slater said.

"You hit him?" Tony demanded, scowling at Slater.
"He's our producer. What is wrong with you?"

He flashed his palms. "I get asked that a lot."

Turning, he walked up the block, past the box trucks,
toward the Continental. When he pulled out his phone
he saw that he'd missed a call earlier. It was an 818 number with no name attached. He read the transcript of the
voice mail:

"Hello, Mr. Ibáñez. My name is Hugo. I work for Big
Mike. I wanted to make arrangements with you for your
Santa Fe trip. The aircraft is available Saturday, if that
works for you." He recited a phone number, the same
one that showed on the caller ID.

That was tomorrow—he needed to get on it.

Climbing into the Continental, he was startled at
the sight of his own face in the rearview mirror, for a
split second thinking it was a different person sitting behind him. He looked like a cartoon character. The hat

too — he was still wearing it. They weren't getting it back now. Pulling it off, he tossed it on the passenger seat.

There was also a text from Andy:

Lunch? I want the ramen at the central market.

Slater texted back:

Meet you there in thirty.

Before he started the engine, he texted Lunelle in Santa Fe:

Are you available at ten a.m. tomorrow for that interview?

He was halfway downtown on the freeway when her response popped up on the screen:

Text me when you're on the plaza. I'll be nearby.

Tapping at the screen, he called Big Mike's staffer.

"Thanks for calling back," Hugo said when he picked up.

"Are you Mike's assistant?"

He laughed. "I'm his pilot. What time would you like to leave tomorrow?"

"That's up to me?" Slater said. "I have to be at a meeting in town at ten."

"That's ten mountain time, correct? Let me check the numbers."

Slater could hear the clacking of a keyboard, and eventually Hugo spoke.

"To get you there on time, it's wheels up at seven."

"That works."

"Big Mike said you wouldn't need a flight attendant. I hope that's OK."

"I don't care about that," Slater said. "I just need to get there. What's the flight time?"

"Eighty-four minutes. I'll text you the address of the office we use. It's at Van Nuys Airport."

"How far ahead do you want me to show up?"

"That's up to you," Hugo said. "We'll leave when you get there."

When he ended the call, he had to grin. The guy obviously thought Slater was somebody important.

When he got to the market, he pulled into the parking structure next door, then walked into the big hall. He found Andy on a stool at the ramen place, his walking sticks propped against the counter next to him. As Slater sat on the adjacent stool, Andy did a double-take.

"You went a little heavy with your ... makeup today."

"The camera loves it," Slater said. "I was an extra on *Snap Out of It* this morning."

"Sweet. Did you meet the actual crazy hoarder?"

"We don't use that word on set."

The server came over and set a bowl in front of Andy, then eyed Slater. "What'll it be?"

"Bring me the vegan version."

As she stepped away, Andy lifted his bowl to slurp the broth. Watching him eat was always entertaining—it was messy, and despite how chaotic it looked, he usually achieved his aims. Even though he'd spilled soup on the counter, he got most of it, and all of the noodles, into his mouth.

When Slater's bowl arrived, he grabbed a pair of chopsticks and made quick work of it.

"About your drone photo," Andy said, pushing his bowl away. "I can't find any of the usual ... signs of photo editing or AI manipulation."

"So it's legit."

"I also can't prove a negative. I can't say ... for sure it wasn't edited. It might be some technique that doesn't leave ... the same kind of traces. The AI bullshit factories are evolving fast."

"Can you try something else for me?" Slater said. "I want to get into the files at Desert View Rocketry."

"They do defense work. That's … risky. It's going to cost you."

"It always does." He frowned. "Don't I always pay you?"

"You do," Andy said, "but when I bring it up, you … always get steamed."

"So why do you bring it up?"

"You owe me for what I've … done already. Eight yards."

"That seems high," he said, but reached for his wad of cash.

"Don't pay me here," Andy said. "I'll get jacked on the way home."

Rising, he notched his arms into the cuffs of his sticks.

"Do you want me to walk you home?" Slater said.

"I don't need a bodyguard."

"That's not why I offered. I actually like spending time with you."

"You'll just slow me down, normie."

That made him chuckle, and he watched Andy stride away toward the Broadway entrance. He actually made pretty good time on those sticks.

Slater walked in the opposite direction, toward the parking structure. He needed to talk to Redge Black later today, and Lunelle was tomorrow. Thinking about it, why hadn't Sybil mentioned either of those names? It felt like she hadn't dug that deep, and just took what Desert View told her at face value. He thought about what Goh said about Sybil. She was physically fit, he knew, despite the pneumatic boob job. Not just lanky, Sybil had some muscle tone, like a runner. And she'd been wearing workout clothes when he saw her a couple of days ago.

When he climbed into the Continental, he phoned Ben.

"Does Sybil go to the gym?" Slater said when he picked up.

"Yeah, almost every day. Did you see her there?"

"Which gym?"

"Uh … it's on Fig by the metro station," Ben said. "I can't remember the name."

"When does she usually go?"

"After lunch."

"So right now."

"That sounds right," Ben said. "Why?"

"No reason."

Slater ended the call and fired up the engine, then drove to his house, and nosed into the garage. Toward the back of the garage was where he stored his illicit surveillance gear. Built to look like a cheap sheet-metal office-supply cabinet, but hardened and bolted to the floor, it was actually a gun safe that could hide in plain sight. He didn't have any firearms, but his gear was too illegal to leave lying around.

Pulling open the cabinet door, Slater took out the lock-reading probe, and the heavy key binder that went with it, and loaded them into his canvas satchel, then set it in the trunk of the Continental.

The makeup, he remembered. It made him way too memorable. He hustled up the stairs and spent a minute in the bathroom washing his face. At least the stuff wasn't greasy and came off easily.

FOURTEEN

I N THE GARAGE AGAIN, Slater backed into the street and waited for the door to roll down, then drove to Sybil's building, and parked around the corner. Grabbing his ball cap from the back seat, he pulled it low over his brow, then switched on the stealth glasses and put them on. He didn't need to bother wearing gloves—he'd already been to her place, so his fingerprints had a legit reason to be there.

Slinging the heavy satchel on his shoulder, he walked around to Sybil's building. This whole block was high-rises now, the street starting to look like Chicago or Manhattan. When he was a kid it had all been low-rise commercial structures and surface parking lots. The neighborhood was getting busier too. When these towers had first gone up they were mostly empty, and it felt like a ghost town. Now there was a coffee place on this block, and a chain pizza joint, and a woman pushing a stroller.

Slater walked down the ramp into the garage under Sybil's building. There was no walkway, but there was enough room to step around the barrier arm. He knew there were cameras in the elevators, but he hadn't seen any in the garage, and there weren't any in Sybil's hallway.

The stairwell would be make-or-break: if there were cameras inside, he'd have to abort. When he pulled open the door to the stairs, he saw there were none here either. He kept an eye out for them as he climbed past the first few landings, just in case, but there were none.

It was a long climb, and he had to take a break half-way up to catch his breath. As he started trudging upward again, he was breathing hard, his heart pounding. His shoulder was aching from the weight of the satchel when he stepped out on 28.

At Sybil's door, he knocked hard, and paused to listen, then pounded with his fist. There was no response. He looked around the hallway to make sure he was alone, then pulled the lock-reading probe out of his satchel. It could assess most standard locks, and he knew that's what Sybil's deadbolt was, as he'd cased it when he'd been here before.

The lock reader had a key-shaped probe at one end of a cable, the other end with a connector for his phone. When he plugged it in, Svetlana's app took over the screen, turning it black with the word "готов." Crouching in front of the handle, he inserted the probe into the lock. At first the screen went red, but after a moment of subtle adjustment, it flashed green with a number: 325.

Tucking the phone and the probe away, he pulled the key binder out of the satchel, and set it on the floor. He could feel the sweat trickling from under his cap onto his neck. It would look really suspicious to be seen doing this, and he worked quickly, flipping through the heavy pages of little numbered pouches with the ghost keys. When he found the one marked 325, he pulled it out, and tucked the binder back into the satchel. Rising, he slung it on his shoulder, then tried the ghost key in the lock.

The cylinder twisted freely, retracting the bolt with a muted *thunk*. Thank you, Svetlana. He eased the door open and was instantly struck with a piercing high-pitched electronic shriek—an alarm. He pulled the door closed again and bolted it with the key. With his shirt sleeve he quickly wiped off the handle where he'd touched it, then walked to the stairs.

As he reached the stairwell, he could still hear the alarm, faint and distant now but blaring insistently. It was easier walking down, even though he was still breathing hard from the climb.

There was no alarm panel inside Sybil's door—he was sure of it. He'd looked for one. Maybe the panel was hidden somewhere, or it was some new kind of alarm system he hadn't run into before. At least he wasn't on camera, if she had one inside, as he'd only cracked the door an inch before the alarm sounded.

Eventually he was almost down to the lobby level. Half a flight below him a door swung open, just as he stepped onto the landing, and a uniformed security guard stood looking up at him. He had an officious badge on his shirt but no sidearm. Beefy, with his black hair slicked back, it was hard to tell whether he was muscular or just flabby. As Slater descended, the guy didn't step out of the way.

"Where are you coming from?" the guy said.

"The fuck business is it of yours?"

"Were you on 28?"

"Move it or lose it, toots," Slater said, and started to push past him.

The guard grabbed his arm and yanked him back. With his free hand Slater swung at his face, managing to strike his jaw. Unfazed, the guard shoved him back, then punched him hard, right in the kisser, knocking his glasses off.

The glasses clattered on the concrete floor as Slater stumbled backward. His heels hit the bottom step, and the weight of the satchel pulled him back, and he fell onto the stairs on his ass. He sat there for a moment and touched his lower lip, finding blood on his finger.

"That hurt, you dick."

The guard stood in front of him with his fists balled. "I asked you a question."

Slater stood up slowly, and feigned grogginess, squinting and shaking his head and working his jaw with his hand. The guard fell for it, taking a couple of steps back, and Slater took the opening to lunge at him. With the advantage of facing him head-on, he easily blocked the guy's attempted punch, and struck him hard on the jaw.

"Why do you make me do this to you?" Slater demanded, and struck again. "Why do you do it?"

Eyes glassy, the guy stumbled backward until his back hit the wall, his hands clawing at empty air. Knees buckling, he slumped downward. He wasn't out, Slater decided, watching him. He was just momentarily dazed. He'd come around soon.

Scooping up his glasses, he hustled down the stairs, and walked into the garage, and strode across to the ramp. He stepped around the barrier arm, and when he got to the sidewalk, he slowed his pace to a normal commuter gait.

As he came up to the Continental, he casually looked around the street, but nobody was following him. Climbing in, he fired up the engine and pulled into the traffic.

That had been a fricking stupid thing to do, strolling in there like a damn tyro. He'd nearly got himself caught. Was he getting soft? The narrative complex was a huge distraction, but he needed to stay sharp, and not make the kind of mistakes that could land him in the hoosegow.

A few blocks away he pulled in at a meter, and shifted into Park, then checked his face in the mirror. He dabbed at his bloody lip. It wasn't too bad—a cut that would heal eventually, and maybe the makings of a bruise.

Digging out his phone, he called Duarte.

"I want to buy the Continental," he said when the guy picked up.

"That's great news," Duarte said. "I know you're a responsible parent. You can wire me the dough."

"Can I come out there? I have cash."

"I'm around all day."

Pulling back into the street, Slater drove to his office, and took his canvas satchel from the trunk, and went upstairs. Max wasn't here, he saw, and flicked on the lights as he stepped in. Eyeing the statue of Rey Pascual, he clicked his tongue in greeting.

In the corner behind his desk sat a squat antique safe, painted black with faded gold lettering that read MONTCLAIR SECURITY. It was as old as this office building, and fit precisely on the bolts set in the concrete floor, designed to hold it down. A century ago it would have been used to store cash and sensitive paperwork, basically the same as what he and Max used it for. He dialed in the combination and pulled open the door.

They'd been trying to shift their cash earnings into bank accounts, but it was a slow process, keeping the deposits small enough to avoid the scrutiny of the tax people and the FinCEN goons. There was still plenty of dough in here. Pulling out three racks, he stuffed them into his satchel, then pulled out the accounting envelope they used to keep track. On the back he wrote:

Slater −30G. auto.

O'Dowd was going to love that.

———•———

DUARTE'S PLACE WAS ON Whittier Boulevard, past the 710 in unincorporated East LA, and Slater drove toward it. The yard was surrounded by tall steel pickets with razor wire coiling along the top. The gate was open, but

Slater parked on the street out front and walked in.

There were a trio of garage bays and an office, and the surrounding yard was filled with classic cars in various states of restoration. Slater found Duarte in the garage, clad in dark blue coveralls and working under a vehicle that was up on a lift. It was the red Polara. He'd driven this one before.

"I love that car," Slater said.

He chuckled and gestured toward the office. "Come inside."

The place wasn't cluttered, but there was a thin layer of grime on everything, the result of years of car exhaust and oil and fluids getting tracked in. Duarte wiped his hands on his coveralls, then went behind his desk and pulled open the top drawer of a file cabinet, eventually pulling out a folder and setting it on his desk. It was the vehicle title, Slater saw, when he folded it open.

"It makes me happy to be selling it to you," Duarte said. "It's in great shape. I know you'll take care of it."

"I didn't do so well with the last one."

"That's inevitable." He waved an arm. "You know what they say: all love stories end eventually, one way or another."

Digging in his satchel, Slater pulled out the racks and set them on the desk.

Duarte's eyebrows shot up. "You don't mess around."

"They're all used bills, so they're not traceable."

He dropped them in his top desk drawer, and waved at the grubby chair in front of the desk. "Sit down."

They both sat, and took a minute to do the work of signing over the title. For Duarte it was routine, and he explained what Slater had to do for the DMV.

Vera walked in, and stood next to the desk, and pushed her hair back with a hand. "So you fell for her."

Slater sat back and met her gaze. "You know, Vera, I

think this was the Lincoln Continental Mark IV 385 V8 that was in my heart all along."

She laughed. "I thought you two might be a good match. Have you heard of the designer Mark IV?"

"What's that?"

"For the '76 Continental, they had different designers do a version of the paint job and the interior. There were Mark IVs by Givenchy, and Cartier, and Emilio Pucci."

"How cool is that?"

"I had one of the Givenchy models in here," Duarte said, "but the Pucci is pretty rare."

"Enjoy your new rig," Vera said, and walked out.

Slater took the title and got up. "Any insight on the Thunderbird's brakes?"

"I haven't looked at it yet. It's complicated because it's so messed up. You hit the ground hard. The frame is bent all to hell."

"I don't really remember it happening. I think I got knocked out."

"I'll get to it early next week."

"I doubt that anyone's gunning for me," Slater said, "but if they are, it would be good to know."

He walked out to the street and climbed into the Continental, grasping the wheel with both hands.

"We belong to each other now," he said aloud. "Be good to me, and I promise I'll be good to you."

Digging out his phone, he looked up the number for the deli on Melrose and dialed.

"Is Reggie on the bar tonight?" he asked the woman who answered.

"Who's asking?"

"I'm a friend of his. He left his hat at my place. I wanted to drop it off."

"He starts at four."

It was close to four now, he saw as he ended the call.

Pulling into the street, he got on the freeway and drove to the Fairfax neighborhood, nosing into the little parking lot next to the deli. The place had been here forever. When he was a kid he used to eat here sometimes with his parents. They'd always get black-and-white cookies from the bakery to take home.

He knew the bar too—a small afterthought tacked onto the side of the sprawling dining room. It was divey, and if he remembered correctly, smalls were two for one if you came early enough.

Stepping into the bar, the place wasn't crowded, with just one of the booths occupied and a couple of lone patrons on the stools. The guy behind the bar matched the photo of Redge Black that Andy found. He still had the beard, and tonight he was wearing a black beret instead of the straw hat, and a black T-shirt with a band logo on it.

There was entertainment too—past the end of the bar and facing the booths was a little stage space. A guy sat playing an electronic keyboard, and next to him a torch singer in a long black dress was performing without a mike.

Slater sat on a stool at the end opposite the other drinkers, and Redge soon stepped over.

"What'll it be?"

"Whatever bourbon is in the well," Slater said. "Neat."

Redge turned to the wall of bottles and set to work.

His booze rules said he could have one with other people when he was working, but this was an exception—he had to drink to do the work. Redge set down a lowball glass with a generous finger of amber liquid in it, and as Slater set a sawbuck on the bar top, the torch singer hit a painfully off-key high note.

Slater winced. "Isn't it a little early for live music?"

Leaning toward him, Redge spoke quietly. "She's the manager's mother-in-law."

"Good thing the booze is cheap."

"It looks like you need it. That cut is fresh."

Slater absently touched his lip. "Yeah, I walked into a door."

"I've met doors like that. They're usually liquored up and belligerent. At least here there's a bouncer."

From the other end of the bar, a woman called "bartender," and Redge stepped away.

This wasn't bad stuff, Slater thought, sipping at his bourbon, even though it came from the well. But his standards weren't very high. A few minutes later, Redge came over with his change and set it down.

"You used to work at Desert View Rocketry," Slater said.

His brow furrowed. "Who are you?"

"A friend of Ben Clague."

"OK," he said, and hesitated before he spoke. Slater could see him mentally shifting gears. "I remember Ben. We worked together for over a year."

"What do you remember about him?"

"He was a decent guy. Personable. People liked him. I think the women liked him."

"What did Ben do at Desert View?"

"He worked as an electrical engineer," Redge said. "He designed circuit boards."

"And you manufactured them?"

"I worked in the shop. I was the foreman."

"Why aren't you there now?" Slater said.

"Things were slowing down. Between you and me, that place is on its last legs. I'm actually surprised it's still operating. Layton has been selling off equipment and firing people for a while now."

"They do jobs for the military. I thought that meant unlimited budgets."

"You know the feds. It's all or nothing." Redge

shrugged. "They have lots of rules, and if they don't renew your contract for some reason, suddenly you're making zero."

"Is that what happened?"

His brow furrowed. "I don't know the details."

"What else do you remember about Ben?"

"He worked hard. I remember he acted a little crazy sometimes."

Slater swirled the bourbon in his glass. "Crazy how?"

"He'd chew people out. He seemed stressed."

"That must have been intimidating."

Redge shrugged. "Not really. Ben's not a big guy. He weighs maybe a buck forty. I could have taken him."

That was way off, Slater knew. Ben was much bigger than that. But he'd heard that detail before. Pulling out his phone, he found a photo of Ben and held it out to Redge.

"You're sure it's the same guy?"

"That's Benoni."

He studied Redge's face. Ben had said he never used that name. But maybe he'd told Redge what it was, corrected him when he called him Benjamin. More interesting was that Redge hadn't seemed surprised that Slater was looking to talk about the guy, and more salient, he hadn't questioned why Slater was asking about Ben.

"So why is everyone at Desert View white, except Ben?" Slater said. "It's weird."

"I never thought about it."

"That's the cozy thing about white privilege. You don't have to think about it."

"Maybe it's the local labor pool. Palmdale is pretty white."

"It's actually not," Slater said. "Not at all."

"I can't help you with that one," Redge said, and stepped away.

Draining his glass, Slater left his change on the bar and walked out. On the drive back to his house, his phone buzzed in its dash mount—Sybil. He tapped it to pick up the call.

"I need to talk to you," she said. "Can we meet?"

Did she know it was him that tripped her alarm? She could have pulled footage from somewhere, a camera he hadn't noticed, or maybe she talked to that idiot security guard. Even from a physical description, she could have easily identified him.

"What do you need to talk to me about?"

"Not on the phone."

"How urgent is it?"

"It doesn't need to be tonight," she said.

If she was collaborating with that idiot guard, he could finger him in a heartbeat. No way was he going over there.

"You can come to my office," Slater said, "but it'll have to be tomorrow. I'm tied up until late afternoon."

Once he'd nosed the Continental into the garage, he climbed the stairs, and found Pike on the sofa with the *Odyssey*. He was still wearing dress pants and a white shirt, rumpled now and half unbuttoned. Slater knelt in front of him on the faux turf, and leaned in, and ravished him, mouthing his neck and his chest. Pike sighed with pleasure and met his mouth.

After a minute Slater pulled back and tapped the book. "Are you reading ahead?"

"Just the opposite. I'm going over the parts I fell asleep for." Pike frowned and put a hand under his chin, and touched his lip with his thumb. "What happened here?"

Slater groaned. "Honesty and transparency, right?"

"Always the preferred route."

"A security guard thought I'd broken into his building. He decided to mix it up."

"Did you break into his building?"

"No," he said flatly. Technically that was true—he'd had a key, and he hadn't broken anything.

Rising, he sat with Pike on the sofa.

"Is the guy still breathing?"

"He's fine. I'm the only one who got injured." He leaned down to pull off his boots. "You're off tomorrow, right? Do you want to go to Santa Fe?"

Pike sat back and laced his fingers behind his head. "Santa Fe's fun. There's good food."

"I'm just going for a few hours. I need to interview somebody."

"I don't know if that's even possible. It takes work to get there. You have to fly to Albuquerque, then it's an hour's drive each way."

Slater met his gaze. "It's ninety minutes from Van Nuys by private jet."

"You're renting a jet."

"I'm borrowing a jet. From a satisfied former client."

Pike frowned. "What client?"

"When I tracked down that stolen landscaping. The client's husband is a *gantse macher*."

"And he's going to loan you his jet that costs, like, five grand an hour to operate."

"It's just sitting there anyway. Airplanes are like cars— they need to keep moving. You can't let them sit around and rust out. It's use it or lose it."

"It sounds like you're doing him a favor," Pike said.

"Exactly. I'm leaving first thing. We can be back by mid-afternoon."

Pike massaged the back of his neck. "In that case, of course I want to go to Santa Fe."

FIFTEEN

I T WAS STILL DARK when they climbed in the Continental and headed to Van Nuys Airport, cruising up the 101. There was a lot of traffic.

"Where are all these suckers going at sunup on a Saturday?" Slater said.

"Work, most of them, I suspect," Pike said, gazing out the side window. "It's a big city."

Slater wasn't thrilled that Pike had called his mother. She was going to meet them for breakfast. He'd texted Lunelle to push back their meeting, and that meant their trip would be an hour or more longer than necessary. But Slater couldn't squawk—it was a good opportunity for Pike to see her.

He followed the app's directions to the aviation business the pilot had given him the address for, and parked out front. From the back seat he grabbed his faux leather jacket and pulled it on once he'd climbed out. Pike had convinced him to bring it, claiming it would be cold there. He'd worn a sleeveless navy-blue puffer jacket himself, and it looked sharp on him with the denim.

When they walked into the building, he could see the tarmac through the windows at the far end. The first golden light of early morning was stretching across the hangars in the distance, illuminating the tails of the array of airplanes parked at them.

The clerk at the desk asked for his name, then walked them out to the tarmac. Parked right outside was a small jet, its engines mounted back by the tail. Walking around the wing was a guy in a white shirt and black pants, a pair of dark sunglasses hanging from his shirt pocket. He seemed to be looking over the aircraft.

When he spotted Slater and Pike, he walked toward them. His shirt had epaulets, Slater realized. It was a uniform. He had that East African look, angular, almost Middle Eastern.

The guy flashed a smile and said, "Mr. Ibáñez?"

"You must be Hugo. This is Pike."

Hugo shook his hand, and then Pike's, and looked each of them in the eye. That seemed overly formal. But then Slater wasn't part of this world, and had no idea how it all worked.

"Is anyone else joining us?" Hugo said.

"It's just us."

"Go ahead and get comfortable on board. I'll be right with you."

Near the aircraft's nose the door was folded down to reveal a set of steps built into its inner side. Stepping in, they had to stoop for the low ceiling. A bulkhead separated the cockpit from the cabin, but there was no door. Another pilot sat in the right seat, wearing the same white shirt with the epaulets, and big can headphones.

There were four upholstered armchairs facing each other, and two more farther back. Wood paneling covered the wall below the windows, and the bulkhead, like wainscotting in a tobacco lounge. Slater took the second chair, and Pike sat facing him, settling into the seat.

"You won't get motion-sick riding backwards?" Slater said.

Pike held his gaze for a moment, then laughed.

"What?" he demanded.

"The things you do, forty-niner." He gestured at the cabin. "This. It constantly amazes me."

"In a good way, I hope."

"The best possible way. I love that about you."

Hugo climbed in and pulled up the door, then sealed it.

"Buckle up, fellas," he said, and took his seat.

Soon the engines were running, and then they were taxiing. The engines roared louder as they picked up speed, eventually lifting off the ground. The ascent felt steeper than in a commercial airliner, and it was weird that Pike was sitting the wrong way, almost floating above him now. They both gazed out the little windows, watching the ground drop away.

Slater scowled and waved at his ears. "The engines are really loud."

"You should complain to the owner," Pike said. "Tell him he needs to do better."

He knew Pike wasn't serious, but he nodded. "That's a very good idea."

Once they'd climbed over the mountains, the dusty tans and pinks of the Mojave stretched out below. They rode in silence for a while, both of them idly staring out at the landscape. He didn't feel fully awake yet, even though taking off in a small aircraft got the adrenaline flowing, and Pike had made coffee when they got up.

"That has to be the Grand Canyon," Pike said.

The early sunlight was casting long shadows on the canyon walls, illuminating the myriad reds and oranges of the rocks, the hazy depths fading to purple and then black.

"It's really beautiful," Slater said.

"A-yup. That's quite a hole in the ground."

Watching him, Slater had to chuckle. He was so bright sometimes, so inane at others. He loved both sides of this guy, loved all the variations in between, loved everything about him.

He closed his eyes for a while, half dozing, and sometime later felt the nose dip. Soon the desert landscape was coming up to meet them, the buildings and roads growing larger until the runway rumbled under the wheels.

Once they'd stopped rolling, the engines powered down, and then Hugo got up to push the door open. He stepped down onto the tarmac, and they followed him out.

It really was cold here. He hadn't expected that, even though Pike had told him to wear a jacket. The air felt thin and dry.

"Do you know how long you'll be?" Hugo said.

"No more than a few hours."

"Would you mind texting me when you're thirty minutes out? We'll get things set up so there'll be no delay."

"It's a deal, Hugo," Slater said. "The same number you called me from?"

He smiled. "That's the one."

As they walked toward the little terminal building, Pike said, "It's almost like he works for you."

"Big Mike must have told him to keep me happy."

"That's the owner's name?"

"I don't suppose the 'Big' part is on his birth certificate, but that's what they call him."

"Where does his money come from?"

"I don't even know," Slater said. "I know he's into horses. English riding style, with the jodhpurs and the black jacket and the hat. The whole nine yards."

They walked into the terminal, and through it to the street. As they stepped outside, there was a view of the desert and the distant mountains. The vibe was different from the Mojave. Lighter colors, maybe, and the sky was pale and delicate compared to the Mojave's deep rich blue.

"There's Mom," Pike said, and gestured to a dark-blue

Crown Vic parked at the curb.

Slater had met Esther before, and she made him a little uneasy. As they approached, she climbed out of the car. Her brown hair was styled back behind her ears, and she had some weight on her frame, today wearing trousers and a dark-green jacket. Stepping around the front of the Crown Vic, they both embraced her.

"You're looking especially radiant today," Slater said.

"Aren't you the honey-dripper."

"It might be honey, but it's true."

Esther's brow furrowed. "What happened to your lip?"

"I walked into a door."

"OK," she said evenly.

"Do you want me to drive?" Pike said.

"Great idea."

She walked around to the passenger side, and Slater hustled to follow and pull the door open for her. He gently closed it, then climbed in the back seat.

"This guy," Esther said, and chuckled. "Where did you learn the old-school manners?"

"I went to a boarding ranch in Wyoming when I was a teenager. It was all boys, but they taught us how to work with horses and how to act chivalrous with women. Old West type stuff."

"Was it a summer camp?"

"Something like that."

Pike pulled onto the road and headed away from the little airfield.

"How was the drive up?"

"No traffic," she said. "It's a beautiful morning."

"Esther, I do love this car," Slater said. "Is it a '99?"

"You know your vehicles." She glanced back at him. "Cars don't matter here like they do in California."

"It might not matter to you," Pike said, "but it does break down."

Esther chuckled. "That it does. And when it does, I'm *gornisht,* I'll admit that."

"My mother uses that word too," Slater said, "but she pronounces it *gernisht.*"

"I'll have to meet her one day," Esther said. "I was happy that Zeb took up with a Jewish boy."

"The usual expression is 'a nice Jewish boy,'" Pike said.

Esther turned back and looked Slater up and down. "I'm aware."

He sighed and looked out the side window at the desert rolling by, half listening to them chat. Pike seemed to know where he was going, and made a left onto a busy road. Once they were in the town, he pulled into the parking lot of a diner.

When they walked in, Pike spoke to the host like they were old friends, and she led them to a booth by the window. Pike slid in opposite Esther, and Slater sat beside him.

"Is there anything for you to eat?" Pike said, scouring the menu.

"I'll be fine."

"I remember," Esther said. "You're a picky eater."

Slater met her gaze. "I'll actually eat anything, as long as it's not from an animal."

The server came over, and after Pike and Esther ordered, Slater said, "Can you do oat milk or soy milk?"

"We don't have anything like that."

"So let's do oatmeal with no milk, and hit me with the java."

As he handed her the menu, Pike said, "Bring him a couple of sopapillas."

"Got it," she said, and walked away.

Slater eyed him sidelong. "What are those?"

"A local delicacy. Totally vegan. You'll love them."

"That's so California," Esther said. "The vegan thing."

"It's easy there," Slater said. "You don't even have to think about it. It gets harder when you leave civilization."

Her eyes narrowed. "I worry that Zeb will start to acquire those habits, working in the big city."

"Mother, please. I'm not going to turn into a yoga teacher or a pet psychic just because I live in LA."

"Now I've done it," she said, eyeing Slater. "I'm only called 'Mother' when he's upset with me."

"I'm not upset with you. I know you're upset that I moved away."

"I worry about you," she said. "It's such a violent place."

"I think about that sometimes," Slater said. "My part in it. I know I kind of upended his life."

"I upended my own life," Pike said, and squeezed him around the shoulder. "I make my own decisions." Eyeing Esther, he added, "You know I'm only an hour's plane ride away."

The food arrived, and the sopapillas turned out to be soft puffy flatbread, fried in oil and still hot. Slater took a bite. The white stuff on them was powdered sugar. Pike was right, they were delicious.

"So why did you name your son Zebulon?" Slater said, pulling apart a second sopapilla. "He doesn't really use that name."

She gestured with her fork. "When I was pregnant, I read a piece in the Sunday newspaper about the historical Zebulon Pike."

"That's who comes up when you try to cyberstalk this guy."

"He did some exploring for Thomas Jefferson around the same time as Lewis and Clark. The Spanish were in charge of this part of the world, and they detained Zebulon Pike right here in Santa Fe. They took him to Mexico. Eventually they set him free again."

"Interesting."

"Jefferson's Pike wasn't Jewish, but Zebulon is the name of one of the lost tribes." She shrugged. "I thought it was a good solid name."

After they'd eaten, and chatted a while longer, sipping coffee, Slater made it a point to pay for breakfast, and Pike drove them deeper into the town. He parked at the curb across from the plaza and they all climbed out.

Handing Esther her keys, Pike embraced her.

She kissed Slater on the cheek. "Thanks for breakfast."

"I'll try to send him here more often."

"I'm just glad he has somebody." Esther raised her eyebrows. "I'm coming to visit, by the way."

"Of course." Slater nodded. "You should."

They watched her climb in behind the wheel of the Crown Vic and deftly pull into the street.

Pike gestured up the block. "We can cross to the plaza up here."

As they walked, Slater ran a hand through his hair and took a deep breath.

"You look relieved," Pike said.

"I really don't want to make an enemy of her."

"I can see how hard you're working not to." He squeezed him around the waist. "I've never seen you do that with anyone. It's actually amazing that you could stay on good behavior for such a long stretch. I'm impressed."

"I kind of want to punch somebody right now to compensate."

Pike chuckled. "When is your target due?"

Slater pulled out his phone to check the time. "She'll be here any minute."

They crossed the street to the plaza. Mostly open space, it had some greenery, and patches of lawn, and some cobbles.

"You like the trees?" Pike said, following his gaze upward.

"I think that's an American elm."

"Is that unusual?"

"It's not something you see every day. A fungus wiped out millions of them during the twentieth century. In the East they're basically gone."

"I love that you know that."

"I love how much you love this place." Slater waved his arm at the plaza. "You kind of lit up as soon as we got here."

"All roads lead to Santa Fe. It's the hub of the Southwest. From Missouri, from Mexico City, from California. *Bam*, right here at the plaza."

"You're the hub of the Southwest." Slater punched him on the shoulder.

Pike laughed and rubbed his arm. "What was that for?"

"It's you. You're so damn upbeat. I can't stand it." He put his hands on his waist and pulled him close. "I love you so hard."

Leaning in, Pike met his mouth for a moment, then pulled back, blushing a little.

"Do you want me to fade when your target gets here?"

"Can you sit in?" Slater said. "You're so good at it. Kind of like Doris. You turn on the charm and people go moon-eyed. They don't even realize they're being interrogated."

He stood up straighter. "I'm glad you've noticed my skills."

Looking past him, Slater jutted his chin. "Showtime."

SIXTEEN

P IKE TURNED TO LOOK. Lunelle wasn't very tall, and she was curvy, wearing a denim jacket and black leggings under a gray miniskirt. Slater waved at her, and she came over to them.

"You're Ibáñez?"

"Call me Slater. This is Pike."

"I can't believe you came from California just to talk to me. You really get around."

"Like the monkey and the weasel," Slater said flatly. "Is there somewhere we can sit?"

"The bar in the hotel." Lunelle pointed out an adobe-clad building across the street. "It'll be quiet at this time of day."

She led the way, and Slater studied her as they walked into the hotel lobby. He'd never told her he was from LA—someone else had.

Inside the bar were low ceilings and lots of dark wood. Lunelle led them to a table at the back. Slater sat opposite her, and Pike sat beside him.

A server clad in black and white with a little bow tie stepped up.

"Coffee for me," Slater said. "Do you have plant milk?"

"I don't know what that is."

"Just black."

"Same," Pike said.

"I don't need anything." Lunelle shifted in her chair

as the server left, her eyes darting from Slater to Pike.

"You worked with Ben Clague," Slater said.

She nodded. "That's right. At Desert View Rocketry."

"Why did you leave that job?"

"They weren't getting as many of the military contracts, and they started laying people off." She shrugged. "I earn more now."

"Why are you working at a lighting company?" Slater said. "It seems radically different from what Desert View does."

"I had what you'd call a crisis of conscience. I decided I didn't want to be building world-destroying machines anymore."

Slater waited while the server set down their cups. Lunelle had a nervous tic, he saw, absently rubbing the nails of her thumb and middle finger together, making a subtle *click, click, click.*

"Desert View works on drones and airplanes, don't they?" he said, and slurped at his coffee. "Not nukes."

"They also work on guided missiles. Those kill people. It's on a smaller scale, but they're still meant to destroy somebody's world." She held his gaze. "I hope nobody ever fires one at your neighborhood."

"What was Ben like?"

Lunelle's expression shifted. "He was personable, I'd say. People liked him. He was easy to work with. Women liked him, although he wasn't my type."

"Did you ever see him get angry?"

"I saw him get stressed out, and snap at people. He acted a little unpredictable. I don't think it impacted his work."

"So what did Ben look like?" Pike said.

Lunelle frowned. "You know him, don't you?"

He tilted his head toward Slater. "He does. I've never met him."

"Well, he's a Black guy. Tall, like six feet, but not very big. He weighs maybe one forty or one fifty. About my age."

"What was it like to work there?" Pike said.

"I enjoyed it, I guess. The engineering work wasn't especially challenging or creative. We were making parts that had already been designed. I just had to replicate them."

"You liked Palmdale?"

She smiled. "Not really. The desert is much nicer out here. Santa Fe is old, so it doesn't have the urban sprawl made for cars."

Watching her talk, he knew Pike was softening her up by asking her about herself, and things she was interested in, rather than on-topic questions.

Pulling out his phone, Slater found the drone photo and held the screen toward her. "That's you. When was this taken?"

"A year ago, maybe. We were working on refitting that UAV."

"You spent a lot of time on the base?" he said, and set his phone on the table. Pike briefly picked it up to study the image.

Lunelle nodded. "We were there all the time."

"Redge Black and Cody Layton were on the crew with you?"

"Right. Just the four of us."

"There are five people in the photo," Pike said.

Her face turned red. "That's what I meant," she said quickly. "It was a while ago."

"Who else was at Desert View when you worked there?" Slater said. "Ben and Cody and Reg, obviously. What about Patsy?"

"Sure. She did HR. I didn't know her very well."

"What about the redhead on the front desk?"

"I know Graham, again not very well. He seemed nice enough." She scoffed. "It would suck to work with your mom, though. Can you imagine?"

"Who's his mom?" Pike said.

Lunelle's brow furrowed. "Patsy. She's also Cody Layton's sister. There's a lot of nepotism over there. How do you not know that?"

"I haven't been out to the factory," Pike said. "Slater did those interviews."

"Do you remember why Ben left the company?" Slater said.

"That happened after I left. I have no idea." She sat up. "Listen, I've got stuff to do today. Do you have what you need?"

He sat back. "For now."

She got up, and they watched her walk out.

"Did you know those people were all related?" Pike said.

"I did not."

He chuckled. "You covered it well."

"More interesting is that she didn't ask why I was asking about Ben."

"That implies she already knew why."

"I never mentioned him to her until today," Slater said, and sipped his coffee. "When I first called her she thought it was about an insurance claim on her car. She also knew we were from Cali. That didn't come from me."

"So she talked to somebody you already interviewed."

"That fits. What was your impression?"

"What she said about Ben sounded rehearsed," Pike said. "Like she'd memorized it."

"It was also the same dope everybody at Desert View gave me. Almost the same words."

"I'd say that means they're all comparing notes."

"Did she seem nervous to you?" Slater said.

"I'd say so. The thing with her nails. It doesn't mean she's lying or hiding something. Some people get nervous just talking to strangers."

"Another weird thing—she's the third person who said Ben was thin. The guy must have gained a lot of weight. If he weighed a hundred and forty pounds, he'd look like a scarecrow."

Pike drained his coffee mug. "Are we headed back? You should text Hugo."

Picking up his phone, he sent the text, and they went out to the street.

"Let's go to the other side of the plaza," Pike said, and they walked through the arcades fronting the space, looking in the windows of the art galleries and cafés. "We'll have to come back and spend the night. There's lots to do here."

He'd brought them to a taxi stand around a corner on a side street. Pike really did know this town. Soon they were at the airport, and walked through the terminal building.

Hugo welcomed them with a smile at the steps of the aircraft, and once they were on board, he pulled the door closed. Slater sat facing backward this time. Soon they were in the air, crossing the vast Southwestern dry lands.

Pike gestured around the airplane's cabin. "This just feels so decadent."

"Your department flies you around when you need to."

"That's not untrue. Although we usually fly commercial. On surveillance ops it's four guys in a four-seat Cessna with an empty detergent bottle to piss in."

Slater chuckled. "What are we going to do when Queen Esther visits us? I'm thinking we could put her up at Doris's."

His eyebrows shot up. "Do not call her that. She'll box your ears, and then she'll box my ears. She prides herself on being a regular person. That's why she drives a twenty-year-old Crown Vic."

"I'm not sure she approves of me yet."

"Of course she doesn't," Pike said. "You're never going to be good enough for her golden boy. No one is."

Watching him, Slater frowned. "Well, that sucks."

"It doesn't mean you won't get along. Eventually you might even enjoy each other."

He looked out the window at the endless desert mountain ranges stretching toward the horizon. "She does have good taste in cars."

———◆———

WHEN THEY LANDED AT Van Nuys, Hugo made a point to shake their hands again. He seemed relieved to say good-bye. Once they were out on the street, Slater stood and looked around, trying to spot his car.

"Your new baby is right there," Pike said, pointing out the Continental.

"So it is. Cloud blue. It's going to take some time to get used to."

Traffic hadn't slowed down yet on the 101, and they made good time on the drive back to the house. Slater dropped Pike, then drove to his office.

On the elevator ride up, he got a text from Sybil:

Are you available now?

He texted back:

I'm in my office.

Upstairs, he sat at his desk, and eyed the statue of Pollux. It always made him think of Pike. Sweet beautiful Pike. So hot and smart and sly. He'd caught idiot

Lunelle contradicting herself, and the way he'd pointed it out to her made her step in it even more.

Leaning back and swinging his boots up onto his desktop, he texted Andy:

Any progress on those files?

His response came a moment later:

Still working. No developments.

Next he dialed O'Dowd's number, glad that she picked up.

"When you asked around about Sybil Álvarez," he said, "did your source mention where Dragan has his gambling halls?"

"I can find out. You're not thinking of going there."

"I need to look around."

"I'd strongly advise you not to do that," O'Dowd said. "These are scary people, Slater. They have a lot of valuable down-low stuff to protect."

"I'll go in incognito."

"Do you even know how to do that?"

"Discretion is my middle name."

"Just don't punch anybody," she said. "Let me make a call."

A while later came a knock at the door. He got up to pull it open, and Sybil stepped in. Even though it was Saturday she was wearing a gray suit with a sheer blouse that flattered her breasts, open a few buttons to show her cleavage.

"Nice place," she said, glancing around. She pointed to the statue of the skeleton on the front desk. "That's Rey Pascual."

"Nobody ever recognizes him," Slater said. "People assume he's Santa Muerte."

"Santa Muerte is a woman. Rey is the king of the

graveyard. I guess they share that thing about not being judgmental."

"Come in." He stepped behind his desk and waved her to the guest chair. Once they were both sitting, he held her gaze. "You were in a romantic relationship with Ben."

Her eyebrows shot up. "That's no secret."

"So why did nobody tell me?"

"Because it doesn't matter. It has nothing to do with his employment or his time at Desert View Rocketry."

"So Ben is bi?"

Sybil sighed. "He says so. He told me that when he broke it off. I thought he was just trying to avoid being gay. You know, hoping he'd snap out of it." She snapped her fingers.

"You have to take people at their word," Slater said. "If he says he's bi, he's bi."

Her eyes narrowed. "In your job, do you ever take people at their word?"

"Never. Everybody lies to me all the time. It's the only constant in my world. But sex is different."

"You apply a different set of standards?"

"I'd frame it that with sex, all bets are off."

Sybil held his eye. "So where were you all day?"

"Why does that matter?"

"I'm curious about the status of the case, and who you've interviewed."

"You're not my client." He waved a hand. "I talked to some witnesses. I think I'm getting close to some answers."

"Witnesses? What did they witness?"

"It's not like in your business, with depositions and court cases and contracts. For me witnesses just means saps who might know something. People like to talk."

"So what answers are you closing in on?"

"No comment." He raised his voice. "Why are you here?"

Sybil shifted in her chair. "I have some work that needs doing. I figured you were the man for the job. I need you to pick up a package from a client."

He shook his head. "I don't do courier work."

"It's easy money. You just have to meet the delivery guy and retrieve the item."

"You should swing by the post office. They do packages."

"This one is being delivered at the convention center. In the men's room."

"That means you don't want the pickup recorded on video," Slater said. "Restrooms are the only public places that don't have cameras."

"Can you blame me? We live in a surveillance state."

"It's more than that. The convention center is a busy place. It must be about anonymizing it, so that nobody can spot the couriers, or notice the handoff." He watched her for a moment. "I didn't see any cameras in your office."

"Of course not. The last thing my clients need is to be recorded."

"Why can't you go into the men's room yourself? People aren't uptight about that anymore."

"The client involved is a little paranoid," she said. "He thinks he might be under surveillance, and by extension, I might be too. I can't discount that."

"Who's surveilling him? Local PD, or the feds, or some syndicate rival?"

"That's not something you need to know. Like you said, it's a busy place. There's a fashion trade show there all week. You'd fit right in." Her eyes flicked over him. "The men's room part, obviously, not the fashion crowd."

"I can't do it anyway. Courier work is small potatoes.

You need to find yourself a nickel rat."

"I'll pay you whatever you ask."

He chuckled. "That's not a smart opening bid. It has to be something illegal, right? I'm thinking drugs or weapons or cash. What else could it be? Something hot and easily identifiable, maybe. Somebody else's jewelry?"

"Never mind what it is," Sybil said. "That's none of your business."

"Unless I get arrested carrying it around."

"How often do you get stopped on the street and searched?"

"It might happen if someone is following the person who's doing the handoff."

"That's why we chose a crowded place. Nobody will be able to piece it together on camera later. They can't follow everybody in that place." She huffed. "I'll pay you five hundred."

"Five yards for a few minutes' work. It must be extremely illegal."

"There's no risk to you, unless you get sloppy."

"I guess I could do it for a grand."

"That's a lot of money."

Slater waved a hand. "That's my rate."

"Fine," she said flatly.

"Payment is due in advance. Meaning right now."

Sybil scowled and pulled open her bag, and dug out a wallet, and riffled through its contents. She set a sheaf of C-notes on his desk.

Reaching for the pile, Slater scooped them up, not bothering to count them.

"Once you have the package, you can hold it for me until I'm ready for it." Sybil gestured to the safe in the corner. "Does that thing work? You can keep it in there."

"Why would you trust me to hold it? I could just open it and sell the dope or the guns, or keep the cash."

"I don't think you're that guy. Even if you were, my client is a powerful man. He'd want to talk to you."

"He'd hunt me down and grease me, you mean."

Sybil chuckled. "Such a colorful expression. He's definitely not someone you want to mess with."

He already had messed with the guy—she had to be talking about Dragan.

"When is this going down?" Slater said.

"In the next few days. It has to be during the trade show, when it's crowded."

"Tell the delivery guy I'll be wearing a blue ball cap and eyeglasses with very colorful frames."

"That works," she said, "but you won't know him without a code word. I'll let you know what that is once I pin down a time."

"It's like a damn spy movie," Slater said. "Can't he just recognize me from the glasses and the cap?"

She held his gaze. "We always do it this way. It's called double-blind security. You've never met, but you each have a key to identify the other person."

"Whatever." Slater sat up. "You have to leave. I'm ex-hausted."

"Long day?" she said as she rose.

"I'm not going to lie to you, Sybil. I work and I work till I'm half dead, doing what I have to do to keep all this going." He waved his arm at the room. "The banks and my mechanic and all the moving parts. And it still feels like I'm climbing a never-ending slope in the Sierra. With every step I'm sliding backward in the scree."

"That's actually what most people call life, you big drama queen," she said, and walked out.

SEVENTEEN

S LATER HEARD THE DOOR latch, and sat listening to the silence for a minute. It was quiet—the sewing factories had cleared out for the day. His phone had buzzed in his pants a minute ago, and he pulled it out to check. O'Dowd had called, and he tapped her name to call her back.

"Dragan has a couple of gaming places," she said. "My contact knows about one in Buena Park. It's in the back of a smoke shop. They run card games and some slots."

"Can I just walk in?"

"Usually you need to be invited by someone who's already known there. It's all on the down-low. My contact said if you say Rosie invited you to play cards, they should let you in."

"Who's Rosie?"

"She manages the place," O'Dowd said. "Knowing her name should get you in the door. Take cash with you. You'll need it."

"Is there a dress code?"

"It's a sleazy strip mall in Orange County, Slater, not Monte Carlo. I'll text you the address."

"Thanks for the info," he said.

"It's billable hours. You're going to pay me for it."

"I wouldn't have it any other way."

Once he'd ended the call, his phone buzzed with the address from O'Dowd. When he copied it to his navigation app, it said it would take almost an hour, even though it was right down the 5. That had to be about Saturday traffic. It got heavier as the day wore on.

He really was tired, and he rubbed his eyes. Flying had sucked the life out of him. But he needed to work. Thinking about it, the phrase to get him in the door at Dragan's illicit casino was about card games. That meant poker and blackjack. He wasn't going to take the time to learn poker, but blackjack was manageable.

Pulling his keyboard toward him, he did a search for how to win at blackjack. There were several similar strategies on when to take a card and when to stand based on what cards the dealer showed. Slater spent a minute trying to memorize the advice, then went down to the Continental and got on the freeway.

Buena Park had a low-income vibe, and wide boulevards with churches and body shops and liquor stores. He pulled into the strip mall at the address O'Dowd had sent and spotted the smoke shop. The lot was too crowded—all these cars would get in the way if he needed to leave in a hurry. He drove out and parked on a quiet side street.

Since it was Dragan's business, there was the risk that he might be here. If he was, Slater would have to fade. Of course Dragan would remember him—Slater had punched the guy in the face.

Walking back to the strip mall, he went into the smoke shop. It was a narrow space, with a wall of shelves crowded with vape pens, a colorful array of bottles of flavored vape juice, and on the top shelf a row of glass bongs. The opposite side was a plexiglass barrier fronting the counter, with a little cutout at the register to pay through.

The place was deserted except for the clerk, a chubby guy with saggy jeans and a scruffy beard, his unctuous black hair tied back. He was parked on a stool near the register.

"Rosie invited me to play cards," Slater said as he stepped over to him.

"Fine by me. The door's open."

"Where's the door? I've never been here before."

The guy frowned. "You go in through the Frigidaire." He jutted his chin toward the back of the shop. "I'll unlock it. Listen for the click."

Slater walked over to it. The tall white door had a chrome handle. With rounded corners and the surface bulging outward, it looked old, dating to the middle of the last century. From inside it he heard the snap of an electric lock disengaging, and he pulled on the handle. It wasn't actually an icebox—it was way too deep, and not cold inside. This was a little room with black walls and low blue lighting, and no obvious way through.

"There's nothing in here," Slater said, looking toward the clerk.

The guy glanced toward the parking lot and lowered his voice. "It's like an air lock. Just close the door behind you."

Stooping to step through the door, he saw there was a handle on the inside, and he pulled it closed. The moment it latched, the back wall of the little room swung open. He was greeted with a sudden wave of noise and smoky air as he stepped into the card room. The place was really well soundproofed—he hadn't heard a hint of the din from outside.

Under a high unfinished ceiling with exposed beams, a row of slot machines clanked and flashed along one wall, every one of them with a player perched on a stool and engaged with it. There were three blackjack tables, two with games in progress, and half a dozen people crowded around a roulette wheel. At the far side was a long narrow table. Nobody was using it now, but he knew that was for shooting craps.

It wasn't nearly as sad and seedy as he'd expected. This was a full-on casino and it was hopping with players. Just like in the legal casinos in Nevada, a haze of tobacco smoke hung in the air. It made sense that management wouldn't enforce that law, seeing as the whole operation was illegal. Looking around, he realized that O'Dowd was right, in a way—Slater stood out in this crowd. Most of the clientele were Asian and over fifty.

Near the air-lock entrance a beefy guy was standing against the wall, his head shaved, wearing a dark dress shirt with a necktie. As he stepped in, the guy briefly looked him over, his expression glazed, then looked away. That was a very good sign. This guy was the muscle, and the optimal reaction from him was disinterest.

He was armed, Slater saw, with a big old .38 semi-automatic on his hip. He wasn't even trying to conceal it. That was likely the point, so that the customers knew there'd be consequences for misbehaving.

Along the wall a few feet past him was a window with solid brass bars over it, and Slater stepped over and leaned in. The cashier was a twenty-something guy with spiky hair.

"What's the buy-in for blackjack?" he said.

"Right now it's five."

Digging out his wad of cash, Slater handed over two twenties and a sawbuck, and the clerk slid a rack of chips toward him. Looking them over, he saw that this would be easy—they were clearly marked with $5.

Carrying his chips, he made a circuit of the room, taking it in. There was no sign of Dragan, and just the one security guy. All the dealers were wearing the same black vest over a white shirt.

He took a stool at a blackjack table where two other people were sitting. The green felt tabletop had outlines for each player's cards and was marked PAYS 2 TO 1 in yellow letters. The guy on the next stool, wearing a rumpled gray suit, was playing two hands at the same time.

"It's five to play," the dealer said, and Slater slid over a chip. The deal happened fast, and Slater hesitated when his cards dropped. "Uh … stay."

The guy next to him double-tapped a finger on the table to get another card rather than asking for it, and once he said "Stay," the dealer showed her cards, and took all their chips.

On the next hand he tried to remember the strategy, and lost another chip. A few rounds into it he actually won a hand, but then lost several more. He was able to get into the pace of the game, and won again, but in the end he lost more than he won, even using the strategy he'd memorized. Once all his chips were gone, he got up and stretched his back.

The guy in the rumpled suit eyed him sidelong. "You're bad luck."

"And you're a patsy for not walking away," Slater said.

Over by the slot machines he stood at the wall to look over the room. He wasn't even sure what he was doing here. This wasn't a central part of his case, just a gut feeling that he should check it out and see what Dragan was doing, and where his money came from.

A woman appeared at his elbow, petite and only as tall as his shoulder. In her fifties, her dark hair was in a tight bundle around her head, and she had smoker's lines under her eyes. She was wearing the black vest of the staff, but he hadn't seen her dealing.

"How's your luck going?" She had a slight accent—Mandarin, maybe, or Tagalog.

"Freezing cold. I went bust."

She laughed. "Take a breath and hit it again. I'm sure things will change."

"You must be Rosie."

Her brow furrowed. "Correct. I haven't seen you here before."

"I do some work for Mrs. Wang," Slater said. "She told me about this place. She's not here tonight, though."

"I'm not sure I know her."

"Has Dragan been in today?"

Rosie stepped around to look him in the eye. "What do you know about Dragan?"

"I know this is his place. He has to pick up the cash at some point, right? The house always wins."

Her eyes hardened. "You're with the bunco squad."

"I'm not the cops," Slater said. "I'm just asking you a simple question."

"You can't hang around my place to spy on the boss."

Looking toward the cashier's cage, she snapped her fingers, and the burly enforcer stepped over.

"Is there a problem?" he said.

Rosie took a step back. "This pigeon is sticking his nose in where it doesn't belong. It's time for him to leave."

The guy reached for Slater's arm. "Come on, *payaso*."

Slater shrugged out of his grip. "Keep your paws to yourself."

"It's time to go."

"Unless you're going to draw down on me," he said, gesturing to his sidearm, "you don't get to tell me what to do."

The guy groaned, and slowly shook his head, then threw a fast right. Slater hadn't anticipated that, hadn't been ready for it, and took it on the jaw, his head snapping sideways. Before he could recover, the guy grabbed his wrist. Slater tried to twist out of it, but this guy was strong, and fast, and he shoved his arm up his back.

Slater knew a wrestling move to get out of this hold that involved flipping the opponent over his hip. But this guy was big—he might break his own arm in the effort, and with that weapon on his hip it didn't make sense to escalate. He let the guy frog-march him toward the back of the room, opposite the door from the smoke shop. A few people looked up from the slots, but most either ignored them or didn't even notice.

The guy hustled him through a doorway with an emergency exit sign above it, and when they got to the fire door, he shoved Slater into the crash bar, and the door snapped open. This was outside, a gritty alley with ancient broken asphalt and lined by cinder-block walls.

Once they were through the door, the guy pushed him hard, and Slater stumbled and lost his balance. He managed to direct his momentum lower, to roll sideways, so that he landed on his butt rather than on his palms or his knees. He sat up and massaged his manhandled bicep.

"Did you really have to do that?" he demanded. "You could have just shown me the door."

The guy jabbed his finger at him. "Don't show your face here again." Turning to the fire exit, the door had swung shut, and when he tugged on the handle, it was locked.

"Oopsie," Slater said, watching him from the middle of the alley.

He turned and jutted his chin at him. "Fuck you," he said through his teeth, then walked toward the side street at the end of the building.

"Any time, *cabrón*," Slater called after him.

The guy actually was kind of hot, his chunkiness more muscle than flab.

Getting to his feet, he brushed the grit off the seat of his jeans. At least he hadn't ripped them when he landed. He rolled his neck and walked the same direction the goon had gone, swinging his arm to rotate it and get the blood flowing again. It hurt but it didn't feel like anything had torn or dislocated.

Why hadn't he anticipated that first punch? He'd let the guy get the drop on him. He could have taken him if he'd been smarter about it. But then again, the person with the gun was ultimately going to win any disagreement.

It was getting dark out, the streetlamps winking on as he climbed in behind the wheel of the Continental. Pulling out his phone, he saw a text from Big Mike:

How was your trip?

He twisted the key in the ignition, firing up the throaty engine, then texted back:

Didn't Hugo fill you in?

Mike's response came soon after:

You owe me.

Slater thumb-typed a reply:

I can't wait. I'm getting a stiffy just thinking about you. When and where?

It didn't take long for him to answer:

Tomorrow evening at the stable?

Slater wrote back:

That works. You have to wear the boots.

He sent another text:

Have to.

Thinking about it, he sent another:

I want you to imagine me rock-hard and deep inside you, my arms wrapped around your sweaty body, my hot mouth on your neck.

He wasn't really that turned on by the guy, but he knew anticipation was a big part of sex.

————◆————

WHEN SLATER GOT BACK to his house, he found Pike upstairs in the kitchen with a takeout bag on the counter.

"These are from that new dumpling place," Pike said. "I hope they're good. Ready to strap on the old feed bag?"

Slater embraced him and mouthed his jaw. "You're not even horsey and you're using horse language."

"Some of my neighbors in Albuquerque are horsey." He ran a hand into Slater's hair.

"And you knew every one of them, didn't you." He met Pike's mouth and lingered in it.

Eventually Pike pulled back. "Come on. It's getting cold."

They sat at the table to eat, and Pike looked him over as he dug in a little white box with his chopsticks. "You look tired. I guess we had a long day."

"I also went behind the Orange Curtain after."

"The scintillating heights of affluent Irvine?"

"Buena Park. It's at the opposite end of the economy. Gritty like LA but not as crowded."

Pike set his chopsticks down. "It's Saturday night. It feels like we should go out somewhere."

"Even though we were up before the sun and flew across three states and back?"

"I'm tired too. But again, it's Saturday night."

Slater chuckled as he set down a takeout box. "What did you have in mind?"

"There's a queer line dancing class. It's over in WeHo. There's also a dance hall that has swing lessons."

"All these options seem to involve dancing."

"We could also just go listen to jazz at that hotcha place on Crenshaw."

"I want to do what you want to do," Slater said, and folded his arms. "Doris used to swing dance. I know what it looks like. Let's do that."

Pike beamed. "I'll see if there's room for us."

"My only demand is that you buy me a shot of espresso on the way."

Before they left, Pike made him change out of his jeans into trousers and dress shoes. He said he'd be able to move better. The pants felt weird and light, like the kind of sheer clothes Dragan wore, and with the thin little shoes he could feel every pebble underfoot.

Pulling up on the dance hall, Slater recognized the place. It had been here forever, its pink stucco fronting the street, the bare wooden rafters inside arcing high overhead.

"I used to come here with Doris," he said as they walked in. "It looks exactly the same."

There was no music on, but two straight couples were messing around with dance moves on the floor. A woman in a billowy blouse caught sight of them and stepped over. Her blond hair was tied back, and she introduced herself as Janie, the instructor.

There were only a few other people in the class, and Janie started them off with a triple step, making them practice it over and over. Pike was already good at it, of course, and Slater struggled to catch up as they practiced.

Next Janie taught them how to turn under the partner's arm. It was actually easy once you got the knack of it. Pike made it look fluid, and Slater just felt awkward, but it got easier as he started to commit it to muscle memory.

When Janie called a break, they grabbed bottles of water that someone had set out and sat on a bench at the side of the room.

"Do you have any idea how hot it is to watch you dance?" Slater said. "You're so confident. It looks so natural."

Pike laughed. "You're the only person who sees that."

"I'm not so sure. At one point Janie was totally giving you the big eye."

"I'm not actually that good at it. You're doing OK, though. I can tell you have athletic sense."

"It actually reminds me of wrestling and fistfights," Slater said.

"In what possible way?"

"It's the same idea. You have to move in a specific pattern, and you have to think fast. This is more predictable—you know what the other person is going to do."

"And there's a lot less likelihood you'll wind up bleeding."

———◆———

BACK AT THE HOUSE, as he followed Pike up the stairs, Slater said, "One-two-three, one-two-three. Come on, boy, hustle."

Pike chuckled and stopped on the landing. "I'm sweaty. I should shower."

He grabbed the sides of his belt and pulled him close. "You should fuck me first. I want you on top of me. The way your body moves. You're like the boss of dancing."

"I love that you see me that way." He leaned in to mouth Slater's neck.

Pulling him into the bedroom, they were soon naked. Pike was already hard as he climbed onto the bed. Slater sprawled on his belly, and Pike straddled him, pressing his cock into his thigh.

"Man, I love your body."

He grabbed the lube and stroked himself, then penetrated him, slowly at first. He lowered his weight onto him and shoved his arms under Slater's. As he worked up to pounding him, he kept a firm grip, and strained into him as he climaxed.

They lay that way for a while, hot and sweaty and intense, with Pike's breath gradually slowing. When he rolled off, Slater sat up and stroked his raging woody.

"Sit behind me," he said, and Pike knelt at his back, reaching around to squeeze his cock.

Slater pulled his other arm up and folded it around his neck, notching his throat in the crook of Pike's arm. Pike stroked him, and squeezed his neck tighter as he got close, but not enough to cut off his air. It was enough to send him over, and Slater came, his body shuddering.

Afterward he stretched out on his belly and started to drift off. Pike got up and went to shower. When he came back and got into bed, Slater stirred.

"I feel like I'm winded," he mumbled. "Like I've been slammed to the mat with my lungs emptied."

Pike caressed his back. "Did I squeeze too hard?"

"It's not that. That was fucking hot. It's a metaphor. Like when Agamemnon says his soldiers roared like the waves crashing on the rocks. It's what you do to me. You knock the wind out of me."

EIGHTEEN

W AKING ALONE, SLATER DOZED for a while,
slowly coming up to consciousness. He could
hear movement upstairs, the rattle of a knife
or a spoon on crockery. Pike was making coffee or having his breakfast.

He needed to talk to Cody Layton, or Patsy, or Graham today to find out whether what Lunelle told him was true. They wouldn't be in the office on Sunday. But he had a connection to Graham.

Grabbing his phone from the bedside table, he opened Svetlana's app and checked on the vehicle tracker on Cody's Silverado. The battery had died last night. The map showed a gray dot with the last known location, at Desert View. He saw that Sybil had texted earlier:

I have some information for you. I'm in my office.
Be here by ten.

Slater sent Graham a text:

Can I see you today?

His reply came a moment later:

It's a long drive for you, city boy. Want to meet me in Newhall? It's about halfway. There's a great park with some hiking trails.

He didn't really need to go hiking, but less time on the highway was appealing. He wrote back:

Send me a map link. Give me a couple hours.

Forcing himself out of bed, he showered and then pulled on his jeans and a long-sleeved shirt. Upstairs, Slater poured himself a coffee and went to look for Pike. He was out on the deck despite the cool of the morning, sitting at the patio table, eating a bagel and looking at his phone. He went out to join him.

After he felt sufficiently awake, Slater got up from the table. "I'm out today. On my case."

"I was thinking I might clear the leaves off the roof," Pike said.

"That's a great idea. Use the leaf rake. Otherwise you'll poke a hole in the surface and we'll get wet when it rains."

"I think I'll be able to figure it out."

"Flat roofs are a real bear."

Pike chuckled. "And you're a real control freak."

He dropped to one knee and pressed his face into Pike's belly. "I'm not telling you what to do."

"I don't mind."

Slater kissed him and then rose. "There's leaf bags in the garage."

On the drive to Sybil's, his phone buzzed in its dash mount. It was her—he wasn't going to pick up, as he'd be in her office in a hot minute.

"Idiot," he muttered, and swiped it away. She needed to chill out.

Nosing the Continental into the underground garage, he parked and rode up to the twenty-eighth floor. Sybil pulled open the door soon after he knocked.

"Finally," she said, and waved him in, and went behind her desk.

As he walked in, Slater scanned the walls for an alarm panel, but he couldn't see it anywhere. Maybe she controlled it from her phone. At some point he'd need to find out how these new systems worked.

As he dropped into the chair across from her, Sybil said, "How is the case going with Ben?"

"I'm pretty sure I know what's happening. Just not who's behind it."

Her eyebrows shot up. "What is it that's happening?"

"That's privileged information, sister. Why am I here?"

"You have a job to do. The delivery person will look for the blue ball cap. He'll ask you about Shorty Wilson, and you reply, 'That guy is a bum.'"

"The fuck is Shorty Wilson?"

"Some baseball player."

"You could have told me that on the phone."

"I told you my client thinks we might be under surveillance. We're avoiding electronic communication."

Slater studied her face. The client had to be Dragan. Rosie said that too, the thing about Dragan being spied on. Dragan and Rosie had both thought he was on the bunco squad. They all sounded paranoid.

"When is the handoff going down?"

"Now," she said flatly, and picked up her phone to glance at it. "Actually in ten minutes."

"No pressure though," Slater said.

She frowned. "That's on you. I told you to get here earlier. But you've still got time. The convention center is two blocks from here."

"That place must have half a dozen men's rooms. Which one?"

"I'm told the largest one is near the entrance to the south building. On the left side, close to Pico."

"And you don't want me to bring the package back here."

"I don't know if my office is being watched," Sybil

said. "Just keep it in your safe. I won't need it for a day or two. Text me to let me know you got it. But don't say that. Just say you've filled out the form."

"I actually know how to do this stuff," Slater said, and rose. "Can you validate me?"

"*Este pendejo*," she said, but opened a desk drawer to grab a little parking card with a bar code on it, and handed it to him, flashing a fake smile.

Slater didn't know exactly what that expression meant, but he heard it a lot. It was definitely an expression of contempt.

Once he was behind the wheel of the Continental, he switched on Svetlana's camera-jamming glasses and pulled them on, then drove up the ramp and over to the convention center. There was no street parking, only paid lots, and he turned in to one, irritated at the inflated cost. Grabbing his blue ball cap from the back seat, he pulled it on, then climbed out. He opened the trunk and took out his empty satchel, slinging it over his shoulder.

At the main building several tables were set up right inside the doors. He spotted one of the people seated there who wasn't talking to anyone else, a woman with a bowl haircut, and approached her.

She looked up and smiled. "Do you have a pass?"

"This is the first time I've been here. I'm a buyer."

"If you just need a day pass, it's twenty-five."

Slater dug out his cash and set down a twenty and a fin.

"Your name and your company?" she said, plucking the bills from the table.

"John Slade. Amalgamated Textiles."

She typed that on a keyboard and then pulled a sheet of cardstock off her printer, deftly folding it and inserting it into a clear plastic sleeve. Clipping it onto a lanyard, she handed it to him, and he looped it around his neck as he stepped into the exhibit hall.

The place was massive, he saw, looking down an aisle with vendor booths lining either side. It seemed to stretch for miles. He'd never seen so many clothes together in one place.

Checking the time on his phone, he saw he was running late, and looked for signs pointing to the restrooms. He followed the arrows to the side of the hall. This was a huge room too, he saw, walking into the men's room. There were a dozen or more stalls and a whole row of urinals along one wall. Sybil was right—the place was busy, with a constant stream of people walking in and out.

Slater stood at the sink and looked at his face. This mirror was a lot less kind than the one in his bathroom, the harsh lighting showing dark circles under his eyes. He tapped at his split lip. It still looked scabbed and ugly. Twice this week he'd let some lowlife get the jump on him. He heaved a sigh. What a freaking mess.

A guy stepped up to the next sink and started to wash his hands.

"I like your cap," he said. "How about that shortstop? Shorty Wilson."

"That guy is a bum," Slater said, meeting his eye in the mirror.

He chuckled. "I hear you, brother." He looked down at Slater's boots, then turned away and stepped into one of the stalls behind them.

It took a second for Slater to realize what was going on. He went into the adjacent stall and closed the door. A moment later a package appeared under the divider, and Slater reached down to take hold of it. Wrapped in brown paper, it was the size of the boxes they used for four takeout doughnuts at Nathan's shop, and it had the same shape. It felt solid—too heavy to be drugs, and not weapons either. This was definitely cash.

As he tucked the package into his satchel, he heard the delivery man unlock the stall door and walk away. Slater waited a minute, then walked out. He made a circuit of the convention hall, not really focused on what he was seeing, the clothes and the fabrics and the displays, but he had to do it in case he was being watched.

Eventually he walked out the front entrance. On the way to his car, he checked to see if anyone was shagging him, but there was no sign of that.

Climbing into the Continental, he drove across Downtown to his office. The surface lot was almost empty—nobody worked in the building on Sunday. Upstairs he flicked on the office lights and stuck his head into Max's office to make sure he really was alone.

In his own office he knelt in front of the safe, and dialed in the combination, and pulled open the heavy door. Feeling the heft of the package, he hesitated. Why was he doing this? Maybe he should cut the damn thing open. But he already knew what it was, and in the big picture it didn't really matter. It was a tight fit, but he got it positioned inside, then closed the door of the safe, and twisted the handle, then spun the dial to lock it.

He sat at his desk for a minute and texted Sybil:

I completed those forms. Let me know when I can drop them off.

Once he'd locked up the office, Slater went down to the surface lot and got on the freeway. The roads were busy all day Sunday, but at least it was moving, and in less than an hour he was in Newhall.

The location Graham had sent was in a gravel parking lot, on a hillside at the edge of town. As he drove in he saw the sign marking it as a state park. He pulled up next to the dull-red Wrangler and climbed out, stretching his back as Graham stepped over.

"How many classic cars do you have?" he said, looking over the Continental.

"Just this one. I wrecked the Thunderbird on the Newhall Grade. Right after I saw you on Wednesday."

His eyebrows shot up. "Well, that sucks. You weren't injured?"

"Only my wallet."

"This one looks to be of a similar vintage."

"A little older. It's a '73."

"I can't believe such a massive car only has two doors."

"It wasn't meant to haul kids around," Slater said. "It was meant to look cool."

"I can't deny that it still does."

"So you're a hiker."

"Not really," Graham said. "But this is a fun walk. Uphill at first, then a loop in the canyon. About an hour total."

Graham chatted as they started off, but soon fell silent, as they were both breathing hard on the ascent. At the top they stood for a while and took in the view over the mountains and the town below. A train was snaking along in the middle of the urban sprawl and slowing down.

"Is that a commuter line?" Slater said.

"It goes all the way to Lancaster."

"Who knew."

"Everybody who lives around here," Graham said.

That made him laugh, and they started into the canyon, where the trail was wide enough that they could walk abreast. There was a little elevation gain but nothing like the climb at the beginning. It wasn't so bad to be out in nature, Slater decided. Even though the chaparral was dull and dry from the summer heat, waiting patiently for the winter rains, it felt like when he worked on landscaping, getting his hands in the dirt, and it was definitely recharging his batteries.

"So Cody Layton is your uncle," Slater said.

"That's right."

"Why didn't you tell me that? Why didn't Cody mention it?"

"Why would anyone point that out? It doesn't matter."

"It seems to me like you're obfuscating. I just can't figure out why."

"There's no secret, but we don't advertise it either," Graham said. "Cody doesn't want Desert View to look like a mom-and-pop family business."

"Even though that's kind of what it is, with your mom working there."

"My dad works there too. In the shop." He waved a hand. "The feds have expectations about how businesses are run. To get one single contract you have to go through hundreds of pages of disclosures and rules and acknowledgments."

"What about Ben?" Slater said. "Did he ever flirt with you?"

Graham eyed him sidelong. "I thought you came out here to see me. I didn't realize I was going to be interrogated."

"You're a witness in my case."

"I didn't witness anything."

"You knew Ben."

Graham huffed, and they walked in silence for a while.

"I didn't know Ben very well," he said finally. "People come and go."

"Except your relatives. They seem to stick around."

When they got back to the parking lot, Graham said, "There's a coffee place near the station. You want to follow me there?"

"I'm up for java," Slater said.

When they got to the coffee joint, there were two parking spots right in front, and he pulled in behind the Wrangler.

"I love the Doris Day parking," he said to Graham as they climbed out. "That never happens in the city."

"What's Doris Day parking?"

"In her movies she's driving around Midtown Manhattan in a car the size of mine, and when she pulls up at the place she wants to be, there's a spot for her to park right out front."

Graham chuckled. "One of the perks of living in a small town."

Inside he ordered a soy latte, and sat with Graham on the stools at the bar along the front window.

"So how serious is that ring on your finger?" Graham said.

"Serious as a heart attack, brother. It's part of a whole narrative complex."

"I feel like we have a connection, Slater. I thought maybe we could try something. Step out together. You said I was a slab of cream cheese. And you liked my hair."

"Red means stop." Slater held his gaze. "You're not seeing me, Graham. I'm bad news. Real bad. I'd ruin your life."

"I'd be willing to take that risk." He looked away. "How long are you going to be investigating Ben Clague?"

"I'm not investigating Ben. I'm investigating Desert View and the supposed NDA. So far it's just vapor. Cody and Patsy refused to show it to me. That alone says a lot."

"You don't believe them?"

"I don't believe anybody. But I have some theories. I'm close to figuring out what they're up to." That was pure bluster, and he watched Graham's face to see if it sparked a reaction.

His eyebrows shot up, but then his attention was

pulled away. Outside the window, a woman paused, and peered in at them, and waved. Her dark hair was styled around her ears, and she was wearing a lot of makeup, and a colorful print scarf.

She stepped inside and approached them. "Graham," she said in a singsong voice. "How are you?" She reached for Slater's hand and gave it a squeeze. "I'm Marion."

Graham was red-faced now. "Sorry—this is Slater."

"Do you work at Desert View?" Marion said.

"He's dating my sister," Graham said quickly.

Her eyebrows rose. "I see."

Slater frowned at Graham. "That's right. Because I'm so into women."

"Cathy, right?" Marion said. "I haven't actually met her."

He folded his arms. "Yeah, we got it bad, and that ain't good."

"I know Cathy was a Bruin. Did you meet at UCLA?"

"Something like that."

"So are you a child therapist too?"

"Oh, hell, no. One of those in the family is plenty."

"We should catch up," Marion said, eyeing Graham. "Let me get a coffee."

Rising from his stool, Slater said, "I was just headed out. Cathy wants me to pick up tampons."

"Such a gentleman," she said, and squeezed his forearm.

Walking out, he got in behind the wheel of the Continental. He was due at Big Mike's stable, and he probably should have made time for a shower after hiking. But Big Mike probably wouldn't mind if he was a little ripe.

NINETEEN

W HEN SLATER GOT TO Downey, the parking at the stable was almost full, and when he went inside the main building, there were lots of people around. He asked for Big Mike at the front desk.

The clerk peered at her computer screen. "You're here for a meeting? Mike booked event room B." She pointed down the hall, in the direction of the stables.

The door marked B was half open, and he rapped on it as he stepped inside. There was a long conference table, and a credenza, and big windows looking out onto the show ring. The only occupant was Mike, wearing his riding outfit, the tan jodhpurs and the tall boots, his white shirt open halfway down his chest.

Mike took a deep breath. "You made it."

"You wore the boots," Slater said, looking him over as he closed the door.

He stood up straighter. "It didn't seem like I had a choice."

The guy seemed jittery. Not tweaking, Slater decided. Maybe just nervous with anticipation.

"How was Santa Fe?"

"I accomplished what I needed to. I don't think Hugo knew what to make of me, though. I'm sure I don't look like your usual business associates."

"I wasn't about to tell him you were a ruffian."

"Even though that's essentially the truth," Slater said. "So where do you want me to rock your world? Is there a stall with fresh straw in it that's not in use?"

"We'd be seen. There's a lot of people here today. This is the only private space I could find."

"It's not very private with all these windows."

"Right." Mike stepped over to the corner and pressed a wall switch. The windows instantly turned milky-white and opaque.

Slater put his hands on his hips. "How cool is that? The things you can do when you have money."

"The problem is the door," Mike said. "I assumed I'd be able to lock it, but it doesn't have a bolt."

"I can fix that."

He stepped over to the row of armless chairs along the wall, upholstered in the same forest green as the wheeled ones around the conference table. Lifting it up, he carried it over and angled the back under the door handle, then stomped on the front of the seat, shifting the legs to the floor. Leaning in to tug on the sides of it, he found it was wedged in tightly.

"Nobody's coming through this door without a battering ram or a grenade," he said.

"You have such useful practical skills."

Stepping over to him, Slater slid his fingers inside Mike's belt buckle. "You want to see more?"

Mike stood up straighter, and put his hands on Slater's biceps, and squeezed. "You're warm."

"Ninety-eight degrees, baby."

"I wanted to ask—are you always the saddle, or does it go the other way sometimes?"

"You can fuck me, big guy, if that's what you want," Slater said. "I can take it like a man."

"I do want. Very much. But maybe you could do me first."

"The big guy wants it all. I guess that fits with your social status."

He put a hand on Mike's shoulder, then grabbed the hair on the back of his head and pulled on it to expose his neck. Mike flinched but didn't pull away, and gasped as Slater mouthed his Adam's apple, then his jaw, and his ear. At some point he got a nasty mouthful of Mike's cologne.

"You're so hot," Mike said.

Slater groped his pants. "You're already hard."

Unbuckling his belt, he yanked down the jodhpurs, and knelt, and took him into his mouth. Mike ran his hands into his hair. After a minute Slater pulled back.

"You need to get out of these pants."

Mike pulled a chair out from the table, and sat to pull off his riding boots, and ditched the pants.

Unbuttoning his shirt, Slater jutted his chin. "The boots stay on."

Mike grinned and stepped into them. Moving close, Slater grabbed his butt and boosted him onto the table.

"Up here?"

"The geometry works." Slater dug a little tube of lube from his hip pocket and pushed Mike onto his back. Lifting his knee, he worked a thumb into him. Mike winced, and Slater leaned in to meet his mouth, exploring it as he probed deeper.

Eventually he pulled his cock out of his jeans, and found a condom in his pocket, and rolled it on. He pulled Mike to the edge of the table, and lifting his boots onto his shoulders, pressed into him. Starting slow, he was soon pounding him.

Pausing, Slater massaged his thighs. "This is your rodeo. I can pop now or do it later."

"Can I still fuck you?" Mike said, panting.

"Affirmative with either option."

"Then do it. Fuck me."

Slater grabbed his ankles through his boots and

pressed in, pounding him, and strained and grunted as he climaxed. Leaning in, he rested on top of Mike for a moment, and licked a drop of sweat from his neck, then mouthed his chest.

When he pulled back, Mike said, "Do you have any idea how hot that was? You didn't even take off your pants."

"I'll have to now," he said, and pulled off the condom, then dropped to one knee to untie his boots. He kicked them off and stepped out of his jeans.

Mike slid off the conference table, stroking himself, and walked over to the armless chairs, and pulled one out from the wall. "Here?"

"Works for me," Slater said, and once Mike sat down, he ripped open a condom and rolled it on him. "You're so damn hard."

"I've had some chemical assistance."

"Right on." He straddled him, and eased down onto him, moving slowly. Mike put his hands on his thighs, pressing him downward. "Oh, man." Slater winced and groaned, then shifted around to get into it.

With his hands on Mike's shoulders, Slater rocked back and forth. When he met Mike's gaze, there was intensity in his eyes.

"You cheap little thug," Mike said through his teeth.

"You love it."

Mike grasped at his thighs. "Fucking lowlife."

"You love that too."

He could see Mike was getting close, and increased his pace. Finally Mike grimaced and strained into him. Closing his eyes for a minute, he could hear Mike's breath slowing.

"My leg is falling asleep."

"Suck it up," Slater snapped.

He laughed. "Such a hard-ass."

Slater rose and watched as Mike sat up, flaccid now, and pulled off the condom.

"It's nice that there's a clear end point with men," Mike said. "With women it's more nuanced. I find it kind of annoying."

"I wouldn't know."

"I wish we could do this again."

He snatched his shirt up from the floor. "Why not? You're a hot little horseman. And those boots kind of seal the deal."

"I'll look forward to that." Mike stepped into his jodhpurs, yanking them up. "Maybe you and I can go to Santa Fe, instead of you and your boyfriend."

"So you did talk to Hugo."

His expression sobered. "I hope you don't mind me calling you names. In the heat of passion it just came out."

Slater was buttoning his fly. "You can call me anything you want, big guy. Besides, none of those names were technically inaccurate."

"I meant no disrespect."

"When it's part of sex, I don't take it too seriously."

"Because sex doesn't matter to you?"

"It matters," Slater said, "but it's like a parallel space. A different set of rules."

Mike buttoned his shirt and smoothed the front. "Do I look like I just had sex? I know a lot of the people out there."

"You totally have that look. But nobody who notices is going to care, and anybody who cares isn't going to notice."

He nodded. "Would you mind leaving first?"

Slater stooped to yank on the legs of the chair that he'd wedged under the door handle. It took a couple of hard pulls, but eventually it came loose, and he set it aside. Eyeing Mike, he double-clicked his tongue, then stepped into the hall and closed the door behind him.

It was dark out as he climbed into the Continental, and twisted the key in the ignition, and flicked on the lights. At his house, when he pulled into the garage, he took the lanyard from the textile convention, still sitting on the passenger seat, and climbed the stairs.

Pike was on the sofa in the living room with his nose in a novel. He set it aside as Slater came in. Dropping the lanyard on the coffee table, Slater knelt in front of him.

"Is the roof still intact?"

"Intact and leaf-free," Pike said. "I even hosed off the built-up grime. In New Mexico it's the color of the desert, but here it's black."

"Because it's soot, not dirt," Slater said. "All those tailpipes and tires."

Reaching for the lanyard, he read the card. "John Slade from Amalgamated Textiles."

"That's me. I had to go to a trade show."

Leaning toward him, Pike met his mouth, and mouthed his neck, then pulled back, his brow furrowing. "You don't wear cologne. Where were you all day, exactly?"

"I told you—at a trade show. You know you don't have to be a cop all the time, right?"

"How did you get cologne on your neck?"

"Don't ask."

"Why not?" he said, raising his voice.

"I'm not going to lie to you."

"That's great, Slater. True progress. But not telling me is equivalent to lying."

"Why do you need to know about my work?"

"Let's call it part of our narrative complex."

Avoiding his gaze, he sat on the sofa and leaned down

to untie his boots. "I had to fuck that idiot rich guy who loaned me his airplane. It didn't mean anything."

"Sex in exchange for goods and services," Pike said. "That's the technical definition of prostitution."

"It's just sex." Pulling off his boots, he sat up and met his eye. "We agreed I could fuck people for work if I needed to. It's one of the rules."

Pike was breathing hard. "I wish I was enough for you."

He closed his eyes for a moment, and tried to swallow the lump forming in his throat. "I don't want to hurt you. You know I'm crazy. You know I'm no damn good."

"I can handle all that."

"Maybe it's like Davis. Is he enough for your social life? He's fun to watch a ball game with, and play poker with, but I know you hang out with other people."

"I'm not in love with Davis," Pike said. "I'm not living with him, and I'm not embroiled in a multidimensional narrative complex with him." He held up his left hand and waggled his fingers. "I'm not wearing a ring that symbolizes my commitment to him."

Slater looked away. "I don't know what to say."

"Pick me." Pike thumped his own chest with his fist. "Have sex with me."

"It's all about you. Everything is about you. You get me up dancing. I've never done that. It makes my heart soar because it's with you. You're the only person on the planet for me. You know that. Everything else is just ..." he gestured helplessly. "Bullshit."

Pike watched him for a moment, then leaned in, and pulled him back against his torso. Reclining on the sofa, he kept his arms tight around Slater's chest. Slater could feel his heart beating, feel his breath on the back of his neck. They sat that way for a while, not talking, Pike's iron grip saying a lot without words.

Eventually Pike let go of him. "You're going to suck my dick."

"Now?"

"Right now. If you have stamina for the airplane guy, you can put out for me too."

Slater reached for Pike's belt, but he swatted his hands away.

"Downstairs."

He got up, and Pike waited for him to go first. As if he might make a run for it. Like he was a perp. It was actually kind of hot—something about the implicit distrust. In the bedroom Pike got undressed, and Slater followed his lead. Propping himself on the pillows, Pike sat back on the bed, and raised his eyebrows, and pointed to his junk. Slater stretched out in front of him, and took him into his mouth. He was flaccid but soon got hard. When he looked up at him, Pike was watching him, an intense look in his eye. Anger, definitely, but also something more.

Eventually Pike pushed him off. "I'm going to fuck you."

Slater shifted up the bed as Pike rolled to the nightstand to grab the lube.

"On your belly," Pike said, and when Slater flipped over, he straddled him, and pressed into him. Moving gently at first, he built up the rhythm, sliding his arms under Slater's and holding him tight.

"Hooligan," Pike growled in his ear, and then louder, "You fucking hooligan." Straining into him, he climaxed.

Slater could feel Pike's muscles relaxing, the sweat dripping off his neck, his weight settling onto him. That was the second time today he'd been trash-talked in the middle of the act. Why was it so damn complicated? He wanted the good parts, not the sharp points, but they seemed to be inextricably intertwined.

Still breathing hard, Pike rolled off him. "We should do you."

"I'm OK."

Pike caressed his back for a while, but Slater couldn't look at him right now. The lump in his throat was starting to hurt. Eventually he fell asleep, still on his stomach.

Later, in the darkness, he stirred awake when Pike spoke.

"Why did you call me back?"

"What?"

"Why did you want to get into this? Get into us."

Fully awake now, Slater felt his heart start to pound. "I knew this would happen at some point. You're questioning it. Regretting it. I've blown up your life."

Pike shifted closer and wrapped an arm around his chest. "Not even a little. I'm in. Totally in. You know that. I'm just trying to understand it. The six-dimensional aspects of our narrative complex. The things happening in a direction you can't point. I'm wondering about the start of it."

Slater thought about it. "You sent me that statue of Pollux."

"And then you called me, and told me you were trash, and that I'd be crazy to get into it with you."

"Essentially, that's still accurate."

"It was a while after you'd been to New Mexico," Pike said. "What changed?"

"The day we met, I felt it. I knew you could … change everything. Demolish me, or make me want to be a better man, or burn down my world, or build a six-dimensional love that burns with the intensity of the desert sun. Make my heart swell, or trash my heart beyond repair. I knew it. I avoided it for a while. Then I decided I needed to see what would happen."

"You saw all that the day we met."

"I don't know how I knew. I just knew."

Pike was quiet for a while. "I think I get it. I thought about you a lot before you called me. I was crushed out on you from day one. I guess I felt it too. The potential. Like a big rock perched at the top of a ridge. One little nudge and so much would start to happen. So much would change."

"From that first day?"

"Actually way before that," Pike said, and squeezed him tighter. "It's always been about you, forty-niner. Even before I met you, it was you."

TWENTY

PIKE WAS GONE WHEN Slater woke in the morning, the sheers muting the sunlight, and he lay in bed for a while as his mind swam up toward consciousness. Scrabbling for his phone, he saw a text from Sybil:

I need those documents today.

He sent her a reply:

You know where to find me.

Closing his eyes again, he started to doze, until the phone rang. It was Sybil. He growled in frustration but picked up.

"Where are you?" Sybil said.

"I'm not in my office yet. Cool your jets."

"How can I get those forms if you're not in your office?"

"Yesterday I was supposed to just hang on to them, and now it's an emergency?" Slater said. "Make up your damn mind. If it's that urgent, my business partner can get to the documents and hand them over."

"What's his name?"

"It's on the office door."

"Well, let him know I'm going to come by."

"Done. Now quit bugging me."

Slater ended the call and dialed Max.

"Are you in the office today?" he said when Max picked up.

"I will be, sure."

"There's a brown paper package in the safe. I'm holding it for a crooked lawyer named Sybil Álvarez. She has her underpants in a twist and wants it today. She might come by the office to pick it up."

"What does she look like?"

"Latin, wiry, shoulder-length hair. You can ask her for ID."

"She sounds hot," Max said.

"Gams for days," he said, and ended the call.

He hadn't actually noticed Sybil's legs, but saying that might inspire Max to be more amenable to the intrusion.

Forcing himself out of bed, he went upstairs and found Pike had left half a pot of coffee, lukewarm now since the heating element had timed out. He grabbed a bagel from the bag by the toaster and sat at the dining table to munch on it and slurp from his coffee mug.

Pike had been pissed last night, but it wasn't world-destroying pissed, like he was going to move back to Albuquerque, or throw Slater's stuff out the second-floor window, or go after the Continental with a sledge hammer. Slater had assumed the worst, that Pike's anger was an IED exploding on the road and upending everything, or one of Lunelle's guided missiles, turning it all into twisted burning wreckage. But Pike made out like it was just a speed bump—he wanted to understand it, and ask some questions, not blow it up or burn it down.

What was he missing? It felt like there was something he was supposed to figure out. That stupid twelve-step book for sex addicts that Pike made him read talked about catastrophizing. Maybe that's what he was doing—blowing a manageable thing way out of proportion.

His phone buzzed, and when he looked at it, he found a text from Graham:

We need to talk. I can tell you more about Ben.

Slater wrote back:

What changed since yesterday?

His reply came a moment later:

Can you meet me at my family's place? I'm there for a couple days. Santa Cecilia Island.

Scowling, Slater thumb-typed a response:

The fuck is that?

Graham responded:

Between Catalina and Santa Cruz. It's a private island, so you have to hire a water taxi from the Marina. It takes an hour or so to get there.

He wrote back:

Why there?

A moment later, Graham replied:

I'll tell you when you come out.

He was going to have to call him. A quick search for the island showed that it was a real place, just a speck on the map. The overhead views showed a dock and a few structures among the scrubby landscape. Most of the big Channel Islands were a national park, but he knew some of the small ones were privately owned.

It was always colder at the coast, and in the closet downstairs he found a navy-blue windbreaker and pulled it on. On the drive to the Marina, he thought it through. It was a lot of traveling for a meeting, and he'd just seen him. Graham had avoided talking about Ben yesterday. Why did he want to do that now? Slater knew the guy had a crush on him. That was his own fault—he needed to keep his dick out of his cases.

He dialed Graham's number, and it went to voice mail. He ended the call without bothering to leave a message.

At the Marina he parked in a surface lot and walked down to where the boats were. Lining the walkway were some food stands, and he stepped up to the counter at one that was open and spoke to the chunky woman working there, clad in a white apron.

"Do you know where I can get a water taxi?"

She gestured toward the docks. "Across the way, in Basin C."

"Can I walk there?"

"I wouldn't. It's far. It's where that hotel is. The one with the gold windows."

Back in the Continental, he drove around the perimeter of the Marina, and eventually saw signs for the hotel, and Basin D, and then Basin C. He parked in a lot and walked down toward the docks.

There were so many apartment buildings here, chockablock and right on the water. The Marina covered a lot more ground than he'd realized, and he had no idea it was so densely populated.

On the walkway he saw a sign for Shanghai Joe's water taxi, and he followed the arrow down onto the dock. The boat moored there was white, with a canopy over a couple of rows of seats, and two big engines on the stern. A guy was standing in the back of the boat, with the cowling of one of the engines open, doing something inside it.

"Are you Joe?" Slater called to him.

The guy was in his fifties, Slater saw as he straightened up and looked toward him. His face was lined like he'd spent too much time in the sun, and he was wearing a winter jacket and a black captain's hat.

"That's Shanghai Joe. What can I do for you?"

"I need to get to Santa Cecilia," Slater said. "It's an island."

"I know what it is. That's private property."

"I have an invitation. What'll it cost me?"

"One twenty."

"Do you get paid for waiting time?"

"I'm not going to wait for you," Joe said. "Your hosts can bring you back, or radio for a pickup."

"Can we go now?"

"If you've got the cash."

"I've got it," Slater said, "but I'm not going to pay you until we get there."

He laughed. "You think I'd strand you on a rock if you paid up front?"

"It's just business."

"Let me finish up here." He gestured to the seats. "You can climb in."

Stepping aboard, Slater watched as he closed up the engine, then moved to the front, and cast off.

"You should sit down," Joe said as he sat at the wheel, and once Slater was in one of the seats, he started the engines and pulled away from the dock.

Soon they were cruising toward the mouth of the marina, and around the breakwater, and out on the open ocean. Joe cranked up the engines until they were roaring. Moving fast now, the boat bounced and dropped again as it hit each wave. The speed was great, far preferable to dawdling, but he was going to be pissed if he got seasick from this ride.

Keep your eyes on the horizon, he remembered. That was supposed to forestall getting nauseous. Catalina was off to the left, a dry scrubby mass rising from the water, seemingly pristine. It looked really close, but he knew that was illusory.

Joe sat inert at the wheel, facing the ocean ahead. Slater wanted to ask him where he got the Shanghai moniker, but he couldn't be heard over the engine noise.

After a while a dome-shaped chunk of scrubland appeared ahead, gradually growing larger. That had to be Santa Cecilia. Even though it was on the water, it looked dry—the grass was yellow, the bushes and scrub the dark green of drought. The land rose steeply from the waterline, and from here no buildings were in sight. They must be up top.

It hadn't even taken an hour to get here. As Joe approached the island, he veered to the right, following the shore. The dock came into view partway around it.

Joe idled the engine and drifted up to the dock, connecting with a gentle bump. He got to his feet and deftly tied a mooring line to a cleat. Another boat was moored on the opposite side of the dock. It looked a lot like this one, although it sat higher in the water.

Digging out his wad of cash, Slater handed over the bills.

"Thanks, friend," Joe said, and once Slater had stepped onto the dock, he cast off.

As he walked up the dock, he heard the engines roar to life again as Joe left.

At the foot of the dock was a little boathouse. It looked derelict, with the bush at the shore growing right up to it. The doors were closed, but there was a big gap between them, and Slater paused to peer inside. It was just a storage shed—coils of rope and a pile of lumber and a couple of yellow kayaks.

It wasn't a very big island. Graham should have heard Shanghai Joe's boat. Why hadn't he come down to meet him? Clearly he was going to have to find his own way to the house, somewhere up top. Only one path led away from the dock, a dirt double track up the steep hill, and he started climbing. The overhead view had showed the structures clustered on the east side, the same as the dock, facing the coast. That made sense, as east was the leeward side most of the time, sheltered from the Pacific. It couldn't be far.

The climate was different here than on the mainland, with a lot more diversity of flora than where he'd been yesterday. The land was dotted with scrub oaks, and yarrow, and sage brush. There had been a lot of growth with the heavy rains last winter, but it was all dry now, waiting for the wet season.

Trudging upward, he was breathing hard from the steep ascent. As the path started to level out, he spotted a dark plant among the scrub. It stood out, darker even than the dormant scrub oaks, like it was sucking up all the daylight that struck it, creating a void. Was that black sage? It only grew out here on these islands.

"Look at you," Slater said, and stepped off the path to examine it.

At that moment, from somewhere up the hill, he heard a loud *crack,* and in the same instant a dull *snap* on the bare earth of the path. Slater froze. It took a second to clue in. That was a rifle shot, and the bullet had hit the ground where he'd been standing a second ago.

He dived into the brush, dropping to all fours just below a stand of sage. His heart was pounding, and he was breathing hard. It wasn't an automatic weapon. If it were, he'd be dead already. And the shooter couldn't see him right now or they would have taken another shot.

Looking around, he assessed the curve of the hillside. He might be able to stay out of view if he angled away from the path, downhill to where the terrain was steeper. At first he moved on all fours, then crouched behind the bushes, keeping his head down as he moved from the shelter of one to the next.

The brush was sparser here as he moved downhill, gaining more distance from the path, and he crouched as he moved across the open ground between sage bushes and scrub oaks.

Another shot cracked the air, and he flattened himself to the ground. He hadn't felt anything. That meant it hadn't hit him. But it also meant he wasn't out of view.

On all fours he crawled downhill, under a bush, and then weaved in the opposite direction. Another shot sounded, and he flattened himself on the ground again.

"Fuck," he hissed.

Not far below him, the hillside was a lot steeper. If he could get a little farther down, he might be out of view. Crawling forward, he positioned himself below a scrub oak and then slid down a steep section on his butt. He was almost at the shore now, he saw, no more than a dozen yards.

He looked up the hill. It felt safer here, as the topography sheltered him from anyone higher up. They'd have to get awfully close to see him now. The dock was in sight, and he studied it, thinking about what to do next. He might be able to start the engine on that boat, but he couldn't walk out onto the dock to board it. He'd be completely exposed, an easy target. Swimming to it was just as risky, plus he'd freeze—the water was way too cold.

Making his way along the shore toward the dock, pushing prickly scrub oak branches out of the way, he had to heave himself up on a big rock, then hop down on the other side. As he got closer to the boathouse, he looked up the hill. The shooter would be coming down the double track sooner than later. They knew Slater wasn't armed—if he were, he would have returned fire.

A patch of unnatural blue caught his eye, in the water next to the boathouse. As he got closer, he saw that it was a tarp, covering something half buried in the brush right at the waterline. He lifted the corner. A boat. Pulling up more of the tarp, he found it was a little runabout, with two seats and an outboard engine. Someone had tried to hide it here.

Glancing up the hill, he worked to pull the tarp off, and threw it on the shore, then climbed in the boat. The right seat had a wheel in front of it and a simple throttle lever, but there were no other controls, no starter.

His heart pounding with adrenaline, he dropped to his knees behind the seats and looked over the engine. It was a basic two-stroke with a pull cord. Slater yanked on it, and the motor rumbled, but it didn't catch.

The shooter would hear him, and know what he was doing now, and know exactly where he was. He pulled the cord again, and again, but he could tell it wasn't going to start—there was no life in it at all. He huffed in frustration.

The boathouse, he remembered. There were kayaks and paddles inside. Stepping onto the shore, he went to the decrepit structure and pulled open one of the doors. Grabbing a kayak paddle, he hustled back to the runabout, and untied the nylon mooring line, and knelt in the bottom of the boat, as low as he could get.

He pushed off with the paddle. The bottom scraped audibly for a few feet, resisting the rocks below, but then it was drifting free. With the paddle Slater pushed against the rocks on the shore. He needed to get away from the dock and hopefully stay out of view. The boat bobbed in the waves, and soon he was too far from the shore to reach it. He started to paddle, first on one side, then shifting to the other. The waves moved the boat around more than the paddling did, but he was making slow progress in distancing himself from the dock.

Pausing his efforts, he looked up at the hillside. There was no sign of movement. The shooter would have to get awfully close to the shore, and far off the path, to get a bead on him now.

He took a breath and set the paddle across the seats, then turned to look at the engine again, scanning the bulky cowling. On one side was a black line with a simple twist valve on it. The fuel shutoff. Old-fashioned leaf blowers and string trimmers had controls like that too. He'd been too stressed out to see it before.

Slater twisted the valve open and pulled hard on the cord. The engine instantly caught and roared to life.

"Yeah," he shouted, and lost his balance as the craft jerked forward. Lurching sideways, he steadied himself with a hand on the gunwale, then moved to the seat with the wheel. The throttle was already halfway up, and he pushed it to the max. The engine roared, and the bow rode higher in the water.

TWENTY-ONE

WITH ONE HAND ON the bottom of the wheel, Slater lay sideways, across both seats, keeping as low as he could. Once in a while he lifted his head to peer over the bow, making sure he was still headed toward the mainland, visible in the distant haze. Looked back, he was relieved to see that the speedboat was still moored at the dock. It wasn't coming for him. At least not yet.

As he got farther from the island, the boat bounced more as it hit the waves. It was a little unnerving, but he had to believe it wasn't really unstable. It was a boat, he reasoned—it was built for this.

He was still a sitting duck, but the farther he got from the island, the harder it would be to hit him. If there were more rifle shots he wouldn't even hear them over the engine noise. Looking back again, he saw that the white speedboat still hadn't moved.

Eventually he sat up. Unless the shooter had a military-grade sniper rifle, he was out of range of the island. The runabout wasn't nearly as fast as Joe's water taxi, and that meant the speedboat could easily catch up if the shooter decided to pursue him. It would be impossible to escape on the open water. But when he looked back again, there was no sign of a craft, and Santa Cecilia was receding into the haze on the horizon. With any luck the shooter hadn't even heard him start the runabout and was still stalking him on the island.

Up ahead he could see a patch of white on the water's surface, and as he got closer, he saw that it was waves breaking on a little pile of rocks that jutted a few feet out of the water. He hadn't seen it on the ride out, but it didn't matter—he didn't need landmarks. He knew he was headed in the right direction, with Catalina looming at one side and the mainland in the distance beyond.

He planned to give the rocks a wide berth, but then he saw movement on top of them, above the whitecaps. It had to be pelicans or gulls. But it was too dark. It almost looked like one of the rocks was moving back and forth. As he got closer, he realized it was a dog—a dark-gray pit bull with a white chest, standing there on the rocks, looking right at him.

There was no one there with it, and no other boat anywhere near. He slowed the engine to an idle as he got close. The waves were rough here, and if he hit the rocks he could easily smash the hull and sink. The motion of the water was carrying him toward the outcrop, he realized. He stood up in the boat and eyed the dog. It was just standing there—there was nowhere else it could go.

When he was just a few feet away, he felt the hull connect with submerged land. The boat was still heaving in the waves, and he stepped one foot out onto the dark rocks. But he couldn't get a foothold, with one foot still on the boat, and its motion threw him off balance. He managed to shift his weight so that he fell back into the boat, landing on his butt.

"Damn it," he muttered, seeing that he was drifting away from the dog now.

Taking the pilot's seat, he opened the throttle and made a wide circle. He could drift in to the rocks at a different angle, where there was a flat place to step on at the waterline. Once he throttled down, the boat crept in, and made a sickening scraping noise when it met the rocks below. Slater left the motor idling to keep the boat pressing inward, then stepped on the bow, and planted one foot on the flat rock.

Instantly he felt the cold and wet creeping into his boot as the water lapped over his foot. He could almost reach the animal now, and he held out his arms. A bigger wave crashed on the rocks, splashing up his legs and soaking his jeans. The dog seemed to understand what he wanted it to do, and stepped as close as it could get to the edge of the rocks.

Still a few feet out of reach, Slater beckoned with both hands. "Come on."

The dog hesitated, and walked in a quick circle, and then leapt toward him. Almost not ready for it, Slater grabbed at the animal, its momentum knocking him backward onto the boat. He tumbled on his back on the bow with the dog on top of him. Moving onto his knees, he lifted the animal into the bottom of the boat, then stepped in himself and sat in the pilot's seat. His skin near his ear was stinging, and he dabbed at it with a finger, finding blood. The dog had nicked him with its paw.

"I know you didn't mean it," Slater said, eyeing it. "How the hell did you get out here anyway?"

With the kayak paddle, Slater pushed back from the rocks, relieved when the bottom was floating free again. He lifted the dog onto the seat next to him. Soaking wet, it smelled of salt water and dander, and didn't resist being picked up.

"Let's get out of here, yeah?" Slater said, and pushed up the throttle, steering away from the rocks, and aimed for the mainland.

There were a couple of sailboats in the distance, and the ubiquitous string of freighters on the horizon, but still no sign of the speedboat from Santa Cecilia when he looked back. With one hand on the wheel, he looked over the dog. It wasn't wearing a collar, but its coat looked healthy, and judging by the junk, he was male. He was shivering, Slater realized. He put an arm around him and lifted him onto his seat, shifting over to make room, then opened his windbreaker to fold it around him. The dog let him do it, and pressed against him, not resisting the proximity or being swaddled.

As they got closer to the coast, Slater focused on finding the Marina. There was a breakwater, he remembered, and then he spotted the little lighthouse at the end of Ballona Creek. Piece of cake—he knew exactly where that was.

He kept the boat at full throttle as he navigated into the channel. Someone on a sailboat shouted at him as they passed. He must have broken some rule. Of course he had—he didn't know what the hell he was doing. At least the fuel had lasted long enough to actually get here.

Basin C was where the Continental was, and he followed the sign for it and pulled up to an empty stretch of dock. He killed the engine as he got close, but he'd waited too long, and the boat hit the dock hard, jolting him almost out of his seat. He stood and tied the mooring line to a cleat, then untied the nylon line on the opposite side and knotted it into a leash for the dog. Looping it around his neck, he left it loose enough that it wouldn't chafe.

Once he'd climbed onto the dock, he knelt and lifted out the dog. "Terra firma, buddy."

As he got to his feet, a golf cart rolled up and stopped a few feet away.

"You can't dock your boat here," the driver called to him. Wearing a nylon jacket and dark sunglasses, he had no weapon, no gear or insignia to imply he was security.

"That's not my boat," Slater said, and walked toward the land.

Trotting beside him, the dog seemed happy to be on solid ground. The golf cart was following him, he realized, as he could hear its electric motor in close proximity.

He looked back at the driver. "Quit shagging me with that thing."

"Sir, you need to stop."

"Get a horse," he said, not breaking his stride.

At the end of the dock, the guy rolled past him onto the walkway, then turned sharply in front of him to cut him off. Slater had to yank on the leash so the dog wouldn't get clipped by the tires.

The guy stepped off the cart. "You have to move your boat."

"Unless you have a badge or a gun, you know you can't actually make me do anything, right?"

"I represent the boat owners."

Slater scoffed and sidestepped him, but he stepped in front of him again.

"I'm not done with you."

Dropping the nylon-rope leash, Slater threw a hard right at his face. It struck his jaw, and the guy spun sideways, and fell back onto the golf cart, sprawling across both seats. Slater watched him for a moment, massaging his knuckles. The guy wasn't moving.

He stepped around to the other side of the cart and leaned in, pressing two fingers to his neck. The guy had a pulse. At least he hadn't killed him. Probing his jaw, that wasn't broken either. He grabbed his knee and maneuvered him into the crash position. It took some effort because the guy was big.

"Idiot," Slater muttered. "You shouldn't be picking fights when you have a glass jaw."

The dog was waiting for him nearby, sitting on the asphalt, seemingly unperturbed by it all. Slater scooped up the rope, and the dog trotted beside him to the parking lot. When he opened the passenger door of the Continental for him, he knew what to do, and jumped up on the seat.

"You're no slouch, pup."

He closed the door and walked around to the driver's side. Nobody seemed to be following him, he saw, looking back toward the docks. Hopefully nobody had seen him deck that moron. Climbing in behind the wheel, he started the engine and drove out of the lot.

He'd swung too hard, he knew that. He shouldn't have thrown a haymaker. But the guy was being a dick, and it had been an intense morning.

On the other side of the marina he parked at a red curb, close to the food stands he'd seen earlier. Taking the dog with him, he went up to the counter where he'd asked directions a few hours ago.

"Give me five hot dogs," he said, "and hold the fixings."

"Separate plates?" the woman asked.

"You can put them all together."

While he waited, the dog went to the red water bowl on the ground at the end of the stand, taking a tentative lap at first, then drinking loudly for what seemed like a long time.

After he'd paid the cook, he walked over to the picnic tables at the side of the lot, and pulled the hot dogs out of their wrappers. Piling them on the paper plate, he set it on the ground. The dog eyed them, then looked up at Slater.

"Go on. They're for you."

He stepped closer and started in. Slater had to grin, watching him wolf them down, buns and all.

When they got back in the car, the dog sat on the passenger seat, tongue lolling, panting contentedly.

Slater dug out his phone. He hadn't even considered that it might have gotten wet along with his jeans. But it had survived, and he phoned Etta, an operative he and Max used sometimes. They were helping her learn the trade, and in exchange she'd decorated their offices. Etta worked as a middle-school teacher, so she might be in class, but to his relief, she picked up.

"You're involved with that lesbian dog rescue, right?" Slater said.

"That's not what it's called, but yes, a friend of mine runs a rescue."

"I have a very sweet pit bull who needs a foster home."

"Where did you get a pit bull?" Etta said.

"It's too complicated to explain right now."

"I guess I can call some people."

"I need to offload this dog pronto. Can I bring him over?"

Etta groaned. "I'm not set up for a dog right now."

"I'll pay you. He already had his dinner, and a salt-water bath. Just give him some water, and a blanket to sleep on, and you're golden."

"All right. I'm still at school. I'll be home in an hour."

"It'll take me that long to get there," he said, and ended the call.

On the drive to Etta's, the dog seemed comfortable on the passenger seat, looking around at the stop-and-go freeway traffic. Slater gazed absently at the sea of brake lights. It was so stupid to fall for that. Sailing out to an island in the fricking Pacific. It had sounded hinky from the start. He should have talked to Graham first.

His phone buzzed in its dash mount—a text from Graham:

I saw you called earlier. Where you at? Have dinner with me?

He tapped the screen to phone him.

"I was just thinking about you," Slater said when he answered. In truth he was thinking about eight ways to murder the guy, but he wasn't going to say that on the phone.

"I had fun yesterday," Graham said. "I'm actually in the city. I figured we could get dinner."

"I missed you at the island."

"What island?"

"Don't fuck with me," Slater shouted.

"What are you talking about?"

He roared at him, a lungful of visceral, guttural frustration. The dog looked over at him, concern in his eyes.

"What is going on?" Graham demanded. "You sound crazy. Are you up for dinner or not?"

"Where are you?"

"Somewhere around Downtown. Where all the warehouses are. I have a couple of errands, but I'll be done in an hour or so."

"Look for me in the parking structure at the central market. Fourth floor."

"I know that place. Can I just meet you inside the market?"

"In the parking structure," Slater said, and ended the call.

Etta lived in a crowded neighborhood along the Arroyo, with lots of apartment buildings, and her street was jammed with parked cars. He found a space in the next block, then texted her:

We're here.

With the rope leash in hand, he walked back toward her place with the dog. The boundary between it and the next building was a thick hedge, and he looked it over as they passed. Morning glory vines ran all through it. People let those go wild because they produced lots of flowers, but it was basically a damn weed, and it wasn't doing the hedge any favors.

"Idiots," he muttered, and forced himself to look away.

Etta stepped out the front of her building as he walked up. Curvy, she had her dark hair butched short, and she was still wearing her teacher drag, dark pants and a gray vest over a dress shirt. She crouched to greet the dog, scratching his head and under his chin.

"Hey, fella. What were you rolling in?"

"Seawater," Slater said flatly.

She stood up. "Does he have a name?"

"Probably." He explained where he'd found him, stranded on the rocky outcrop.

"There was no one around?"

"Not when I saw him. I can't explain it. Maybe he fell off a boat."

"Pit bulls aren't good swimmers," she said. "They have too much muscle. They tend to sink."

"He was happy to get to dry land."

Etta reached down again to scratch his ears. "Let's call you Rocky."

"Is he going to be OK?"

She grinned. "You big softy. Rocky melted your heart."

"Your friends aren't going to send him to dog prison," Slater said, "or a labor camp in Arizona?"

"There's no labor camps for dogs. They'll find him a foster family."

"I just can't stand to see him mistreated."

"He's going to be fine. They love dogs, and they treat them well." She raised her eyebrows. "They're always happy to get donations."

He dug out his wad of cash. It was damp, and it took some effort to peel off the C-notes.

"Is three enough?" He handed them over, and before she could answer, said, "Here, take five," and peeled off a couple more.

"This is going to help a lot of pups," she said as she tucked the cash into her pocket. "Including Rocky."

"Thanks for handling this."

Etta's eyebrows shot up. "Pardon me?"

"You heard me."

"I just don't think I've ever heard you use those words before." She waggled her fingers next to her head. "It's causing intense cognitive dissonance."

Slater squatted to rub Rocky's back. "You're going to be OK, buddy."

Rising, he walked back toward his car.

TWENTY-TWO

O NCE SLATER GOT TO his office, he heaved his boots up on his desk and took a minute to breathe, and let his addled mind settle, and think things through. His jeans had mostly dried out, but one foot still felt damp.

Graham was playing innocent, like he had no idea what Slater was upset about. That didn't mean he wasn't complicit. He could have called Slater with the intention to act oblivious when he heard he'd escaped the shooter. But why would Graham try to grease him? Why would anybody? It could only mean he was getting too close to something juicy.

Turning to the safe, he knelt in front of it and dialed in the combination. Sybil's brown paper package was still wedged tightly inside.

"Moron," he muttered, and locked it up again.

She'd been so anxious about it this morning. Maybe she had another angle, something that he wasn't seeing. She said it was too hot for him to bring to her place, that she and Dragan were worried about surveillance. If that really was a valid concern, she was smart not to get it delivered. But it still sounded paranoid.

He sent her a text:

Those documents are still outstanding. We need to finalize that.

Eventually he saw it was time to meet Graham, and

he went down to his car, and drove to the central market. The fourth floor of the parking structure always had lots of room. There wouldn't be anyone around to watch.

As he pulled in to a stall, he saw Graham walking toward him, a grin on his face as Slater got out of the Continental. When he stepped up, Slater slapped him hard, left and then right, a rapid kovac. Graham stumbled back against the SUV in the next stall, alarm in his eyes, and held a palm to his face.

"You can't hit me."

"You'll take it and you'll like it," Slater growled, and lunged at him, grabbing his throat in one hand.

Graham reached up to yank at his wrist. Civilians always did that, and it was totally ineffectual.

"Were you the shooter?" Slater demanded.

He struggled under Slater's hand but couldn't break free.

"What are you talking about?" His voice was distorted by the pressure on his throat. "I didn't shoot anybody."

The look in his eye, Slater realized. It was just fear. Nothing else. He watched him for a moment, feeling the rapid pulse in his neck, then released his grip.

"Show me your phone."

Massaging his neck, Graham scowled at him. "Why?"

Slater slapped him again.

"Stop it," he shouted. "Fuck. What is wrong with you?"

He dug out the phone and handed it over. Slater held the screen toward him.

"Unlock it," he said through his teeth.

Once he had, Slater checked the messages. There were no outgoing texts to Slater this morning, just one about dinner later in the day. Before that was their exchange from yesterday. But that didn't mean he hadn't just deleted it.

"What are you looking for?" Graham demanded.

Ignoring him, Slater checked his location history. The phone had been in Palmdale until the early afternoon, then a blue line snaked through the Newhall Pass, straight through Downtown to Vernon, and now it was here. He handed the phone back and met his gaze.

"I don't know what to believe, Graham. Either you've got ice water in your veins, or you really are clueless."

He raised his voice. "What are you talking about?"

"Let's go eat."

His face was red, and he was breathing hard. "I'm not going anywhere with you until you tell me why you assaulted me."

"I got a text from you this morning asking me to meet you on Santa Cecilia island. When I got there, somebody started shooting at me."

His eyebrows shot up. "I never texted you that. I definitely never shot at you."

"I want to believe that," Slater said. "It's not in your phone, but it came from your number."

"You know it's really easy to spoof a phone number, right? Telemarketers do it a billion times a day. I've never been to Santa Susanna island, or whatever it's called." He threw up his hands. "Why would I want to shoot at you?"

"I can't quite put that together yet." He watched him for a moment. "So do you want to eat or not?"

Graham scoffed and walked toward the elevator. In the market they walked around and picked a burrito stall, then carried the food to the Hill Street side and found a table.

He was hungry, he realized, and ate fast. Like Rocky with the hot dogs.

Graham was watching him as he ate. "Why didn't you call me to ask why I wanted you to go out to some isolated island?"

"I tried," he said through a mouthful of food. "You weren't answering. I thought maybe you'd had a change of heart and wanted to revise your story about Ben. I figured you were going to come clean."

"You have a strange life."

Slater balled up his burrito wrapper and folded his arms. "What was that thing at the coffee place yesterday with Marion? Telling her I was dating your sister. People up there don't know you're a dick hound?"

"It's a small town," he said, and looked down. "I'm mostly out. But I don't need people to know exactly who I'm sleeping with."

"It's none of my business. But then you roped me into it."

"I wish you weren't attached."

Slater watched him finish his burrito. "Let me make a call."

Sitting up, he dug out his phone and called Pike.

"Can I bring a guy over for a three-way?" he said when Pike picked up.

"Seriously?" he demanded. "I just got home."

"He's a redhead. It'll be worth it."

Pike sighed audibly. "It's hard to say no to that."

As he ended the call, Graham laughed. "You didn't actually ask me if I wanted to do that."

"I'd be shocked if you weren't into it."

"What's your man's name?"

"You can call him Reddy Kilowatt."

"What's he like?"

"Pure gravy," Slater said. "All the way down."

"What does that mean?"

"He's everything. The sun and the moon and all the

stars." He shrugged. "You'll like him."

"It sounds like you do."

"You will. Everybody does. It's actually kind of annoying."

———◆———

RIDING UP THE ELEVATOR in the parking structure, Slater texted Graham his address, and as he pulled into his garage, he saw the Wrangler roll past and back in to the curb in front of Pike's SUV. He hit the button to roll down the garage door, then opened the front door.

"Nice house," Graham said, as they walked up.

"I know it's obnoxious. I needed the space."

As they climbed the stairs, Pike called from the kitchen, "I'll be right down."

Slater led him into the bedroom, and a moment later Pike appeared, and introduced himself. He was still in his work clothes—a collared shirt and dark trousers.

"I don't usually do stuff like this," Graham said.

"Neither do I," Pike said, "but for Slater it's pretty routine."

"He must be a handful to live with."

Pike chuckled. "You have no idea."

"Cut the chin music," Slater demanded. He whirled a finger in the air. "Both of you—clothes off."

He sat on the bed to untie his boots, and once Pike had tossed his clothes on a chair, and was standing there naked, he spoke.

"So what are we doing?"

Graham was sitting on the edge of the bed, pulling off his socks, and met his gaze. "I'd like to fuck you. I mean, if that's on the table."

"Sure." Pike chuckled and walked around to the nightstand, where he dug a condom out of a drawer.

Kneeling on the bed behind Graham, he reached

around to caress his smooth chest and massage his swelling cock.

"I can see you're into it," Pike said.

Watching them, Slater could feel his heart pounding. He hadn't anticipated feeling this way, the flash of heat on his neck and his ears, his stomach tightening. But he couldn't say anything. This had been his idea. Once he'd undressed he put a hand on Pike's back, watching as he rolled the condom on Graham's now rock-hard cock.

Shifting onto his side, Pike pulled Slater closer, and mouthed his jaw, and grabbed his cock. Graham maneuvered behind him, an arm around Pike's chest, breathing hard, his face red. Pike winced as he pressed into him.

"Are you OK?" Graham said.

"Bring it on."

Slater mouthed his jaw, and kissed him, and reached for his cock, stroking him as Graham started to pump him. He could feel the force of it telegraphing through Pike's body. Prodding Slater to move up the bed, Pike took him into his mouth, working him leisurely as Graham upped his pace.

It was weird to see someone fucking him, and it made his heart pound, but it was still hot. Pike pulled up, red-faced, breathing hard.

"Put your fingers in his mouth," Slater said.

Twisting toward Graham, Pike caressed his cheek, then probed his mouth with his thumb, then with a couple of fingers. A moment later Graham yelped and strained into him, his face contorting. He pulled away and lay on his back, catching his breath.

"I want to fuck you too," Slater said.

Pike grinned and pushed him back, then straddled his hips and lowered himself onto Slater. Massaging Pike's chest with his hands, he thrust up into him. Graham moved closer and grabbed Pike's cock, stroking him as

Slater pounded him. Pike arched his back and groaned as he climaxed. Seeing that sent Slater over too, and he pressed up into him.

After he'd stopped shuddering, Pike climbed off him, and stretched out between him and Graham, and interlaced his fingers with Slater's.

His head propped on one arm, Graham caressed his chest. "You're so good-looking."

"Back at you," Pike said. "There's nothing like a natural redhead." Pulling his hand away from Slater, he caressed Graham's cheek. "Skin like fresh cream. Lips like raspberries."

Graham closed his eyes and leaned into his hand. "Why is your nickname Reddy Kilowatt?"

"Slater calls me that because the day we met, I had to use a taser on him."

"Ouch." He laughed. "You're so intuitive, the way you touch me."

"This isn't my first barbecue, Red."

They were both way too into it, Slater thought, watching them interact. He folded an arm over his eyes.

A while later, Graham spoke. "Can I shower?"

"Go for it," Slater mumbled.

When he came back, he started to get dressed. "I should go. I've got a long drive."

"Maybe we'll do this again," Pike said, and Slater shot him a look.

Graham beamed. "I'd like that."

He pulled on his sneakers, and they heard him descend the stairs, and the front door close.

"Nice guy," Pike said.

"He was certainly into you. Practically drooling."

"Where did you meet him?"

"He's a witness in my case," Slater said. "He works at that factory in Palmdale."

"Why are you sleeping with someone who's involved in your case?"

"Because I wanted you to have the opportunity to wax poetic. And lo, you found his raspberry lips mesmerizing."

Pike laughed. "You once said you kept your dick out of your cases."

"That's the aspiration, at least." He shifted onto his side. "I had to smack him around today, but then I decided he wasn't actually culpable. I thought I should make it up to him."

"Why did you smack him around?"

"Somebody tried to grease me. At first I thought it was him."

Pike's expression shifted, his brow furrowing. "I'm going to need more information."

"I figured. Can I get a slug of bourbon?"

"Details first, booze later."

Slater huffed but then got into it, and told him about going out to the island, and the rifle shots, and finding the dog. It was probably wise to relate all that with a clear head. The bourbon would still be waiting for him, perched on the shelf, patient and serene. Unlike Pike, who had a lot of questions.

At least Pike didn't point out how stupid he was for falling for it, how stupid it was not to double-check with Graham, how stupid it was to blithely walk into a trap. He already knew that himself.

TWENTY-THREE

▤▤▤▤▤▤▤▤▤▤▤

S LATER WOKE WHEN PIKE came down from breakfast to get dressed for work. Half awake, he watched
him button his shirt, and kissed him when he
leaned in to say good-bye before he left.

As he lay in bed, the bright sunlight helped him wake
up. He finally had some ideas floating around, gradually starting to coalesce, the pieces fitting together. He
grabbed his phone and texted Ben:

We need to talk.

His reply came a moment later:

I'm headed to the central library soon if you want
to meet me there. I'll be in the ESL room.

What was the guy doing in an ESL class? He already
spoke the language. Pushing himself out of bed, he showered and got dressed, in a fresh pair of jeans, since yesterday's were stiff with salty residue from the seawater. He
hustled upstairs long enough to guzzle a mug of tepid
coffee, then drove downtown, pulling into a garage where
Hope dead-ended just below the library.

Slater walked into the lobby and approached the information desk. Through the plexiglass he asked the li-
brarian for the ESL room. Explaining where it was, she
pointed to the escalator up.

It wasn't actually a classroom, he saw when he found
it, but rather a reading room with long tables and

deco-era lamps. The walls and ceiling were painted with an intricate dark forest motif. A few people were scattered around at the tables, reading and staring at screens, but it was quiet. Ben was sitting at a table, engrossed in the blue glow of a laptop.

As Slater approached, he looked up and smiled in recognition. Such a handsome man. So totally fuckable. He sat opposite, and leaned in, and spoke in a low voice.

"What are you doing here? You don't need ESL."

"That's just the name of it." Ben waved at the room. "Isn't this an elegant and inspiring place to work?"

"If you say so."

"So what's the story? Have you been able to get the phony NDA from Desert Sky Rocketry?"

"It's Desert View Rocketry," Slater said. "Listen, have you gained weight recently?"

"Not really. I'm pretty consistent."

"Why do people think you weigh a hundred and forty pounds?"

"I haven't weighed one forty since I was eight years old. I've always been around two twenty." His brow furrowed. "You know, my driver's license says I weigh one forty. That's a DMV screw-up. In the real world I weighed two forty when I first got a license. I lost some of that since then." He patted his stomach. "Good living and exercise."

Slater sat back. "That is very good news."

"How could that possibly matter?"

"I've talked to a series of chumps who claim to know you. I know now they never actually met you. But they've seen your driver's license."

"People at the rocket company?"

Slater rose. "I don't have all the facts yet, but I'm close. We'll talk later."

His phone had buzzed in his pants, and as he walked out, he pulled it out to check. It was a text from Andy:

Drop by.

Once he was sitting in the Continental, he pulled up the photo he'd taken a week ago of Ben's driver's license. Sure enough, his weight was listed as one forty. Why hadn't he noticed that, questioned it, put it together earlier?

"Idiot," he muttered, eyeing himself in the rearview, then started the engine.

He drove the few blocks to Andy's building and parked in the surface lot behind it. When he got up to his loft, Andy pulled open the door, wearing his usual boxer shorts and a tank top. He flashed that smile and beckoned for Slater to follow him in.

Andy sat in his gaming chair. "I can't get into Desert View's files, even though I … tried hard."

"At least I won't have to pay you anything."

He chuckled. "That's not how it works. I did get access to … Cody Layton's personal photo collection."

"How did you manage that?"

"He uses a photo app with pretty … lax security. It's set to back up every photo from his phone. One of those … things he might have used once for a specific purpose, to edit … a photo or to order prints, then forgot about it. He might not even … know it's happening." Andy swiveled to his computer. "Check this out."

A photo popped up on the screen, and Slater stepped closer, and leaned in to look. It was the familiar staff photo with the drone. But this version was different. Cody and Redge and Lunelle looked the same, but where Ben had appeared was empty space between the two men, just dusty tarmac stretching into the distance.

"Mother fucker," Slater said.

"It's possible this is a later photo, and Ben … really was there, and someone erased him. But the metadata says … this was taken two years ago."

"This is the original," Slater said. "They just inserted Ben's head and shoulders to make it fit their story."

"I figured."

"I'm so glad you found this."

Andy eyed him sidelong. "That was almost an atta-boy."

"What do I owe you?"

"Eight dollars from the last job. Let's say … fifteen total."

Slater groaned and pulled out his wad, then counted out the C-notes and handed them over.

"You've basically cleaned me out." He waggled the thin sheaf of bills before he shoved it into his pocket. "I might have enough left for half a tank for my rig and a gas station taquito."

"I know you don't eat those. And you know I'm … worth it." He jutted his chin at the photo on his screen. "Look at that … beautiful thing."

"You're not wrong."

"Damn right I'm not. You have to say it."

Slater put his hands on his hips, and watched him for a moment. "You're good at what you do."

"And I'm worth it. Go on. Say it."

"You're worth it."

Andy threw up a hand. "Thank you."

Slater had to chuckle. "Send me that photo." Holding his gaze, he added, "Bye, beautiful."

Down in the parking lot, he climbed into the Continental and dialed Graham.

"I had an amazing time last night," Graham said when he picked up. "We should schedule that as a regular event."

"Where are you?"

"At work. Why?"

Not responding to that, Slater ended the call and navigated to the freeway, soon cruising through Burbank and Sun Valley. As he was climbing the Newhall Pass, he had a queasy feeling in his stomach. This is where he'd wrecked the Thunderbird. Right over there on the other side of the road. Airborne for a while, then total destruction, and he couldn't even remember it happening.

In its dash mount, his phone buzzed. The caller ID said it was Duarte.

"I got a look at the Thunderbird," Duarte said when he picked up. "It was no accident. Somebody cut into the brake line, right at the reservoir."

"Are you fucking kidding me?"

"They knew what they were doing. They didn't chop it in two, just cut a hole in it. Each time you hit the brake pedal, some fluid would leak out. Then when you started riding them hard, like going down the pass, they would fail completely. Whoever did it probably knew that's where you were headed."

"Can you take some photos of it for me?" Slater said, and ended the call.

Who the fuck would have done that? That loudmouth he'd punched at Desert View would have the know-how, but it was a pretty extreme reaction to a dustup.

His phone buzzed again—Graham.

"I'm on my way to your office," Slater said when he picked up.

"I figured. I'm not there."

"You said you were. What the fuck?" he demanded.

"You sounded pissed off again. I don't need you around my work if you're going to freak out. I came home."

"Where's home?"

"You have to promise not to hit me," Graham said.

"If you don't lie to me, I won't have to."

He huffed and recited his address, and Slater tapped it into his navigation app.

It was a dusty desert neighborhood, and he parked the Continental a block from where the map showed Graham's place. As he walked toward it he saw that it was a bungalow with panel siding. The Wrangler was in the driveway, and pulled in behind it was Cody Layton's Silverado. Had Graham called in his uncle-boss man to defend him?

His vehicle tracker was still in the wheel well of that rig. Retrieving it was risky, as he might be spotted, but those things were expensive. Striding up to the Silverado, he glanced around to make sure he wasn't being observed, then squatted at the rear tire, and reached up into the wheel well. Once he had the tracker in hand he pocketed it and stepped out to the sidewalk.

The chain-link fence between Graham's house and the next one was just a few feet tall, and instead of walking up the driveway, Slater stepped past the palm tree at the curb and strode into the neighboring yard. This one had green turf, but Graham's was unirrigated brown dirt. As he stepped over the fence, he saw there was a garden window on this side. Those were usually at the kitchen sink.

Slater had planned to look inside, but as he approached the window he heard voices, and flattened himself against the wall next to it. The sash was halfway up, he saw, the screen visible above the sill.

"I didn't sign up for this." That was Graham's voice. "Nobody said it would involve murder."

"You don't even know if that's true," Cody said. "It's just what that wetback told you. To me it sounds pretty far-fetched. I'm a lot more interested in what he knows.

On the weekend you said he was close to figuring it all out."

"I don't know what he knows. Listen, he'll be here any minute. You need to leave."

"I'm happy to stay and talk to him with you. That way we can keep the story straight."

"That's not going to work."

Cody raised his voice again. "You don't jump out of the canoe halfway across the lake, Graham. Stay the course. Stick to the story."

It was quiet then. From here Slater could see the side of Cody's vehicle. That meant Cody might spot him on the way out. Slater crouched and walked under the window, around the back side of the house. He heard the Silverado start up, and when he peered around the corner, saw it roll up the street.

Slater walked around to the front and banged on the door. Graham pulled it open, his expression somber, concern in his eyes. The front room had overstuffed lounge furniture and a big TV at one end. Farther in he could see into the kitchen with the garden window.

"Is there anyone else here?" Slater said.

"Just me."

He stepped closer. "You lied to me." Slater slapped him hard, a rapid kovac.

Graham shoved his arms off and stepped back toward the kitchen. "Stop it. You said you wouldn't hit me."

"Time to squeal, little piggy." Slater moved toward him, fists balled, and got into his space again.

"You're acting crazy."

"So squawk," he shouted.

Red-faced now, Graham planted a palm on his chest and shoved him. Slater let it happen, and took a step back.

"My shrink says you shouldn't ask people what's wrong with them," Graham said. "You have to frame it as what happened to them." He raised his eyebrows. "So what the fuck happened to you?"

"Did your shrink also tell you about deflecting, and avoiding the question? You know you're going to talk, and you know I'm going to make you talk."

"What is it with the violence?" he demanded.

"I've dealt with closed-mouth guys before." Slater lunged at him, and managed to land a slap despite Graham's flailing arms.

"I don't know what you're talking about," he shouted.

Slater stepped back. "Everybody in your orbit is lying to me. The only place Ben Clague weighs a hundred and forty pounds is on his driver's license."

His face contorted then, and he squeezed his eyes shut. Watching him, Slater wasn't sure what was happening. Graham sobbed and put his fist to his mouth.

"My mother made me do it," he said finally. "How can you say no to your own mother?"

"What did she make you do?"

A sob caught in his throat, and a fat tear rolled down his face.

"Pull yourself together," Slater demanded, stepping toward him.

Graham shoved him back with both arms, using more force this time. "You're a damn brute."

"I know that." He gestured impatiently. Provoking anger in him was better than the tears—it made it easier to get him to focus.

"Can I sit down?"

"It's your house."

He scoffed and dropped onto the sofa, and Slater sat across from him in an armchair. Graham was breathing hard. But maybe he was calming down. He wiped his cheek.

"It's all made up," he said finally. "Cody paid us to

repeat the story about Ben Clague. I've never even met him."

"Whose idea was it?"

"I wasn't in on the planning."

"Who set it up?" Slater shouted.

"The lawyer," he said quickly. "It was the lawyer. Christ, man, cool it. Apparently she had some kind of dirt on Cody. Mom said it was about business loans. Cody got himself into a jam, and he couldn't very well say no to her."

"Who got paid?"

"My mother, for one."

"And you."

Graham looked away. "Me too."

"What about Redge Black and Lunelle?"

"They got roped into it later. Mom said you'd find Redge and Lunelle eventually because you mentioned their names to me. Cody paid them to tell anybody who asked that this Ben guy worked at Desert View. As it turned out, the only one asking questions was you."

"Lo, the truth revealed. The golden thread that knits the world together." Slater sat back and shook his head. "Finally. You little weasel."

"It's family, Slater. Family has to come first."

"And to think I let you fuck my boyfriend."

"You actually invited me over to fuck your boyfriend," he said, raising his eyebrows. "So what happens now? Are you going to call the cops?"

He folded his arms. "I told Sybil that I'd almost figured it out, even though that wasn't exactly true. That must have triggered her. She's the one who got someone to shoot at me. I can't believe how stupid I am, swinging my dick around like that, bragging to her."

"I only met her briefly when she came to the office. She dealt with Cody."

"I also puffed out my chest and bragged to you," Slater said. "On Sunday I told you I was close to figuring it out. Then you told Cody, and he must have told Sybil. She got worried enough to come for me."

Graham looked down. "I did talk to Cody."

He watched him for a moment. "Do you know Odysseus? He lands on this island and steals food from this giant. The giant locks him and his men in a cave, and starts eating them one by one."

"Gross."

"Totally gross. When the giant asks his name, Odysseus tells him it's 'Nobody.' Later he stabs the giant in the eye with a stake, and when the giant calls the other giants to help him, they ask who blinded him. He tells them 'Nobody.' They all think he's nuts, so they don't help him, and Odysseus and his crew escape."

"Why are you telling me this?"

"When Odysseus leaves the island," Slater said, "he tells the giant his real name. Just as a way to say 'Fuck you—I outsmarted you.' Then the giant complains to his father, Poseidon."

"The god of the sea."

"Right. And Poseidon messes with Odysseus for years and years. Blowing his ship off course at every opportunity. If he'd just kept his stupid mouth shut, it would have been fine. But he got tripped up by his own ego."

"Like you telling Sybil you were close to figuring it out," Graham said.

"And telling you. You ran to Cody the same day to tattle."

"It wasn't like that."

Slater scoffed. "At least you're being honest about it now. I just wish there was some evidence. Sybil can laugh in my face and deny everything."

"Evidence to take to the cops?"

"To take to Ben," Slater said. "You people have been driving him insane. He's friends with Sybil, so I'm not sure he'd take my word that she was behind it all."

"Would a video of her convince him?"

"What video?"

"The security recordings at Desert View. Sybil came to the office to talk to Cody. I'm sure that's on video."

"Do you have access to that? Can you get into it from here?"

"Sure." Graham rose, and wiped his nose with the back of his hand, then retrieved a laptop from the kitchen table and brought it back to the sofa. Setting it on his lap, he tapped the keyboard and peered at the screen.

"I know it was a Friday because I left early. I saw her when she came in after lunch but I left before she did. It was a couple of months ago." He glanced up at Slater. "There's only so many Fridays, am I right?"

There was a spark in this guy, Slater thought, watching him work. It was more than just the raspberries and cream. It was charm, maybe, like what people saw in Pike.

A few minutes later, Graham said, "There she is."

Rising, Slater stepped over, and sat beside him on the sofa, and leaned in. The video frame showed the front office, the camera angle from high on the wall, with the date and time superimposed in the bottom corner. In the image Graham was sitting at his desk, and then Sybil walked in the front entrance. The view of her face wasn't clear, but her lithe frame and that rack were unmistakable, as was her voice. When Graham greeted her, she said, "I'm here to see Cody Layton." They watched as Graham picked up the phone, then rose and led her into the back.

"This might be useful," Slater said. "Can you send me that clip?"

"Let's see when she leaves."

He fast-forwarded through the video. Graham suddenly disappeared from his desk, and then two figures appeared in the front office. Once he rewound it a little, and played it at normal speed, it was clearly Sybil and Cody. Sybil was talking as they stepped out of the back.

"You don't need to worry about whether it's going to work. You say what you're supposed to say, and the tax man will never hear a word about your fiscal skulduggery."

Cody stopped in the middle of the room. "It's a hell of a game you're playing. What did this Ben guy ever do to you?"

"That's not something you need to know," she said, and walked out the front door.

Cody stood for a moment, watching her leave, then turned and went back toward his office.

"Fuck me," Slater said.

"It's pretty blatant, huh."

"This is exactly what I need. Make a clip of that and send it to me."

Once he'd tapped at the keyboard for a minute, Graham said, "Done." He sat back and shifted sideways to face Slater. "That's it—I've betrayed my family."

"More like they betrayed you. They're supposed to take care of you, not drag you into fraud and attempted murder."

Graham looked away. "Still."

"You told the truth," Slater said. "There's value in that. You need to question whether Cody is worthy of your loyalty. I'm pretty sure that fucker sabotaged my car."

His brow furrowed. "What?"

"When you and I went to that shipping container, somebody messed with my brakes. That's why I wrecked the Thunderbird."

"He wouldn't do that. Cody's no killer."

"Who else would have done it?" Slater demanded.

"I don't know why he'd bother. He's got bigger problems. It feels like he's shutting down the company. He's been selling off the CNC machines."

"What are those?"

"Computerized lathes," Graham said. "to make customized parts out of metal."

"Like parts for airplanes and drones and missiles."

"Cody says the business isn't really viable anymore."

"That's hard to believe," Slater said. "Once you latch onto Uncle Sam's nipple, the milk flows fast and large. Cody must have really screwed up for them to cut him off."

"I have to get on with my life anyway. Get a better job."

Slater got up. "You need to play dumb for a few days. Don't talk to your mom about this, and don't tell her or Cody what you told me."

Graham rose. "Fine."

"I'm not messing around." Slater jabbed a finger at him. "You blab, and I'm coming for you."

"I said I'd keep it to myself," he said, raising his voice. "I'm not anxious to be blamed for ruining the whole scheme."

———·———

As Slater walked up the block to the Continental, he thought it through. His instinct was to go punch Cody Layton in the face. But he couldn't do that. If he confronted him about sabotaging the Thunderbird, the guy would alert Sybil. And he wasn't even sure it was Layton who'd done it.

He needed to talk to Sybil. She'd already tried to grease him once—he needed some insurance. As he got behind the wheel, he found the video clips that Graham had sent, and attached them to an email. He started the engine and headed toward the freeway.

On the drive back to the city Slater dictated a long message explaining it all, Sybil's machinations and Cody's complicity, then emailed it with the video clips to Max. He set it to be sent late tonight. That meant he could cancel it later. But if anything happened to him, Max would get the whole story.

It was still early afternoon when Slater found a meter on Sybil's block, and rode up to her unit, and pounded on the door. When she pulled it open, she was wearing dark dress pants and a blue satin blouse that showed a lot of cleavage.

Sybil frowned at the sight of him. "What are you doing here?"

"The jig is up, sister."

"What are you talking about?"

He raised his voice. "You concocted the whole bullshit story about Ben working at Desert View."

"Are you armed?"

"I'm the one who should be asking you that. Although I doubt you'd gun me down yourself, in your own place."

She leaned out and glanced toward the elevators. "Come in and stop shouting at me in the hallway."

Sybil sat behind her desk, and Slater stood in front of it.

"Are you going to sit down?" she said. "You're making me nervous."

He scoffed but took a chair. "You ran a squeeze play on Layton, and got his whole nepotized office to lie for you. What I can't figure out is why."

Sybil sighed and leaned back. She looked tired. "Are you recording this conversation?"

"Should I?"

"It doesn't really matter. Recording someone without their consent isn't admissible as evidence."

"That's lawyer talk," Slater said flatly.

"I was hoping you wouldn't figure it out. You're a lot smarter than you look."

"What do you have against Ben? He seems like a straight shooter. A civilian. He's not down in the cesspool with me, and not a lowlife like you."

"Ben and I were romantically involved before he went gay. I was head over heels—he was my soul mate. But he threw it all away." She raised her voice. "He trashed me."

"So the point was to stop him from getting the job at Ekragen? It seems like a lot of work for that kind of payback."

"When someone routinely lies, and falsifies their résumé, and conceals documents, they get a reputation. It goes way beyond one job. It lasts a lifetime."

"So you were trying to ruin his life."

Sybil shrugged. "Nothing tastes as sweet as revenge."

"You know there's other straight guys in this town, right?"

"I didn't even plan it, really. It all fell into my lap." She sat up, her eyes bright now.

She was reveling in this, Slater realized, telling him how clever she was. He gestured for her to continue.

"I was working on a case and came across information that made Cody Layton completely amenable to working with me," Sybil said. "It struck me that he was in the same industry as Ben. All the pieces were there. I just had to put them together."

Watching her, Slater wished he actually had set up his phone to record this. Admissible or not, she was spilling it all.

"So you forged Ben's signature on the NDA," he said.

"At first it was just pointing out the NDA to Ekragen,

and making sure Layton would confirm it to them. But then that prick Nathan got you involved, and the whole thing snowballed."

"What did you have on Layton?"

"He borrowed money from the wrong guy. He was trying to prop up his business after the feds started to wind down their contracts with him."

"Was it your client Dragan?"

"He knows who you are, by the way. You used an alias to get on his film set, but we put it together. Johnny Slade." She scoffed. "You're like a cartoon character. And you shouldn't have punched him."

"I'm not worried about that degenerate," Slater said. "Although I actually do admire how tits-out he is about his sense of style. It takes a lot of man to wear satin that tight."

"I can't believe you actually stalked him. How did you even find out about Dragan? You're like a pipe that breaks when nobody's home. The water that seeps into everything. All the dark dirty places."

"When you say it snowballed, you mean Lunelle and Redge Black?"

"They learned the script, and they got paid." Sybil chuckled. "I love how you got sticky with Graham. You raced out to Santa Cecilia with a hard-on and your tongue hanging out."

"You're right—it was a boneheaded thing to do. I need to keep my dick out of my work." Slater gestured helplessly. "But how could I not? Graham is a total snack."

Her lip curled in disgust. "And you think I have crummy taste in men."

"Who was behind the rifle on that island? And why there? It was pretty fucked up to try to ice me like that, by the way."

"Attempted murder is a serious allegation, Slater. I

don't know anything about what happened there."

He shook his head. "It doesn't wash. Nobody else had motive."

"Coincidentally, the person who owns Santa Cecilia is a client of mine. It's quite rustic. A couple of cabins, a hand-pumped well for water. His family uses it as a summer getaway. This time of year it's deserted."

"I know you set it up," Slater said, "but I don't think you were the shooter. That would be a little too hands-on for Sybil. You'd have to lower yourself from your twenty-eighth-floor perch. Get your hands wet down in those dark dirty places."

"If I did want you out of the picture, I would have hired one of the many lowlifes I've worked with over the years." She waved a hand. "I don't do criminal law, of course, but I run into lots and lots of thugs." Her eyes flicked over him. "Present company included."

"What about sabotaging my car? Did you tell Cody to do it, or was that his own initiative?"

"I don't know anything about that."

He pursed his lips and thought about it. "I guess that all fits."

"I didn't get around to picking up my package yet," Sybil said.

"On Monday morning you were so antsy to get it. It makes sense now. You didn't think I was going to live to see the sunset."

"I hope you don't think you can hang on to it just because you're angry with me."

"I'm well aware that it's worth more than my life," Slater said. "It's cash, I'm thinking. Not dope. You don't seem like a pusher. It has to be about you stooging for Dragan. Are you chiseling him, or is all that lettuce supposed to get washed by some penny-ante small business?"

"That's not something you need to know."

"Well, you know where it is. Send one of your flunkies to pick it up. Or tell Dragan to drop by. He's hot for a straight guy. I could gaze at his tits all day long."

"So have you come up with some plan to go to the police?" Sybil said. "'Oh, poor me, that mean lawyer was so rude.'"

"You did try to croak me, sister. That goes way beyond rude."

"What evidence do you have of that? Nada. You'll blab to Ben that I lied about the NDA. He might believe you, and he might not. Either way, Ekragen isn't going to hire him. That ship has sailed." A smirk played on her lips. "So I win. Trust me—nothing I've done is prosecutable. I've been careful about that. You can't touch me, *ese*."

Listening to her, Slater's heart started pounding. "Fuck that. You're trash, and you treat your friends like trash."

Sitting up, she jabbed a finger at him. "It's you. You're the trash." And louder, "You."

He stood up, and held her gaze, and slowly pushed a stack of files on the edge of the desk until they tumbled onto the floor, flopping in a pile of splayed paper. He turned to walk out.

"How mature," Sybil called after him. "Tell your business partner I'm coming around for that package. Tonight or tomorrow."

Riding down in the elevator, he thought about it. Forging Ben's signature on the NDA was illegal, but not illegal enough for the cops or the prosecutors to start an investigation. It would get filed away and forgotten. Cody Layton would never implicate himself, and he couldn't ask that of Graham either. It felt like the guy was just a patsy in the whole scheme. And Slater hadn't actually seen the shooter on that island—the only evidence he had of her trying to ice him was his own word. That was less than useless. There was no point in even reporting it. It looked like she was right—there was nothing he could do. And that was absolutely infuriating.

On the walk to his car, he pulled out his phone and called Ben.

"Where are you?" Slater said when he picked up.

"At home. Why? You sound stressed out."

"I'm on my way over."

He drove north to Ben's place, on the other end of Downtown, and found a meter on Grand. The apartment tower had no intercom outside, and when he tried the door, it wasn't locked. Inside was a desk staffed by a guy in a jacket and tie. He looked up as Slater stepped in.

"Can I help you?"

"You have got to be fucking kidding me."

He frowned. "Excuse me?"

"This building has a doorman."

"I'm the concierge." He gave Slater the once-over. "Are you here to do some work for one of the residents?"

"Ben Clague."

"Your name?"

"Ibáñez."

He picked up his desk phone, and murmured into it, then eyed Slater. "Twelve oh four. Left off the elevator."

He rode up and knocked on the door. Ben pulled it open and greeted him with a smile. The front room furniture looked like what they put in hotels—dark wood, boxy, devoid of character. The big windows had a view west, of the hills around his own neighborhood, and sections of the 101 snaking up to Hollywood, the urban sprawl stretching to the hills.

"That's a hell of a view."

"Thanks," Ben said, glancing at the windows. "So what's going on?"

"Is Nathan home?"

"He's at work."

"It's truth time, Ben. The story about you working at Desert View is complete fiction. They faked the NDA, and forged that photo, and had a string of people lie about it to my face."

"I already know that."

"Well, now I have evidence." He dug out his phone. "Can we sit?"

Ben gestured to the lounge furniture, and Slater went to the sofa.

"Sit here so I can show you," he said, and Ben sat next to him.

The guy was big, and Slater felt the cushions sink. With the proximity he could feel the heat of his body and smell his sweat. If things were configured a little differently, he'd be all over this guy.

Slater pulled up the photo of Ben with the Desert View staff and the drone. "The boss had this photo framed on his credenza."

"You showed me that before."

Slater swiped at the screen. "This is the original photo."

"Poof," Ben said. "I was never there."

"You need to watch a video. It's from the security camera in the front office at Desert View Rocketry."

Ben leaned in as the clip started to play. Sybil's voice sounded tinny through the phone's speakers: "I'm here to see Cody Layton."

"That's Sybil," Ben said. They watched it until Graham walked Sybil into the back offices. "She went out there to look at the fictional NDA. She told me she did that."

"Look at the date stamp. This was way before you had the problem with Ekragen."

Leaning in, his brow furrowed.

"Here's the clip when she leaves the office later that day."

He hit play, and they watched her talking to Cody in the outer office.

"You don't need to worry about whether it's going to work," Sybil said. "You say what you're supposed to say, and the tax man will never hear a word about your fiscal skulduggery."

"It's a hell of a game you're playing," Cody said. "What did this Ben guy ever do to you?"

Ben frowned and sat back. "I don't get it."

"Sybil set up the whole thing," Slater said intently. "She's the mastermind. She's trying to mess with you. Derail your career."

He scoffed. "She wouldn't do that."

"The guy in the video who showed her out is Cody Layton, president of Desert View. Sybil ran a squeeze play on him."

"What does that mean?"

"She blackmailed him to say you worked there and had an NDA. He confirmed that fiction when Ekragen contacted him." Slater waved a hand. "That redheaded snack on the front desk admitted to me that he'd been paid off to say the same thing."

"Play it again," Ben said, and took the phone from him to look closer.

Slater could see he was breathing heavily now. After the clip played, he let the phone drop to his lap. His face had gone ashen.

"She's my friend."

"She's also your ex," Slater said. "And she's also fucking crazy."

Ben looked up at him. "I can't believe this."

"Believe it, brother. The video doesn't lie."

"What am I going to do?" he said, half to himself.

Slater took his phone back. "I'll write up a report outlining the whole thing. It'll be on my agency's letterhead. You can take that and the video evidence to Ekragen and explain things. They still might not hire you, but at least you can show them there's no NDA, and you're not lying on your résumé. You just have a crazy vindictive ex."

Watching him, Slater could tell he wasn't really absorbing his words, his gaze fixed on the coffee table. Not a good time to tell him what he owed him, he decided. He wanted to be done completely with this, but Ben wasn't in the head space for his bill—he looked shell-shocked.

"I know it's a lot to digest," Slater said. "Talk to Nathan about it. Will he be home soon?"

"Yeah, OK," Ben said, not looking at him.

Slater walked out, and on the ride down in the elevator, he closed his eyes, and rolled his shoulders, and took a few deep breaths. He really needed to shed this feeling of frustration. There was nothing more he could do—he had to let it go.

In the lobby, the concierge looked up at him from his desk. "All squared away?"

"I managed to fix the dishwasher," Slater said, standing in front of him, "but I was a little surprised."

His brow furrowed. "About what?"

"The appliances, and the fittings, and everything about this building. It's just so …" he paused, and looked the guy up and down. "Cheap."

Not waiting for a reply, he walked out.

TWENTY-FOUR

PIKE'S SUV WASN'T AROUND, Slater saw, when he got to his house. He was still at work. There wasn't a whole lot of daylight left, but he needed to get his hands in the dirt. It grounded him, recharged him, counterbalanced the toxicity of the cesspool.

Once he'd parked the Continental, he phoned Grace, the elderly woman who lived in the ADU next to his garage. She'd been in the life in Vegas and worked as an operative for him sometimes. Gray hair and advanced age were an excellent cover—most people looked right through her.

She didn't answer, so he left her a voice mail: "I'm going to come into your yard to do some work on the hydrangeas, so don't shoot at me."

He knew she didn't have firearms. Not that he'd seen, at least. Even if she did, Grace was too imperturbable to cap him without a good reason.

At the workbench in the garage he pulled on a pair of heavy gloves, and kneepads, and then grabbed a plastic bag of fertilizer and a bucket of bark mulch. Walking around the far side of the house, he went through the narrow gate into the only yard space on the lot. Grace had a little patio table and chairs outside her sliding door, and he wanted the space to be pleasant when she had her morning coffee. The hydrangeas weren't blooming now, but they were well established, he saw, looking them over.

Slater spent some time on his knees massaging

fertilizer into the soil around some of the plants. The earth here was alkaline, like most of SoCal, and that made the hydrangeas produce pink flowers. Adding the acidic fertilizer would make these ones bloom in blue next year. After he'd finished with the fertilizer, he spread a layer of bark mulch around the plants, and then grabbed the hose and watered everything down.

Standing there with the hose running, the kneepads still puckering his jeans, he couldn't see any path to get Sybil thrown in the hoosegow. She was a degenerate, but she was also a savvy lawyer. She would have carefully covered her tracks at every step. He had to believe her when she said he couldn't touch her. She would have made sure of that.

Even though she'd tried to grease him, he wasn't that angry about it anymore. Not enough to do something rash, anyway. That wasn't like him—he was getting soft. Or maybe Pike and the distraction of their narrative complex were filing off some of his rough edges. He could understand why Sybil had come for him, given the circumstances. Icing him was an easy fix to keep her operation rolling. It was harder to figure why Cody Layton would mess with him when they'd just met. But maybe he'd perceived the risk that Slater would figure it out and his house of cards would collapse.

Ben would definitely be upset with her once he'd recovered from the surprise. Slater had hit him with world-altering news. That look on his face. Shock and betrayal. He aimed the hose at the hedge along the back of the yard and let the water run onto it. Thinking about it, why had he left the guy alone? Showing him that video was like cocking a six-gun, and he'd just set it in front of him and walked out.

He turned off the water and quickly coiled up the hose, then ditched the gloves and the kneepads and the bark mulch on the workbench in the garage. Digging out his phone, he pulled up the lock-reading app. He wasn't sure if it kept track of the ghost keys he'd used, and it took a few taps to find it, but eventually, there it was: a list of the dates and key numbers. Thank you, Svetlana.

Opening his gear cabinet, he pulled out the key binder and retrieved the one from the pouch marked 325. Hurriedly locking it up again, he climbed into the Continental and drove fast and hard toward South Park. At one point he punched it to bust an extremely yellow stoplight, and roared through the intersection.

The golden light of the end of the day illuminated the apartment towers as he pulled up to Sybil's building and parked in a loading zone. He'd probably get cited, but he was in a rush. He hustled down the ramp into the garage, where he could get inside fast, then rode up to the twenty-eighth floor, and dug out the ghost key, and let himself in.

The room lights were off, and the alarm didn't sound. At the big windows, beyond the desk and the lounge furniture, the glass door to the balcony hung open. Ben was standing out there, bathed in the golden light, his big frame almost as tall as the windows. Sybil was out there too, sitting on the edge of a planter box and slumped over, her ear to the balcony rail. Her eyes were closed, mouth agape, hair loose and scraggly. She was still wearing the blue satin blouse and the dress pants. As he stepped toward them, he saw that her hands were cuffed in front.

"Don't come any closer," Ben called to him.

Slater stopped a few feet from the doorway. "That blouse she's wearing is way too sheer for November, don't you think? I guess she really wants to show off the rack. I would too, I suppose, if I'd shelled out for it."

Sybil wasn't fully unconscious, he realized, as she

briefly opened her eyes in a slow glassy blink.

"I thought I locked that door," Ben said.

"Do those cuffs have fur on them?"

"They're from a sex-toy shop. Nathan and I get a little kinky sometimes."

"Right on. I have some too, but they're not as fun as those."

"You're not going to stop me," Ben said, raising his voice.

"Why would I do that? This trash bag tried to croak me." He cocked his head. "She looks a little out of it. I just saw her a few hours ago. Before I came to your place. She was in much better shape."

"Sybil is hopped up on ketamine right now."

Slater put his hands on his hips. "Also from your party supplies, I'm thinking."

"For a stone-cold liar, she's way too trusting. I asked her to get me a drink, and I slipped it right into her Fresca." He jutted his chin toward the balcony rail. "She's going to commit suicide right now."

"You should take the cuffs off first. It's a good thing they're padded. They won't leave any marks."

Ben's eyebrows shot up. "You're really not going to try to stop me?"

"You're a pretty big mook, Ben. I'm not sure I could stop you. You'd have her over that railing before I got through the door."

"She tried to ruin my life," he shouted, and shook Sybil's shoulder. Her head wobbled and sagged forward.

"I get that. She came after me too."

"She really tried to kill you?"

"She lured me out to an empty island in the middle of nowhere. One of her lowlife contacts was waiting there to shoot at me."

"That's cold."

"Straight people are crazy, right?" Slater said. "It was my own fault, in a way. It was stupid of me to fall for it. But it's still infuriating."

"She's a menace," Ben shouted.

"I agree. It would be so satisfying to watch her drop. Like a rag doll in the wind. My instinct is actually to help you do it. You could lift the arms, and I'll lift the feet. I want to watch the descent."

Ben's brow furrowed, and he didn't move. "OK."

"The thing is, if you do it, you're not really fixing a problem," Slater said. "You're making things worse. The suicide story is never going to fly."

"It will if you can keep your mouth shut."

"It doesn't matter what I do. The cops will see you on video walking into the lobby today. They'll find your prints in the apartment, and they'll find the ketamine in the soda and in her toxicology report. They'll start to dig into your relationship to this lowlife, and interview everyone you've ever met, and grill Nathan in a windowless room for hours and hours and hours." He waved an arm. "What a mess, right?"

"This has nothing to do with Nathan," Ben said.

"They don't care. They'll do it anyway. The cops are good at this stuff. It's their specialty. I hate to tell you that, because in my heart of hearts I want to see Sybil do the swan dive. But this is my world," Slater said. "I'm the guy who can throw punches and handle the rough stuff, remember? I know what I'm talking about. You'll get caught, you'll get sent up, you'll never get to work for that defense contractor, and you'll never see Nathan again."

Ben's face contorted, and he sobbed audibly. Slater watched him for a moment before he spoke.

"I'm not saying we won't toss her over," Slater said, "but can we bring her inside? Just for a minute. Just so we can think it through and consider the long-term consequences."

He didn't say anything, but then nodded. Slater showed his palms and stepped out onto the balcony. The breeze struck him, and he inhaled sharply.

"It's chilly out here."

The fuzzy cuffs were upholstered with leopard-print fur, he saw. Slater put a hand under Sybil's armpit, and Ben took the other side. Her head lolled forward as they lifted her up and carried her inside, the toes of her shoes dragging behind them on the carpet. They dumped her on the red sofa, and Sybil groaned.

Slater shifted her onto her side, positioning her cuffed hands in front of her crotch. Adjusting her legs, he moved her top knee forward so that she wouldn't roll onto her back.

Rising, he eyed Ben. "Sit down."

Ben sank into one of the lounge chairs, and Slater dropped to one knee in front of him.

"Aren't you going to rescue the poor woman now?" Ben said, and waved an arm at her. "Free her from the tyranny of the fuzzy cuffs?"

He kept his gaze on Ben. "She's in the crash position, so she won't choke on her own vomit. That's as much as I'm willing to do for her. It's you I'm worried about." Leaning in, he brushed the tears off his cheek with his thumb, then pulled back.

"I'm such a fuck-up."

"I don't see that at all. You can only push people so far before they snap." Slater snapped his fingers. "Today, that was you."

"I really, really want to throw her off that balcony."

"I know you do. So do I. But you didn't do it right away. You could have tossed her before I got here. Something made you hesitate. Made you think twice."

"It's murder," Ben said. "Of course I hesitated. I'm not cold-blooded."

Slater chuckled. "It's always the quiet ones who go all out."

"Quiet doesn't mean insensitive." Ben wiped at his face. "I've got as much repressed rage as anyone. You're lucky—you just let the fists fly when it comes up, and you're done with it. Like with that homeless guy at the doughnut shop. *Bam*."

"That hasn't always served me well."

He shook his head and squeezed his eyes shut. "Even the fact that I wanted to do it. That I started to."

"But you didn't. Look at me," Slater said, and held his gaze. "No one is beyond redemption. You proved to yourself today that you're not that guy. You're no murderer. You showed me that too. You took the step back. Focus on that."

TWENTY-FIVE

T HE NEXT DAY, SLATER slept in, then drove to his office. He was going to give Ben and Nathan a day or two before he hit them up for the rest of his fee. Ben definitely needed some time to settle down. He'd spent a long time with him yesterday, after talking him down, and stayed to make sure he didn't change his mind and throw Sybil off the balcony. He'd watched as Ben took off the handcuffs, and they'd left together.

Up in his office, sitting at his desk, Slater's phone buzzed, and he pulled it out to check. The caller ID said it was Conrad, his idiot ex.

"Where are you right now?" Conrad said when he picked up.

"Why are you asking?" Slater said. "When a police detective asks questions like that, it makes me nervous."

He chuckled. "I know your instinct is to hightail it and jump over the back fence."

"What do you want?"

"Your name came up in a case," Conrad said, lowering his voice.

"I know you have a flag on my name in your stupid police computer."

"You're lucky that I do. I can try to keep you out of worse trouble."

"What case are you talking about?"

"The bunco squad busted up an illegal gambling operation. One of those where they hit all the targets at the same time so that nobody gets tipped off and has a chance to flee. That happened this morning. One of the people arrested was a lawyer named Sybil Álvarez."

"Seriously?" Slater said.

"She wasn't working at the card rooms, but she's involved. We've been surveilling her. The charges are illegal gaming and money laundering. The gaming isn't all that serious, but money laundering is a felony, especially at the scale they were doing it. She works with a guy named Dragan. He's in the soup too."

"What's it got to do with me?"

He didn't even have to ask that, but he wanted to know what Conrad knew.

"Sybil hasn't told us everything," Conrad said. "She's being selective about what she remembers. But she told our people that you're holding cash that was supposed to be delivered to a nail salon to be laundered."

"Did she tell you I don't even know what that package is? She hired me to be the errand boy, not the banker."

"That's her version too. She said you were working as a courier."

"It's not a version," Slater said. "It's the immutable unwavering truth. She paid me to pick it up and store it for a few days. I didn't know what was in it."

"You didn't check?"

"It's a sealed package. I put it in my safe." He sighed. "I figured it was probably cash. Did she say how much it was?"

"I'm not going to tell you that. I'm not actually on the case, but I'll get myself on it. Then I'm going to come and retrieve it."

"Well, I'm not in my office right now."

"You'd better be in your office soon," Conrad said, "because Sybil won't be in the jug for long. Lawyers know how to work the system."

"I'll meet you there in a few hours."

Slater ended the call and swiveled to the safe. He dialed in the combination, and twisted the handle, and pulled open the heavy door. The bundle was where he'd left it, and he hauled it out and set it on his desk. It was wrapped in heavy brown paper, like a grocery bag, and sealed with packing tape.

Etta kept office supplies in the drawers of the front desk, and he stepped out to dig through them, and found a box cutter. He cut the brown paper where it was taped together.

When he got it open, it was indeed cash, bound in bundles with blue elastic bands. Flipping through one, then another, they were all C-notes, and all used bills. He didn't count the stack, but from the uniform thickness of each one, these were hundred-bill racks. There were eight of them—eighty grand. Fifty bucks of this was money he'd blown himself in Dragan's card room. Slater held one of the bundles to his nose and inhaled, savoring that sweet heady scent of greenbacks.

On his phone he tapped Ben's number, and listened to it ring, but there was no answer. Next he called Nathan, relieved that he picked up.

"You need to come to my office now," Slater said. "Bring Ben too."

"Is it about your fee?" Nathan said. "Ben told me the whole story. You'll get paid."

"It's not about that. It's about vengeance. Actually, it's even better than that. But you have to hustle."

"I'm at work. At the Broadway store. I think Ben's at home."

"Walk out right now," Slater said, "and get in your dick-magnet Bronco, and pick up Ben on the way. I promise it'll be worth it."

He hesitated but said, "I guess I trust you."

"Get your ass over here," Slater said intently, and ended the call.

Nathan must have literally dropped what he was doing, as it was less than half an hour later when a knock came at the office door. Slater pulled it open to find the pair of them, Nathan in a business-casual dark shirt and chinos, and Ben wearing a red sports jersey. Ben still looked unkempt, bleary-eyed, a little spacey.

"I was working," Nathan said.

"The doughnuts can wait." Slater beckoned them into his office, and dropped into the chair behind his desk.

Nathan's brow furrowed as they sat down. "What's going on?"

"I have some happy news," Slater said, looking from him to Ben. "Sybil is in jail today."

"How?" Ben said. "She laughed in my face when I threatened to go to the cops. She told me no one could pin anything on her. She said she hadn't left any trace of what she did."

"Sybil is smart, but she's a crook in more ways that just gaslighting you. She's been helping a client to launder his illicit earnings. Today she got caught."

Nathan frowned. "Money laundering?"

"I don't know all the details. One of her clients is a lowlife film producer who makes a lot of dough with illegal card rooms. The dope I heard is that she was helping him run the cash through small businesses to legitimize it." Slater waved a hand. "One of their penny-ante partners probably got caught and turned on them."

"She won't be in for long," Ben said. "She's slippery."

"It doesn't matter." He sat up. "Sybil actually hired me to pick up a cash delivery for her and hold it for a few days."

"Why would she do that?" Nathan said. "You were the biggest threat to her operation."

"It was strategic," Slater said. "Keep your friends close, and your enemies closer. I'm thinking it was a way to keep tabs on my investigation."

"I still can't believe she trusted you with cash."

"Sybil knows the rules of the cesspool as well as I do. She knew I'd be smart enough not to mess with it because I knew her client was a lowlife who'd come after me. It's a common-sense rule in my business—you don't chisel dangerous people." He raised his eyebrows. "But she was stupid to trust me."

Pulling open his bottom desk drawer, Slater heaved up the open bundle, stacks of cash spilling onto the desktop.

"Fuck me," Nathan said.

"We're going to divvy this up."

"I'm pretty sure she's going to want this back."

"So she can sue me," Slater said. "It cuts both ways—we can't touch her, but now that she and her client are busted, she can't touch me. Unless she wants to show receipts for this." He set three racks in front of Ben. "Thirty for you. Compensation for Sybil's rat-fink behavior. And thirty for me. My fee for getting shot at, and for being underestimated. It'll just pay for my car. I'm pretty sure Sybil's stooge at Desert View had a hand in wrecking my old one."

"What about the other twenty?" Ben said.

"We have to leave something for the cops."

Nathan eyed Ben. "I'm not sure you should take this."

"It's dirty money," Slater said. "No question about that. Sybil already told the cops about it."

"How do you know that?"

"She gave them my name, and told them I was holding it, and they called me. They're coming over today to pick it up. If we let John Law take it all, it'll wind up collecting dust in some evidence locker."

"If Sybil told the cops it existed," Nathan said, "she

would have told them the amount."

"Whatever she told them doesn't matter. It's not her money. It went through several people's hands between her client and me. I know there's no paperwork on it. Anyone could have taxed part of it. Or maybe she lied to the police about the amount."

"Why would she tell them about it in the first place?" Ben said. "Why would she tell them anything? I know her. She's not easily intimidated. She wouldn't just offer it up to the police."

"Sybil is talking because she's trying to save herself," Slater said. "She knows what they have on her. It must be pretty damning. When you get caught dead to rights, it's smarter to be a cooperating witness than a coconspirator. You'll do a lot less time."

"Are you sure the film producer won't come after you?" Nathan said.

"He and Sybil both know this dough is a write-off. The cops confiscated it. Plus he's going to have bigger problems with the judicial system."

"Let's call it restitution," Ben said, and picked up the racks. Half rising, he stuffed two in his front pants pocket, the third on the other side.

"You can't tell anyone about this," Slater said. "Not even your mama."

Nathan nodded. "Of course not."

"You can't put it in the bank."

Ben frowned. "Why not?"

"Because your Uncle Sam is going to want to know where it came from. Certain transactions trigger their interest. Cash deposits in round numbers, and more than a few thousand bucks without an obvious source. Just spend it—but not too fast, and no more than ten grand at a time. More than that and businesses have to report it to the feds."

"I guess this changes things," Ben said. "It changes how I feel about it all. I still can't believe Sybil would do something so devious and cruel just to mess with me. And now she's ratted out her client." He gestured helplessly. "She's a terrible person."

"You can tell me all about it one day," Slater said. "Right now you have to get out of here. The cops are coming to pick up the twenty grand Sybil asked me to hold for her."

"Will they be looking for eighty grand?" Nathan said.

"I don't care what they're looking for. Sybil had me pick up twenty grand. That's what I was given by the courier. That's what I know."

Nathan nodded. "This is good. You know how to do this."

Slater eyed Ben. "How much cash did I give you today?"

"Nothing," he said, and grinned. "You're the one who did the work, remember? We paid you the rest of your fees."

"Good answer."

"How much did we pay you again?" Ben said.

"You gave me three grand in cash."

"Do you actually want us to pay you?" Nathan said. "I can write a check."

"Sybil already covered it," Slater said, and tapped his stack of racks. "Now, vamoose."

Ben laughed, his tone rich and deep, and they stood up. Slater followed them into the front office.

"It's really good to hear you laugh," he said.

Ben paused at the door and leaned in to give Slater a brief bear hug. "Knowing she's in jail feels like an accelerant. It'll help me get over it."

"He'll be fine," Nathan said. "He just needs to get used to the new reality. To absorb the betrayal."

"Plus there's all that lettuce to soften the blow." Slater waved an arm. "Thanks, Sybil."

Once they'd left, back at his desk, he tossed his racks into the safe, then wrote on the back of their accounting envelope:

Slater +30G. Client fees.

The previous entry was the cash he'd taken to buy the Continental, he saw. It was the same amount. It made more sense that this infusion zeroed out that withdrawal. He scratched out both entries and put the envelope back in the safe.

After he locked it up, he took packing tape and scissors from Etta's desk, and cut the brown paper down to a smaller size, and wrapped the twenty grand in it. Once he'd taped it up, he set it in the middle of his desktop. It didn't look like much anymore.

Reclining, he ran a hand through his hair and took a deep breath. Conrad would be here soon, and he'd probably bring a colleague with him. They knew it was cash, so it wouldn't be left alone with anybody until it was counted and catalogued. The discrepancy in the amount wasn't going to be an issue, even if Sybil told them how much it was. Conrad would just have to settle for his version. It came down to his word against hers, and she was the one who was about to be indicted.

He eyed the bundled cash on his desk. "You can't touch me, *esa.*"

———◆———

www.ingramcontent.com/pod-product-compliance
Lightning Source LLC
Chambersburg PA
CBHW010741310726
48971CB00010B/2896